LIGHT 'EM UP
BY KELLY JAMIESON

LIGHT 'EM UP
Copyright © 2024 Kelly Jamieson
Print ISBN-13: 978-1-988600-86-4
Ebook ISBN-13: 978-1-988600-85-7

BANG BROTHERS HOCKEY SERIES

Meet the Bang Brothers—five hot hockey-playing brothers who are allergic to commitment. The brothers are about to face off against their newly-retired mother...who suddenly has plenty of time to play matchmaker. Add in their baby sister and some secret dating, a single dad, an accidental pregnancy, a marriage of convenience, and a wrong bed—or two—and these siblings are not going to know what hit them!

Lace 'em Up
Show 'em How
Hit 'em Hard
Lock 'em Down
Light 'em Up
Hook 'em Hard

FROM THE JOURNAL OF
STELLA BANG

Dear Diane,

It's hard to believe you're gone. More than hard; it's devastating. Lars says time will ease the band of pressure that cuts across my chest when I think of you. But no amount of time will make me miss you any less. I suppose the passing years will only result in an acceptance of reality.

I lost my best friend.

Just the other day, I picked up the phone to tell you about the twins' mess at school. It involved crazy glue (stolen from the teacher's supply closet) and googly eyes! Needless to say, Jakob was NOT happy. He's been so serious and severe the last few years; it's a good thing he has the twins to make him crack a smile now and then.

Anyway, I picked up the phone to tell you, and then I remembered. Oh, the waves of anguish are unbearable and relentless whenever I remember. My therapist says that's normal. In fact, it was her idea that I write to you. She said it could be cathartic. Healing.

Little does she know we'd cork a bottle of wine and spill our guts, no doubt dissolving in laughter, whenever one of us needed to heal a heartache. Your bad breakup with Joe. My sadness when Jakob divorced. Your mother's passing. Leif nearly being expelled from university. We've seen each other through all the ups and downs.

It's difficult for me to move forward and start a new chapter without you.

But I bought this diary. And now, I'm sitting here, at the kitchen table, writing to you.

The house is quiet. Lars left early for practice. And the kids... they're all grown up. After years of pinching their cheeks and reminding them that mother knows best, they're out into the world. Blazing trails and finding their footing.

That's another reason I can't accept you're gone. You, Diane, with your flashing blue eyes, loud, boisterous laughter, and penchant for mischief — how can you be gone? I contacted your niece and nephews after your funeral. They were kind and gracious. But they don't remember you the way I do. I'm not sure anyone does. And that sits heavy on my chest, keeping me up at night.

What's a life without love? Without friendship? Without family?

Lars and I are coming up on thirty-five years of marriage. I know how fortunate I am to have married the love of my life and then stayed married for thirty-five wonderful years. I'm blessed to have birthed six healthy, beautiful children who all pursued their passions and are making their way in the world.

And yet, I can't help but wonder — are they fulfilled?

None of them are close to family. None of them have found or kept love. They're...adrift. Just like you were before I forced you to join my family. "An honorary Bang," you laughed. But I saw the happiness it brought you. It was the same happiness I felt.

King's in his thirties and hasn't had a serious relationship since college. Jakob is a single parent struggling with raising children on his own. Jensen and Annie are still thick as thieves but on opposite ends of the country. Leif avoids commitment like the plague. And Tanner's living his best life, partying like it's his job.

When will they settle down? Find the type of happiness I've known for over half my life? I don't mean to sound old-fashioned — although I can admit that I am in many ways, but I want more grandbabies. And to know that my children are fulfilled. Happy. In love.

I want them to find what Lars and I share. Love, respect, commitment. Trust.

I want them to have everything I wished for you, Diane. And perhaps the most challenging part of letting you go is knowing you didn't have the great big love you desired.

It's true what they say: life is too short.

Which is why I have an idea. A plan, really, although I haven't told Lars yet. I think the kids — all of them — need help. A mother's touch, so to speak, since I obviously know best. And, with Lars coaching the junior league, he's either at the rink or traveling with the team. Most of the time, I'm on my own. It's lonely without you to come by for a cup of tea or meet for lunch. Depressingly so.

My therapist thinks a change of scenery will help. She thinks I should shake up my routine.

And so... what if I visit them? The kids. I can help them. Cook their favorite meals. Look after the boys so Jakob can go on a date or two. Give them the nudges they

need or, in some cases, the well-placed shoves. It will be an
adventure, Diane! For all of us.

I just need to run it by Lars, but... soon, I'll write to you
from King's place in Oakland. Isn't that grand? I'll be
living my best life in the sunshine well before the first
snowstorm hits Minnesota. If you were here, I know that
would delight you!

I miss you, my friend. I'll write more soon.

Love, Stella

Light 'em Up is book five in the Bang Brothers Hockey series. If you haven't read the others, it can totally be read as a stand-alone, but you'll enjoy reading all "Mama Bang's" efforts to find love for her children! Light 'em Up is also set in the world of my New York Bears hockey team, book so you'll meet up with familiar characters if you've ready those books. Happy reading!

ONE

Annie

Is it possible to be the most experienced skater on an NHL team and also the least experienced when it comes to hockey? Yep, because that's me, a former competitive figure skater hired as a skating coach for the New York Bears this season.

Excitement rushes through me, tingling in my veins.

I know you're probably thinking NHL players already know how to skate, or they wouldn't be there. Which is true. But there's a lot they can learn to be even better, some of them in particular. And that's my job.

I still can hardly believe this has happened. After I had to give up my competitive figure skating dreams, I taught skating for a couple of years, then coached hockey at a D1 college. But I wanted more. I looked for for an NHL job for a couple of years, and now, finally, I'll be working with the New York Bears. They weren't my first choice and living in New York City wasn't my first choice, but I'll definitely take it. I know it'll be a challenge, but I've always loved a challenge.

It's exciting, but also terrifying.

Right now, day one of training camp, we're in Coach Gary Shipton's office going over who's here at camp man by man. I've been watching video, observing some of the players skating informally, learning my way around the practice facility. I've met the staff and even a few of the players.

"There are fifty-four players on the roster," he tells me. "Thirty forwards, eighteen defensemen, and six goaltenders. We'll want your feedback on all of them, which will help us make some tough decisions in the next couple of weeks to get the roster down to twenty-one to be cap compliant."

I nod. I'm well aware of the pressures of training camp for players—I have five brothers who play in the NHL—and I'm learning about the pressures facing the staff as well. We have to pick the best players and develop the best roster we can to give the team a chance of winning. Which means, winning the Stanley Cup.

Just thinking that gives me goosebumps.

When Gary gets to left winger Logan Coates, my body tenses.

Logan and I have a history. A very brief, intense history which I've never shared with anyone. If that one night was the only thing we shared, I wouldn't be so stressed about working with him. But there's more than that.

A few years ago, Logan badly injured my brother in a game. The fury has faded, mostly. But not my hatred of Logan Coates for what he did to Jensen.

I knew Logan plays for the Bears, of course. Which was one of the reasons the Bears weren't my first choice of team to work for. But he's one player on a whole team and chances are good I won't have to have much to do with him.

Besides, I can't let all that bother me. I'm a professional, here to do a job.

I can do this. I had to develop mental toughness as a young figure skater. It takes a lot of guts to launch yourself in the air over and over, knowing you're going to fall hundreds of times, knowing you're going to be bruised and sore and maybe worse, knowing every time you fail you're going to be frustrated and angry. You can't do that without being gangster.

I was criticized over and over and over, by my coaches—it's their job—and by judges—it's their job, too—and my peers. I had to learn to accept that and learn from it and do better no matter how demoralized and discouraged I felt.

So I can handle dealing with some jerk hockey player. With five brothers, I've done it all my life. Ha.

"Logan's got a lot of drive," Coach Shipton says. "Quick release, soft hands, and he doesn't mess around with the puck."

He doesn't mention Logan's reputation as an enforcer.

"Not a great skater," he continues. "But good at finding open ice. Great shooter."

Not a great skater.

Well, shit.

I mean, I should be happy about that because that's why I'm here—to help these guys skate better. But I'm less than enthusiastic about working with Logan Coates.

I focus on Gary's analysis of each player, making notes on my iPad of things for me to watch for.

Next, Gary takes me into the gym where the players are doing their fitness testing on day one of training camp.

"Guys come to camp in amazing physical condition," he says as we watch vertical jump tests. "Almost all these guys work their asses off all summer."

Again, I know this. I know how my brothers train in the off season. And I can see how fit these athletes are as I watch sprints, pushups, pullups, and more.

After the physicals, we all have lunch. The players head to

the lounge and I eat with the coaching staff in the coach's lounge. The Apex Practice Facility in Westchester County, New York is amazing, state of the art with all kinds of amenities. The weight room alone is mind-boggling. I'll be using it myself to stay in shape, now that I don't train eight hours a day.

Then we head to one of the classrooms, set up like a theatre with tiered seating and comfortable chairs. The coaching staff are all at the front of the room, along with the GM, assistant GM, and the new team owners who bought the team at the end of last season. I watch as players file in and find seats, now dressed in street clothes. I catch sight of Logan Coates with his backwards ball cap, and our eyes meet.

His gaze moves over me and a small groove appears between his eyebrows. Those thick eyebrows shoot up as recognition dawns, then draw back down together in a perplexed pucker. His head jerks back.

The play of emotions on his face is almost amusing. *I get it, buddy. I'm not happy either.*

One of his teammates says something to him and he takes a seat and leans in to listen.

I press my lips together and do a couple of deep, calming breaths.

Tag Heller, one of the new team owners, opens the first team meeting of the season with a welcome back speech for the players. He's relaxed and at ease in front of the players, and I can see they're all listening intently. The other Heller brothers, Jase, Logan (a different Logan), and Matt throw in the odd comment, sometimes joking, sometimes serious. I feel respect for them in the room, which is a good thing

Tag turns things over to Brad Julian, the general manager of the team. He, too, seems to be highly regarded by the players, but I sense there's also respect between Brad and the Hellers. It wouldn't be surprising if the Hellers wanted to fire Brad and hire their own GM, but Brad is still here and it's good to have that consistency for the players.

I keep my focus on Brad and not Logan Coates. Even though I'm so tempted to look at him to see if he's looking at me.

"Last year, our season ended too early," Brad says. "We missed out on the playoffs. At the end of last season we challenged players to think about their training over the summer. How they prepare for games." He takes a swallow of water from a bottle he holds. "We're going to continue on that. We all need to do our part to make that happen. A lot falls on the coaching staff, and we've made some changes to strengthen that. I'll let Gary talk to you about that."

He takes a seat and coach Gary Shipton steps forward.

"Thanks, Brad. I'm really excited about this season. And about this camp. We have some great talent here. Let me just say this: I want to win." He pauses to let that sink in. "I want all of *you* to want to win. Here at camp, we're going to set the tone right away of how we want to play as a team. I want you to feel free to play in the offensive zone using instinct and letting skill takeover. But we're also going to work on how we defend. Are we going to play man versus man in our zone? How is our battle game looking in the defensive zone? Do we need to engage in some three-on-three battle drills to elevate our commitment?"

He saunters across the small dais. "Here's what you can expect. We're going to practice fast. We're going to move a lot. We won't spend a lot of time at the boards, in fact, we may not even stop during a forty-minute practice. We'll look at special team strategies in video reviews with our fantastic video coach, Cal Crider." Cal waves. "We'll have time before practices to work on our power play. Mike Clark, our goalie coach, likes to work with the guys before practice, too. So get ready to work hard."

He strolls back.

"This year, we want to emphasize more than just physical toughness. We want to emphasize mental toughness."

He looks around. Everyone's rapt.

"And we want to emphasize skills. Basics, but at an elite level. And that's partly why we have some new faces in the coaching team this year. Viktor's still here, of course." He gestures to assistant coach Viktor Meknikov, who grins and lifts a hand. "Some of you have met our new assistant coach, Scott Meyer."

Scott steps forward and lifts a hand.

"I know a couple of you guys worked with Scott back in the Western Hockey League," Gary says. "We also have someone not only new to the team but in a brand new role. Please welcome Annie Bang as our new skating coach."

Lifting a hand, I smile and step forward, acknowledging the smatter of applause.

"For those of you who don't know Annie, she is a champion figure skater. With her partner Ivan Koskov, she won medals for pairs skating in US championships, Skate America, Four Continents Championships, and I could go on. They competed in the Olympics. When she retired from figure skating, she turned first to teaching..."

Hearing those words "retired from figure skating" still gives me that stabbing feeling in my heart. But I keep my smile in place.

"...then to coaching, and most recently worked the last two seasons at Bayard College with their men's and women's D1 hockey teams as skating coach. We're incredibly lucky and happy to have her joining the team here and you'll be getting to know her better as she works with the team on improving our skating skills."

I'm so glad he didn't mention my brothers. I don't want to be defined by them. This is *my* accomplishment. *My* career.

I look down at the New York Bears track suit I'm wearing. I did it. I made it to the NHL. Now I just have to show them I belong here.

⌣̲⎯

THE NEXT MORNING, I'm on the ice with some of the players and the coaching staff. The players are divided into two groups for training camp, with one group on the ice at nine o'clock, the other at eleven. There's a mix of veterans and newbies in each group.

I catch the looks from some of the guys—the smirks, the eyebrow lifts. I've encountered a lot of sexism in my career. As a young figure skater, I had to share the arena with hockey players. They called us figure skaters pretentious divas who took over the sound system and chewed up the ice. They'd snicker at us and cheer every time we fell.

It made me tough. I can handle these guys.

As they skate laps warming up, I join them. I get low into my knees and push harder. I sail past the hockey players, their legs pumping hard, mine barely moving. When the whistle blows and we gather around Gary at the board, I see them exchanging glances. I love the expressions on their faces as they look at me—identical open mouths and bewildered eyes.

I smile.

The coaches get the guys doing drills, barking out commands and blowing their whistles. I stay out of their way to observe. At one point I glide up to big Dman Jake Colman and say, "Hey, Jake. Can I offer a suggestion? Bend your knees a little more going into those turns...it'll help with your edges."

He gives me a look. It's clearly a what-the-fuck-do-you-know look. He's six-five, two hundred twenty-five pounds. I'm five-two, about one ten now. I hold his gaze steadily and nod encouragingly.

He ignores me.

I'm acutely aware of the Heller Brothers watching from a box above the ice. Obviously I want to make a good impression. But if these players ignore me, it looks worse for them than it does for me. I swallow a sigh.

At the end of the first session, as the guys are leaving the ice, Jake skates slowly past me and taps the top of my head. "Good job, little coach."

"Hey!"

He stops and looks over his shoulder at me.

I glare at him. "Yes, I'm short. But do not ever pat me on the head. I am not a child and I will fuck you up."

Jake's mouth drops open.

I smile.

The other guys are biting back laughter and I catch a couple of glances of interest. Including from Logan Coates.

TWO

Logan

I still get nervous before training camp.

Nobody but me is ever going to know that, though.

This is my fourth season in the NHL. My fourth *full* season; I spent a couple of seasons in the AHL and got called up a few times while there. I've been training hard all summer. Even so, I get nervous about the fitness testing and the risk that some young pup could perform better than me at camp and steal my spot on the roster. Nothing is guaranteed. Especially since my last two seasons have been...unexceptional.

I know I'll never be the best player on the team. I was a fourth-round draft pick and I've had to fight my way up to the majors. I'm still fighting, now for more ice time and a spot on the third line. So I try to ease my nerves by telling myself training camp is an *opportunity*. An opportunity to show the team how hard I've been working, how much I want this.

But I won't let anyone see me sweat.

Okay that's a total lie, I sweat like a horse. I mean, I won't let anyone see me *metaphorically* sweat. Nobody knows how scared I am that I'll always be seen as second rate. A fourth liner forever. Just like my dad. On the outside, I'm confident. Cocky, even. I play with grit. But hitting guys and finishing the check and then being caught out of position doesn't help the team. I need to focus more on taking the puck rather than taking the body, even though my dad keeps hounding me about playing tough.

Just thinking about my dad gives me a bad taste in my mouth. Ugh.

It's day two of training camp and we're on the ice for the first time. And so is Annie Bang.

"I'd like to bang *her*," Beav says in my ear, looking her way.

I slide him a sideways glare. "Shut the fuck up."

His eyebrows rise. But he shuts up and skates off.

Jesus bungie jumping Christ.

Speaking of banging Annie Bang...my palms break out in a sweat in my gloves.

It was six years ago, the night I met her. A long time ago. It still lives vividly in my fantasies, however.

Years after that, I was playing against Jensen Bang in Los Angeles. Everyone knew the Bang brothers—all five of them play in the NHL I didn't know any of them very well; just from playing against them over the years.

That night my desperate attempt to divest Jensen of the puck in the dying minutes of a game went horribly wrong. I still to this day swear I wasn't trying to hit him. I was honestly trying to stop, because he didn't have the puck, but I ended up falling on him. I know how it looked. I got suspended for four games and was crucified in the media and by the fans for a "dirty hit."

When that incident happened, I didn't make the connection between Jensen and Annie right away, but the whole thing blew up on social media and I realized I'd banged Jensen Bang's sister. And then I'd injured him. I'd reached out to Jensen, and I considered reaching out to Annie, but my agent told me I'd said what I needed to say to the media and to let it drop.

I watch Annie Bang lap all of us on the ice effortlessly. Some of the guys are impressed. Okay, sure, she can skate. But figure skating is entirely different from hockey.

I have to ignore her. I have to put in my best effort. I have goals for this season.

I skate my ass off doing the drills the coaches have us working on, focusing on hockey and not Annie. Until the end of our session and we're all leaving.

And she busts Jake's balls.

It's all I can do not to laugh. Especially at the look on his face. I meet my buddy J-Bo's eyes and he's fighting back laughter, too.

Jake stomps off and I risk a glance at Annie. Our eyes meet in a brief but mighty punch to the gut.

She's aware of me, too.

I turn away and head to the locker room. My heart rate slowed a bit after that practice, but now it's racing again. Shit, shit, fucking shit.

I shower and dress on auto pilot, getting ready for my meeting with Coach Shipton, my head full of confusion. I don't want Annie Bang here. She's a figure skater. She can't teach us anything. But also...she's still hot as fuck.

And that move with Jake—ballsy. Bold. Badass.

I fucking loved it.

But I still don't want her here.

"Hey, Logan," Coach greets me when I walk into his office. "How was your summer?"

"It was really good." I slide the glass door closed behind me and take a seat across the desk from Coach. "I did a lot of training but had some fun, too."

We make small talk and then Coach gets into the meat of it. "So. Like Brad said earlier, we made some moves over the summer. As you know, James was traded to Pittsburgh. We got draft picks in return, and we used those to draft some really good prospects, in our opinion."

I nod. James, who we called Red, had been around for a long time. The loss of an experienced veteran, not to mention our second line center, leaves a huge hole.

"Brad also talked about our draft strategy and getting the best players available at the time. Which means right now, a lot of our talent is waiting in the wings. And then there's the issue of Bergie's injury." Our team captain got his Achilles tendon sliced up. "We don't expect him back in the lineup until possibly December."

I bob my head again.

"So our first line from last season is intact. For now."

That's Easton Miller, Jay Bobak, and Brandon Smith. Also known as Millsy, J-Bo, Brando.

"But at this time of year, nothing's guaranteed," he adds. "Our second line last year was Red, Bergie, and Cookie."

Two of those guys are out.

"There's opportunity for some guys to make an impression and fill that line."

Me. That's me. I clamp my lips closed, though.

"We've got two experienced guys here on PTOs. One winger, one Dman. And we're light on experience in our forwards."

"Yeah."

"I also mentioned how we want to focus on our identity. We want to be more than physically tough. We want mental toughness. We want smarts."

"I know I've been known as more of a physical player," I say. "But I've been working on trying to play smarter. I did a lot of work over the summer with Jimmy Bilinksi."

Coach nods, recognizing the name of a former player who now does training. "Good, good. Glad to hear that."

I smile tightly. He just said a lot of stuff but I'm not sure where he's going with it.

"We'd like to see you do well this year." He leans forward. "You've got a few years of experience under your belt. You've got talent. Good hands, good at finding open ice. Great shooter."

"Thanks." My thoughts are darting all over the place.

"What I'm telling you is, there's opportunity here for you. We want you to succeed. We'd love to see you playing more minutes. Maybe even second line with Axe or Morrie. Or maybe with another center."

Gulp. Is he really saying what I think he is?

Top six? I was hoping to move up to the *third* line!

"We give all you guys the opportunity in camp." Coach meets my eyes. "The rest is up to you to show us what you got."

"Absolutely." My breath has gone shallow. "I want to play smarter. I know in the past I've sometimes put myself out of position for the sake of a hit. I don't want to sacrifice my positioning to make a hit that leaves the other guys at a disadvantage."

"But still use your body to force the puck away from players."

"Yeah."

"You're good at that. I love to see the puck knocked off an opponent's stick and taken the other way because of smart body checking. You know who's good at that?"

I think. "Nate."

"Yeah. But I'm really thinking of Jackson Wynn."

He plays for the Chicago Aces. I can see the comparison.

"He's so good at finessing though players and using his stick in unison with his body."

I nod. I admire Wynn.

"He plays the game with his mind, then puts his body into action." He pauses. "You have good hockey intelligence."

"Thank you."

"One thing we would like to see you work on is your skating."

I frown. "What?"

He nods. "We have our new skating coach this year. She's going to be a great asset."

"I know how to skate," I say, trying for humor.

"Of course you do. But it's not one of your strengths." He pauses. "If you want this, you're gonna have to work for it."

I let that sink in, then lift my chin. "That's what I want, too."

"Great." He smacks his hand on the desk. "I can't wait to see what you've got for the rest of camp."

"I'm looking forward to it, too." I stand.

"Your dad must be proud of you."

I pull in a slow breath through my nose. What the fuck do I say to that? My dad's not proud of me unless I'm slamming bodies into the boards or dropping the gloves. "I guess so," I reply awkwardly, feeling like a puck just settled in my gut.

"He was quite the agitator," Coach says with a reminiscing smile. "The game's changed a lot since his day."

"Yeah, it has." Too bad my dad doesn't see that.

Now I'm done for the day. Sometimes I carpool with the guys who live in my building, but today our schedules are different. So I find my buddies Evan Russell (Russ) and J-Bo to go for lunch. At the last minute, Barbie joins us (real name Igor Barbashev). We hit up a nearby place, Hudson Valley

Market. It's great to hang with my buddies again after the off season.

The waitress takes our order with a big smile and flirty glances for all of us. She's new here, I think. The other waitresses are older women who roll their eyes at us.

J-Bo returns her smile with one of his own. His bad-boy appearance—long dark hair, beard and moustache, dark eyes, well-worn leather jacket—always appeals to chicks.

Oddly, Barbie's broken nose and missing tooth also appeal to women. But he's happily married and doesn't notice. Russ also pays more attention to the menu than the flirty waitress, although her gaze lingers on his face and shoulders. He's more of a clean-cut guy, with thick hair the color of maple syrup and an easy smile.

Hell, the waitress even looks at me with interest.

"So Millsy's married off now. Who's going to be next to bite the dust?" J-Bo asks.

"I'm not comfortable with the term 'bite the dust,'" I say. "You make it sound like his life is over because he's married."

They all look at me.

I grin. "What? It's true."

J-Bo nods slowly. "You're right."

"My life is not over," Barbie says in his Russian accent. "My life started the day I married Nadia." We all groan at that and he grins. "Is true. She is my life."

I roll my eyes but inside I'm a little envious. I've had girlfriends, but I've never been in love. I'm not actually sure if I believe in love. In my family, love is something you use against someone to get something from them. "Cookie's next."

"Hmmm. Could be." Russ purses his lips. "Or Morrie. He and Kate seem pretty serious."

"What about you?" I ask Russ. "You and Hannah have been together a while. When are you gonna propose to her?"

I fully expect him to say "soon" or even "I don't know" but instead he frowns, one corner of his mouth turning down. "I don't think that's going to happen." He pauses. "We broke up."

"What!" We all gape at him, everyone making shocked noises. "What happened?"

He makes a face. "Long story."

"Ah, shit, man, I'm sorry." I shake my head.

"Yes." Barbie nods. "Nadia will be sad. She loves Hannah."

"Crap." J-Bo makes a face. "Sorry, man."

Conversation segues to training camp and which rookies we think are going to make the team. Our first draft pick this year seems to be a good player.

"I hear he's going back to college," Murph says. "Boston University."

"Probably for the best," I say. "Get him more experience, a little stronger."

"Yeah. I think Brickards will make it this year," Russ says.

We drafted the guy two years ago and last season he got called up for a few games and played well. "Yeah, I agree." I'm also aware that Brick plays left wing like me and could be my competition for a spot on that third line. Or maybe the second line? "Also it'll be interesting to see how the guys they signed over the summer fit in to the roster."

"Do you think things are going to be different this year, with the new team ownership?" I ask my buddies.

"Hard to say." Russ rubs his chin. "They did say they weren't going to make a lot of changes right away."

"They can say whatever they want," I point out. "It's what they do that matters."

"So cynical," Russ says.

"Realistic," I correct him.

"It adds a little pressure to training camp this year," Russ says.

"Oh, yeah." I'm already putting pressure on myself to do better, and having to prove myself to new owners doesn't help.

"They made some good moves over the summer," J-Bo says.

"According to Coach, that was all Brad," I say. Our general manager, Brad Julian, is a smart guy. "I think we're all glad Brad's still here."

"Yeah."

Russ shrugs. "The Hellers have lots of experience too."

All four brothers had great careers in the NHL. They moved on to other endeavors after they retired from playing. Tag managed the NHL team in Winnipeg for a long time.

"It has to be better than last year," J-Bo says. "All the bankruptcy rumors about Mr. D'Agostino made things kind of tense."

I tried to ignore all that, but yeah, it did play on our minds.

"It made him tense," Barbie says with a rueful smile. "He was a bear sometimes."

It definitely affected our play and despite a desperate run at the end, with several hard-fought wins, we finished out of a playoff spot.

We move on to some gossip about why the coach in Seattle got fired and a big social media disaster that unfolded on TikTok involving a few teams.

"Stay off social media," I say, shaking my head. "It's dangerous."

"Like a field full of land mines," Russ agrees. "We've all seen it."

"Like that picture of Kravchenko with a cucumber up his ass that got circulated all over the socials," I say.

"Christ. Yeah. His girlfriend was a whack job."

"I don't know why it was such a big embarrassment. Nothing wrong with a little back door play," Russ says.

The rest of us remain silent.

"Oh, come on," Russ says. "You all probably like it."

"Maybe so, but having your naked ass all over the internet is never great," I say.

"Also food up the butt is not a good idea," J-Bo adds.

"I saw a post on Reddit from a guy who wanted to put a cheeseburger up there," Russ says.

We all make horrified noises.

"Fuck off." I scowl at my buddy.

Russ laughs. "I swear. But it was Reddit. Who knows."

"That would definitely lead to an infection," I say with a shudder. "Jesus."

"Things can get sucked in there," J-Bo says. "Don't risk a trip to the ER with something weird up your butt."

"Have you watched that show 'Sex Sent Me to the ER?'" Barbie asks. "Holy shit, some people are weird."

"Evergreen comment," I agree.

We're all laughing now.

"I learned from that show never to eat hot sauce before going down on a woman," Russ says, to more laughter.

"I once gave a woman an orgasm so intense she ended up in the ER," J-Bo says.

We guffaw. "Bullshit."

He laughs. "Okay, it wasn't me. I saw it on TV."

"One chick got appendicitis from swallowing a condom."

This gets a roar of laughter loud enough to have other patrons in the restaurant looking at us.

"Okay, change of subject," Barbie says. "Let's talk about tart cherry juice."

I narrow my eyes at him. "Is that some kind of sex euphemism for virginity?"

He gives me a what-the-fuck look. "What? It's juice."

"Loco has a dirty mind," J-Bo says. That's my nickname. "Okay, what is it?"

"It's good for recovery," Barbie says. "Tons of nutrients. Helps with muscle soreness and strength."

"Huh." Russ tips his head. "Have you been drinking it?"

"Yes. I am a believer."

"I'd try it," I say.

"Make sure you get the kind with no sugar," Barbie says. "I read a book about recovery this summer."

"That's important for a guy your age," Russ deadpans, then cracks up when Barbie nails him with a glare.

"What else did it say?" I ask, always interested in doing better. "Anything new?"

"Whole foods rich in antioxidants, whole carbohydrates, and lean protein," Barbie says. "Also sleep. Lots of sleep. Seven to nine hours."

"I love sleep," I say with a sigh.

"You love being in bed," J-Bo corrects me.

"How do our conversations always come back to sex?" I demand.

"You're the one with the dirty mind." He shrugs.

It's tough to argue with that. I do have a dirty mind. I do like sex.

And now I'm thinking about Annie Bang again.

THREE

Logan

Later, I get home to my apartment on the eleventh floor of a newish high rise in the Lincoln Square neighborhood. It's easy to get to the practice facility in Westchester County from here, and also easy to take the subway to the arena on game nights. It's not a super swank building, but it's modern and spacious for New York. I like that it's close to the river with a walking path and lots of green space.

When I walk in my door, I'm attacked by a killer dog. Just kidding, Teemu isn't a killer, he's a goof and he's excited to see me. I've had him for about a year now. He's some kind of mix of terrier and poodle, we think, so not very big, with crackhead hair. He's really smart and cute. I'm not biased; this is objectively true.

I need to take him for his walk but first I head to my office and sit down in front of my laptop. Soon I'm googling Annie Bang. The pictures that come up are way different than the image she presented today, wearing a baggy black Bears track suit, sneakers, a ponytail, and no makeup. There are tons of photos of her in skimpy, glittery costumes with bright lips and false eyelashes. Her blond hair is up in a bun in some pics and long and loose in others. Wow. Stunning.

Fuck. That's irrelevant. This is a problem.

She's a coach.

It's still hard to wrap my head around it, but she's a fucking *coach*. I can't be leering at her tits and ass. I can't be thinking about putting my hands on her again. Definitely can't be thinking about kissing her and tasting her and—

She hates me.

And that pisses me off.

I don't know why. Yes, Annie Bang is hot. Like, set things on fire hot. I already knew that. Jesus, we spent basically a whole day and night together in bed, burning up the sheets, burning off athletic energy in sweaty, lusty games.

I close my laptop and turn to Teemu. "Okay, buddy, you've been patient. Let's go. Walk? Wanna go for a walk?"

Teemu knows those words and goes bananas, yipping and spinning while I grab my phone and my keys. I clip his leash onto his harness and take him for a nice long stroll along the river.

I'm skeptical of what Annie can teach us. I know there are a few other teams who've hired figure skaters as skating coaches, but we sure as shit don't need to know how to do triple axels and camel toe spins or whatever. I find myself unreasonably irritated by the prospect of learning how to skate. I *know* how to skate.

Put her out of your head.

Sure, sure.

"Okay, let's go home!" I say to my dog and we turn around.

In my bedroom, I throw myself down on the bed to nap and

Teemu joins me. I love napping. I love sleeping. It's my superpower.

I awake to my phone pinging. I fumble around for it and find a the group chat has blown up with dinner plans. I add my message that I'm in, then rub my eyes and check the time. Shit, I really crashed. It's nearly five.

Another text arrives.

> RUSS: Wanna play ping pong until we go?

> LOGAN: Okay Meet you down there in ten.

This building has a recreation room, as well as a gym, although I rarely use it since we work out at APF, the practice facility.

I strip off my clothes, scrub my face with cold water, and change into a pair of dark jeans and a fitted button-down shirt that'll be okay for dinner. I check my phone for any other messages—oh hey, there's one from Mindy, who I went out with last week. *Just saying hey.*

Do I want to respond? I'm not sure. I shove my phone into my pocket.

Russ and I get into a heated game of ping pong, smashing the little plastic ball back and forth across the table. Neither of us are that good, but we have eye and hand coordination and I also have a killer instinct, so I deliberately drive the ball into places that are hard for him to get to. I'm thrusting my arms into the air in triumph when Millsy and his wife Lilly walk in. They also live in the building.

I do a victory dance and Lilly laughs. "You guys," she says. "Not competitive at all."

"I play to win, baby," I say, moving toward her. "Hey, gorgeous."

"Hi, Logan." Her eyes sparkle up at me. She's really pretty and super nice and Millsy's a lucky guy.

"Want a turn?" I ask her, handing her my paddle.

"Sure!"

Russ turns his paddle over to Millsy and we watch them battle it out until the others show up—Josh Heller (Hellsy) and his wife Sara, Owen Cooke (Cookie) and his girlfriend Emerie —and we head out for dinner in the new restaurant the girls want to try.

"This place is fancier than I thought," I say as we're shown to a big, curved booth. The restaurant is called Brunswick Grill, so I expected something casual, but crystal chandeliers hang above us, the walls are all paneled in wood, and velvet drapes separate different parts of the restaurant.

"As long as the food is good." Millsy opens his menu.

The girls order wine but my teammates and I stick to water. There's a lot of seafood on the menu, as well as a lot of spicy dishes, and I debate what to have. I don't want anything that's going to slow me down tomorrow. I end up ordering grilled halibut, which comes with Mediterranean beans (protein and fiber) and something called salmoriglio, which I have to quickly google. It's a condiment made with lemon juice, olive oil, garlic, salt, and herbs. Sounds delicious. Hopefully it's not too garlicky or I'll reek on the ice tomorrow when I start sweating. Did I mention that I sweat a lot?

"So whaddya think of this new skating coach?" Millsy says after we've ordered.

"We've never had a skating coach," Russ says.

"And she's a figure skater."

"Right?" I say, ignoring who this coach is. Am I the only one who's figured it out? Not that they know Annie and I banged in Pyeongchang; but they know her brother. "What is a figure skater going to teach us?"

"Figure skaters have to be good skaters," Lilly ventures.

"Well, yeah, but it's different." I shrug.

"You know who her brothers are, right?" Millsy says.

Shit. I'm *not* the only one who's figured it out.

The guys all look at each other and the silence is dense.

Finally Russ speaks. "The Bang brothers." He nods. "Kingston. Jakob. Tanner. Leif." He pauses. "Jensen."

Millsy slants a glance my way, as do the other guys.

They all know Annie probably hates my guts for what I did.

My face tightens.

"You okay, Loco?" Hellsy asks, concern notching his eyebrows together.

"Oh yeah." I give a dismissive roll of my eyes. "Whatever."

"Why?" Sara looks around. "What happened?"

"I'll tell you later," Hellsy says in a low voice.

"It's not that big a deal," I say, striving for casual. "I got suspended after a late hit on Jensen Bang a few years ago."

"Oh." She blinks and nods. "Ohhhh. And she's his sister."

"Right. But she won't last long," I add confidently.

"Why do you say that?" Russ picks up his glass of water.

"Just a feeling. She looks pretty soft. She won't survive around all of us."

"She has five brothers who play hockey," Russ reminds me.

"Yeah, but this is a job. It won't be easy."

Russ makes a face. "Coach already told me I'll be working with her."

"Me too," Cookie admits.

I sigh. "Me too." Well, I won't be the only one. Especially the only veteran player. But this is a clear sign that things will definitely be different this year.

Ugh. I'm less than enthusiastic about this whole thing.

And it's not just because of who the skating coach is.

I can skate just fine.

Although…I do want to play better. I came to camp in the best shape of my life, with the goal of showing the team I can move up and play more minutes, that I can play faster and smarter.

I'm impatient for our scrimmages before season starts, and I'm impatient for the regular season to get going. I need to position myself to show them I'm good enough.

But I'm not convinced it's going to be because of a cute little blond figure skater.

FOUR

Annie

"How is Ivan?"

"He's good." I'm on the phone with my mom as I grab breakfast before heading to the practice facility. "Why?"

"Just curious. I'm so happy you two are together again."

I narrow my eyes at the way she says "together."

Ivan's my best friend. My former figure skating partner. And now my roommate in New York. I needed a place to live and he offered me his spare bedroom which was perfect until I can find a place of my own.

When Ivan and I skated together, after we won a few competitions and got somewhat known, especially after our first (and only) appearance at the Olympics, figure skating fans started shipping us. People loved our chemistry together on the ice and fantasized about our relationship off the ice. We could never understand why they cared that much, but apparently we did a good job selling the "romance" of our programs. Even though we denied we were in a relationship

LIGHT 'EM UP   33

and insisted to the media we were just friends, the shipping continued.

And one of our biggest shippers was my mom. In an interview, she once told a reporter that we were so close, our relationship was basically like a marriage.

She loves Ivan. I mean, looooves him. What's not to love? He's gorgeous, talented, charming, brave, disciplined, loyal, and respectful. I love him, too! Just not like "that." Not like my mom wanted me to love him.

"Mom..."

"What?" Mom replies.

"You're not getting ideas about us again, are you?"

"What do you mean?" The innocence in in her voice is clearly fake. She knows exactly what I mean.

"Just because we're living together doesn't mean there's any romance developing between us."

"Hmmm."

She doesn't sound convinced.

"Seriously, Mom."

"Living together in such close proximity can trigger other kinds of feelings. Romantic feelings."

"No. It's not happening."

"Well. We'll see. So, when can I come visit?"

I make a face that she luckily can't see. I love my mom, I do, I just can't handle a visit from her right now. "We only have two bedrooms here in Ivan's apartment. One bathroom. There's not even a bathtub!"

"Oh no! I know you love a nice long soak in the tub."

"Yeah." I sigh. "Anyway, there's not a lot of room for visitors."

"Oh that's okay! I can stay in a hotel. I don't want to barge in on you. I just want to see you."

I bite my lip. "I'm a little stressed, starting the new job. I've been super busy. I haven't even finished unpacking. Maybe next month sometime?"

"I could come sooner and help you!"

I laugh. She probably could. She's a diehard hockey mom. "Just give me a little more time to settle in."

She sighs. "Okay, fine. I don't want to make things harder for you. But I can't wait to see Ivan again!"

I repress a scream. "I'm sure he'll love to see you, too."

He will. He loves my mom as much as she loves him.

"Have you heard from your brother?"

"Which one?" I ask dryly. I've heard from all of them in the last couple of days, wishing me good luck at my new job, wanting to know how things are going.

"Jensen! You need to meet Bailey! She's absolutely perfect for him and he's so happy."

"I did talk to him the other day. And yeah...he does sound happy." And I'm happy for him. "Okay, Mom, I have to go to work."

"Well, call me later then. I want to hear more about the new job!"

I end the call as Ivan saunters out from his room, bare chested, wearing low-slung sweatpants. His thick, sun-kissed brown curls that are his trademark hang onto his forehead and cover his neck.

"Who were you talking to, Banger?" he asks around a yawn. He opens the fridge door and pokes his head in.

"My mom. She wants to come visit."

"Oh, nice."

"I put her off."

"Of course you did."

I frown. "What does that mean?"

"When your mom told you not to do something, you did it twice. And took pictures."

I snort-laugh. "That's not true."

"Oh, come on, it is. You've rebelled against your parents your whole life."

I pout. "Well, you know I couldn't play hockey, much as they wanted it."

"I know."

"They thought figure skating was ridiculous. They were wrong."

"They were. In that case. How about the illegal tattoo you got when you were sixteen? And the times we were traveling, and you refused to check in with them because 'you were fine.'"

I roll my lips in.

"Smoking weed?"

"Oh, come on, everyone does that now."

"Not so much ten years ago. And your parents hated it."

I can't stop my smile. "Yeah."

"You painted your bedroom walls black without them knowing."

"Every teenager pushes boundaries. It's part of growing up."

"Okay, what about the time you almost got suspended by the figure skating club because you got drunk at a party?"

I drop my gaze. "Scared straight," I mutter. "My parents were so pissed, but the threat of getting suspended or kicked out scared the shit out of me." I sigh. "Okay, you have a point. But I'm not like that anymore. I'm all grown up."

"Okay."

"Really! It's just not a good time for her to visit! And fair warning...she's getting ideas about us again. Because we're living together."

"Stella's so cute." He backs out of the fridge with a quart of milk in his hand. "Is this still good?"

"I don't know, it's yours. I hate milk. Unless it's in coffee."

He sniffs it. "Seems fine. So when is she coming?"

"Not until next month. This isn't a good time, in the middle of training camp."

"Okay. It'll be fun to see her again."

"She's excited to see you." I roll my eyes. "I think she wants to see *you* more than me."

He laughs and pours cereal into a bowl. "Doubtful."

I toss my orange peel, slide my dishes into the dishwasher, and wash my hands. "Okay, I'm outta here."

"This is the perfect job for you."

"Right?" I wiggle excitedly. "I loved coaching at Bayard, but this is the NHL! Finally, I'm at the same level as my brothers."

He cocks his head to one side and gives me a gentle smile. "It's not a competition. I've always told you that."

"Oh, come on. Everything's a competition." I jerk my chin at him. "Mr. Competitive."

He laughs. "Okay, yeah. But now my killer instinct is for the kids I coach, not myself."

Ivan coaches too, but it's figure skaters.

"I'm not home for dinner tonight," he reminds me.

"Right. Hot date."

"Let's hope." He asked out another figure skating coach for the first time.

"You need to have a girlfriend by the time my mom comes. That'll stop her."

He grins and reaches over to tug my ponytail. "Or you could have a boyfriend."

"Ha ha. Like that's going to happen. Okay, gotta go."

HEADING TO MY OFFICE, eyes on my phone as I rush down the hall, I don't see the big body in front of me until we bash into each other.

"Oof!" I stagger backward and drop my phone. Luckily the cement wall is right here and I fall against it instead of the floor. "Jesus Christ!"

"Whoa!" The deep male voice has my head jerking up as large hands grab my arms. "Watch where you're going, there."

"What the—" My eyes fly open in outrage and I see Logan Coates standing before me.

"Mini Bang," he says quietly.

Oh God. Why did I ever tell him my family called me that?

Heat floods my veins as I stare at him, transfixed. My knees quiver. "*You* watch where you're going," I snap. "And don't call me Mini Bang." I bend and snatch my phone to inspect it for damage. Luckily the protective case is a heavy duty one, because my phone takes a lot of abuse.

Logan steps back, lips quirked. "But it's so cute." He pauses, one corner of his mouth lifting more. "But I guess I should call you Coach Bang."

Is he serious? Or yanking my chain? I give him a bright smile. "Coach Bang is *perfect*."

And I step around him and march to my office.

Asshole.

I've got a little adrenaline rush going from that collision and in my tiny office I pace around, doing some deep breathing, talking to myself to settle myself down. Okay. Now we've run into each other. Literally. No big deal.

Mother of cake, he's still hot.

I close my eyes and go very still. It's okay. I can do this.

From the first time we met, that last day of the Olympics, there was a connection between us. We flirted. It was so easy and fun with him. He found out I was a figure skater and teased me about it not being a real sport. He looked at me like I was beautiful and fascinating.

I haven't felt that tug of attraction for anyone for a long time. I scrunch my face up, forced to admit I haven't felt that kind of magnetism since the first night I met him.

I didn't date much while I lived in Ridgedale. And when I was competing, I didn't really have time for boyfriends. My life was practices, competitions, and trying to keep up with school-work. Now, I'm trying to focus on my new job. And suddenly I'm derailed by thoughts of hot, sweaty, physical sex in the athlete's village.

He's the *last* man I can be attracted to, after what he did to Jensen.

I head to the ice, following the players as they make their way down the rubber mat from the dressing room. These practices are open to the public and a bunch of kids have gathered along the line control barriers set up. Some of the players tramp right by them, others slow down to acknowledge them. Logan Coates makes a point of fist bumping every kid who sticks their hand out. His smile is disturbingly engaging. The kids all notice it too, buzzing amongst themselves and their indulgent parents who also respond to Logan's grin.

He's a real charmer.

This pisses me off.

I glare at his retreating back with the big number 17 on it.

He took my brother down so hard he ended up in the hospital and was out for months. It looked bad. It looked dirty. Social media went nuts about it, vilifying Logan. I couldn't believe it was the same guy who'd...well, let's not go there. I was pissed that he'd hurt my brother and ready to do him harm if he ever came within punching distance of me.

The guy who did that shouldn't be blithely fist bumping and smiling at little kids.

I was worried sick about my brother and furious about what had happened, and I was even more pissed off because it happened the same day I was competing in the Four Continents event in Seoul. I considered withdrawing, but my family and Ivan and our coach convinced me to stay in the competition. I didn't know how I was going to go out there and focus on our routine when my brother was in the hospital in Los Angeles, but somehow I did. It took every bit of discipline and focus I'd learned over the years. We didn't win or even medal and we probably wouldn't have anyway, but I always wondered if that had impacted my performance.

Jensen got better and did play again, with no permanent damage from that ugly hit.

But now here I am face to face with the man I now consider a monster. And that old rage and resentment are gouging at my insides again.

I have to get my emotions under control. This is my job. I have to prove myself. I can't do that hating on one of the players. I have to be able to work with this guy.

AFTER A FEW DAYS of training camp, the exhibition games begin. Not every guy plays in every game, so I'm watching all of them. By this point, we have a good idea which players will make the cuts, and that starts formally happening the day after the first game, when three players are released. A few days later, eleven more guys are cut. I think they did what they needed to—they got on our radar, showed us what kind of player they are, and then when we need to call someone up, we'll know who.

I have to say I'm reluctantly impressed with Logan. He's not a rookie, he's got a few seasons of experience, and is probably a lock to make the team. But he gives his all out there every time he gets on the ice. I can't fault his work ethic.

Now it's time for the tough decisions. We're all in the big meeting room at the practice facility, sitting around the long table. Some of the guys are old school with papers strewn in front of them. I've got my computer with all my notes.

"He's played center and right wing," Gary says about one of the young guys who has been playing in the AHL. "He did some great things with the puck."

"Do we think he can be a full-time center?" Brad Julian asks.

"I think so," Gary says.

"Yeah, I do, too," Viktor says. "He's got confidence with the puck and a nice set of hands."

"But if we needed another winger, he could go there," Scott says.

I nod along with this, in agreement.

We move on to another player, Jack Wasylyk, who was given a professional tryout.

"I've been impressed by his—" I start.

"He doesn't have a lot of experience," Scott interrupts me.

I blink at him, then glance around the table. Everyone's listening to Scott. Ooookay.

I try again. "I think with a little—"

"I like him," Brad says. "But what about Lavoie?"

They debate the two players and which one should get a chance.

"I think Wasylyk has the advantage—"

Brad cuts me off again.

Frustration is an expanding balloon in my gut. I inhale a deep breath, straighten my shoulders, and make eye contact with Brad. "Brad, I'm going to finish my point," I say firmly, leaning forward. I'm not apologizing for talking. I'm not asking if I can talk. I'm *telling* him. "These two players have different skating abilities and based on what I've been learning, I can see Wasylyk fitting in with our vision a lot better than Lavoie. He's relentless pursuing the puck, he has great stick skills, and with a bit of coaching, his skating skills could make him a really great forechecker."

Silence descends. I catch Tag Heller's raised eyebrows, then Jase Heller's lip twitch.

"Go on, Annie," Tag says.

I make my point, outlining my observations, sounding confident, and this time nobody interrupts me.

"HOW DID TODAY GO? Did you axe people?"

"There was a lot of manterrupting." I twirl my fork into the spaghetti Ivan made for us for dinner. "Ugh."

He laughs. "Manterrupting?"

"Yeah. I'm sure I don't have to explain that to you."

"I guess not, no."

"For some reason I didn't expect to have to deal with this here. They knew they were hiring a woman. Why wouldn't they listen to me?"

"Fuckers," he says. "They should totally listen to you."

"Right?" I stab a piece of tomato in my salad. "Eventually I did get them to listen. I had to learn to deal with it at Bayard. You have to be assertive. Use strong body language. Sound confident." I roll my eyes. "Men."

"Yeah, men suck."

I laugh. "Also, we don't 'axe' players."

"Fire them?"

"We *release* them," I say.

"Wow, that sounds so much better."

I roll my eyes, trying not to laugh. "It's hard because all these guys want it so bad. There's one guy I really feel for—he's young but a couple of years ago he got cancer and couldn't play."

"Oh, wow. That's awful."

"Yeah. He beat cancer, though. He's on a PTO."

Ivan tips his head.

"Professional tryout. It's for unsigned players. It gives them a chance to show their skills and hopefully earn a full-time contract."

"Is he going to make it?"

"I think so." I smile. "He seems to have really worked hard to get healthy. I really feel for the guy."

"You have to make decisions on their ability though, right? Not on how bad you feel for them."

"That's true. It's a business." I make a face. "And that meeting was all business."

FIVE

Logan

I'm alone on the ice when Annie jumps out and joins me. I shoot the puck at the empty net, then skate toward her. It's our first "skating lesson."

We've encountered each other a few times over the last couple of weeks, since the day I crashed into her and knocked her phone out of her hand. And each time, I've met with cool aloofness. It wouldn't bother me, except I've seen her interact with the other guys with easy joking and smiles. Clearly, it's just me she hates.

I glide closer, holding my stick in both hands. "This is bullshit."

She blinks. "Excuse me?"

"I don't need to learn how to skate," I grit out. "Why am I here?"

Her jaw tightens "You think *I* want you here?" She leans closer to spit out the words in a low voice. "Get over yourself, Loco."

We glare at each other.

She glances up at the box where Coach Shipton is watching us and sucks in a long, slow breath. "Look, I get it," she says quietly. "You know how to skate. That's not what this is about. It's about getting *better*."

My back teeth grind together.

"*Easier*," she adds emphatically.

"I'm gonna talk to Coach."

She appears unfazed. "You can talk to him if you like. He and I and Viktor made the decisions about these coaching sessions together."

I feel like bashing my stick over the boards.

"I see you're frustrated." She keeps her voice low as the other guys appear and jump onto the ice. "I'm only asking that you keep an open mind and give it a shot." She lifts a hand in greeting to the others and pushes back on her blades. "Morning, guys!"

We're all in full gear, skating leisurely around. Annie's in her Bears track suit and hockey skates, wearing pink mitts. Jesus.

She gathers us near the boards before starting.

"Okay, guys, you're the lucky ones who get the first session!" She gives us a cheeky grin. "But don't worry, you're not the only ones! I want to say a couple of things because we haven't worked together before. I am not here to teach you how to skate. You all *know* how to skate. You play in the NHL. I'm here to make things *easier* for you. And yeah, it might be a little hard learning some new things and doing things differently, but I get results and I promise you if you work with me, your skating will be easier and better."

None of us say a word.

"I know some of you are skeptical about what a figure skater can teach you." Her gaze slides over and collides with mine. My eyebrows draw together as I meet her eyes. "Figure skating is a very technical sport. Every turn you do is marked— your entry to a turn, your exit from a turn, whether it's an inside edge or an outside edge. Speed and execution are so precise and so technical. That kind of technical ability really can help hockey players. At the end of the day, it's not figure skating, it's just *skating*."

The rookies, Adam Wong and Garret Brickards, nod.

"We're going to work on basic elements. Forward and backward skating, crossovers, your edges, and your turning. First let's warm up and do a lap. Let's go!"

We all take off skating, me bringing up the rear with a decided lack of enthusiasm.

"Faster!" she yells.

With an eye roll, I pick up the pace.

Annie joins us and then my eyes widen as she sails past us. My legs are pumping hard. Hers are barely moving. And she's flying by me. What the fuck.

After a turn around the rink, she comes to a halt with an aggressive two-foot hockey stop and grins at us. "Okay, great! Come on over here." She moves over to a faceoff ring and starts skating backwards around it, demonstrating what she wants us to do. "Starting with backward crossovers. Keep your body lined up over the line on the ice. Your knee, hip, and shoulders should all be in line..." She uses a hand to draw an imaginary line up the side of my body. "And we're going to start with little half swizzles, so with your outside leg pump...out...and in. Out...and in." She shows us. "Make sure you're looking back but not turning your body. Okay, go!"

We get in a line and follow her, then she glides away from the ring to watch.

I don't fucking want to do this. It's infantile and pointless. "Too easy," I mutter.

"Back in Peewee again," Jake the Snake says with an eye roll.

"We never even did this in Peewee hockey," I reply. "Jesus, we're not kids."

Annie shoots us a tight, cold smile. It's a little terrifying. She skates over to Jake. "Hold on. The key is body alignment. Your alignment is off. And that means the entire kinetic chain of movement is off." She corrects his posture. "Knee, hip, and shoulder all in line...like this."

He scowls.

She corrects me, too, and I can't stop my scowl.

We circle one more time, then she stops us and has us go the other direction, progressing to lifting one foot, then moving on to crossovers. I heave a sigh.

"No need for speed!" Annie calls to me as I get going faster. "This is about being steady and aligned."

I shoot her a black look.

"Okay, watch me again." She joins us on the circle. "See how I'm really reaching with my inside leg? And then sweeping under..." She does it again, and again, then gets us doing it, once again with impatient looks from all of us.

"Come on guys, enough with the attitude!" She laughs, making it a joke. But not really. "Okay, Adam...make sure you're pushing with that outside edge...there...yes, like that. Do it again..." She watches until satisfied, then moves to guide me. "Let's practice a spiral..."

"What the fuck? I'm not doing any spins."

"No, not a spin, a spiral. Hold yourself on one foot...keep that leg up...lean in a little...like that." I glide on one foot. And fuck me, I wobble. Just a bit. "Exactly. Practice doing those."

She moves to the other guys and gives them some one-on-one pointers. "Slide that outside foot across horizontally," she tells Garret. "Like this." She slows the motion to show him what she means. "Heel turns in aaaand...slide across. You got it!"

She watches us more, then says, "Okay. Let's focus on really *reaching* with that inside leg...really reach! That's where your power comes from. Reach! Reach! Yeah!" After a few minutes where I'm not really reaching, she stops us. "Okay, did you feel that? Did you feel the power when you focused on that inside leg?"

"Yeah!" Adam says. "I did."

Jake and I give him a cynical look.

Annie glares challengingly at us. "You didn't feel it?'

I shrug.

Her lips thin. "Okay, when figure skaters head into a jump, we skate backward. Mostly. Watch."

She heads across the ice then skates back toward us, backward, lengthening her stride, getting low, and then propels herself off her inside edge, makes one full rotation in the air, and lands smoothly. In fucking hockey skates.

When she sees our expressions, she looks like she's trying not to laugh. I hurriedly school my features into unimpressed boredom.

"See when I was going backward...can you picture Kingston Bang lining someone up for a filthy open-ice hit?"

We all bark out out surprised laughs. Yeah, I can see it.

She grins. "Let's practice it again. Imagine that's what you're doing."

I see some of the other guys waiting to come on the ice. It's time for our regular practice. Thank God.

It's hard to believe a pretty little blonde with long pink fingernails and pink lip gloss and pink mitts is going to teach us how to skate. We're hockey players, for fuck's sake.

But she's already set us on our asses when she lapped us skating. Jesus, it didn't even look like she was trying hard. Then she jumped in the air and twirled, landing on one foot so grace-fully it kind of made my heart stutter. What the fuck.

But still, figure skating is entirely different from a hockey game. And I still don't want to be here, no matter how sexy the coach is.

And there it is again...she's a coach.

"Deeper knee bends, Garret!" she calls. "Yeah!" She pumps her fists in the air, appearing genuinely delighted at his performance.

"Okay, we're done for today," Annie tells us. "If you have some extra time to practice those backward crossovers, that would be great. I'll see how you're doing on Thursday. Thanks, guys!"

Annie glides away effortlessly, greeting the other guys as she leaves. They all swarm onto the ice. As I skate past the bench, Coach waves me down. "Logan!" He jerks his head, signalling me to come over. I stop at the board and look at him inquiringly.

I'm sweating.

I always sweat, but today I'm *really* sweating.

"Look, I was watching you out there."

I smile. Yeah, I saw him about halfway through the session. He's going to tell me I don't need to worry about this.

Keeping his voice low, he says, "I need you to have a better attitude about this. It's not respectful to Annie, and it's not respectful to your teammates to be rolling your eyes and making smart ass comments."

I freeze and stare at him. Then heat flows up my neck and into my face. "Uh..."

"Nobody's going to take this seriously if our veteran players don't. Those rookies out there are looking to you as an example."

I swallow.

"You told us you have goals this year. That you want to play better, get more minutes. This is a way for you to do that and you didn't look like you even gave a shit. Did you mean what you said?"

"Yeah," I croak out, my face burning.

"Because talk is cheap. Actions speak louder than words. Hold on, I can probably think of a few more clichés."

I try for a smile.

"It's true though. We're looking to see how you follow up those words with actions." He pauses and meets my eyes. "Got it?"

I nod. "Yeah." My voice rasps again. "I got it."

"Good." He slaps the dasher board. "Okay, guys let's go!"

I skate over to join the boys gathered around Viktor who's got a white board out.

Shit.

I work to focus on what our assistant coach is telling us, trying to shut out my anger. Bad enough that I have to do these "skating lessons" never mind that Coach called me on my attitude. Yeah, I'm pissed.

I throw myself into practice, skating my ass off, shooting hard, aggressively fighting for the puck in battle drills. My thoughts are circling at the back of my brain the whole time, but I blow off adrenaline physically and by the time we're done and I'm collapsed onto the bench in the locker room, my mind is quieter. I slowly take off my gear and let myself think, blanking out the guys yakking.

Earlier, I was pissed. Now I'm embarrassed. Maybe a little ashamed.

Under the spray of the shower, I can admit I felt insulted by the fact that I've been told I need to improve my skating. Resentful. I blamed Annie for that. And I acted juvenile.

I'm better than that.

Now the one I'm angry with is myself.

"Come on, Loco!" Cookie calls to me. "My grandma runs backwards faster than you move."

I flip him off and slam my locker shut. "I'm coming. Jesus. What's the rush?"

He and Millsy give me similar looks, with a raised eyebrow. They exchange glances.

"You seem crusty," Cookie says.

"Was your skating lesson that bad?" Millsy asks. "It sucks to have to learn to skate all over again."

I glare at him.

He laughs. "I get my lesson tomorrow. Come on, man. We all have stuff to learn." He slings an arm around my shoulders and herds me out of the locker room.

"How was it?" Cookie asks.

I shrug. "It was fine.

I don't tell them that Annie Bang skated circles around us. They'll see that for themselves. I also don't tell them that Coach gave me shit for being a dickhead. I'm definitely not letting on how shitty I feel. I'll sit with that a little longer until it doesn't sting so much.

Goddammit, I'm such an idiot.

I beat myself up the entire ride home, sitting in the back seat while the other guys yammer on about our season opener tomorrow night. Why am I even trying to do better? I'll never get more ice time. I'll never make the second line. Probably not even the third. If I don't even try, I won't feel so bad. I should keep playing the way I always have. But even that was never good enough for my dad.

I LINE UP WAITING for Murph to take the faceoff. I'm on a line with him and Burr—the third line. A step in the right direction.

Except...Brick is playing on the second line. The new guy. Coach is trying some new line combinations for our season opener, and he had to juggle things because Millsy's out tonight puking his guts out with some kind of flu bug, but I'm a little pissed that the new guy is playing with Cookie and Axe, who moved up from the third line as well to fill the holes left by Bergie and Red.

Sanders on the Condors' defense plants himself next to me and gives me a sneer. "You think you're as tough as your old man. You're not."

He's said shit like that before. It pisses me off. I don't know how that motherfucker knows what to say to get under my skin. It's *his* superpower, I guess.

I'm already irritated and I have to fight to ignore him.

Murph wins the faceoff and gets the puck right to me. I've got it on my blade and ready to shoot at the net, but before I can do it, Sanders knocks me off it and steals it. *Asshole!*

He passes to another Condor and they're off down the ice toward our end. Luckily Jammer and Nate are on them, keeping them to the outside, taking away a chance to shoot. Sanders has the puck again and I go at him, laying a hard hit on him against the boards.

The fans cheer.

Murph snaps up the puck and heads back toward their net and I start off after him when Sanders whacks his stick across my legs.

"Fuck!" My first instinct is to stop and go back at him. But somehow my second thought kicks in and I keep skating after Murph. The crowd is roaring for a penalty but the refs are fucking blind. Murph passes to Burr, who passes to me. I get it back to Murph now on the Condor's blue line, ready to go to the net, but as I do, a Condor player comes between us and intercepts the puck.

Fuck!

He grabs it and he's off, flying down the ice. I take off after him as do J-Bo and Barbie. I'm pushing so fucking hard but there's no way I can catch that guy. J-Bo is a fast skater and almost catches him, and Barbie's too late. I trip over the blue line (not really, fuck me, it just feels like it) sliding flat and uselessly on my chest as the Condor player shoots the puck and scores.

We lose the game three-one.

The mood in the room is gloomy after. I know from experience I can't beat myself up over a mistake, but it's hard not to. My turnover cost us the game. And I've never felt like such a shitty skater as when I tried to chase that Condors forward. My limbs feel heavy as I shower and change, and the sour taste in my mouth lingers.

Then I check my phone and see the texts from Dad.

> You should have gone after that asshole Sanders. You gotta toughen up.

Guess I should have known he wouldn't like that, even though Sanders ended up taking a penalty. I know I did the right thing, but it sucks that Dad always has to criticize.

And another one.

> Watch where you're passing!

Like I don't know that. My shoulders slump and my gut cramps. This one he's right about. I fucked up and I know it. Everyone knows it.

SIX

Annie

A knock at the door of the video room has my head popping up from where I'm staring at a computer monitor. Two women about my age are standing in the open doorframe—one taller, her long brown hair rich with red highlights, her eyes a dark blue, the other with wildly wavy long brown hair and stunning light greenish-blue eyes. They're both smiling at me.

I tilt my head. "Hi."

"You're Annie Bang, right?"

"Yes, I am." I push back from my desk and smile.

"I'm Sara Heller." The one with messy golden brown hair steps forward, hand outstretched. I rise and shake it. "Josh Heller's wife."

"Ah. Of course. Nice to meet you."

"And I'm Lilly Miller, Easton's wife."

"Good to meet you, too."

"We wanted to pop by and meet you," Sara says. "You've got these guys all befuzzled."

"Befuzzled?" My eyebrows shoot up.

Sara laughs. "Yeah. Sorry. Josh always makes up new words out of two. Now I'm doing it."

"I get the meaning."

"We think it's so funny that a woman coach has caused so much mayhem for these guys." Lilly chortles. "It's hilarious. They're so confused."

"Um...okay." I bite my lip, both amused and uncertain.

"We had to meet the girl boss who's kicking their butts." Sara grins. "You're not what I expected."

"No?" I grin.

"I knew you were a figure skater, but somehow I expected someone big and tough, the way Josh talks about you."

"I am tough."

"I bet you are." Sara laughs. "Sorry, you know what I mean."

"No worries, I do."

"You're just a little thing," Lilly says. "That makes it even better."

They seem highly amused by this.

"Can we take you for coffee?" Lilly asks. "Josh and Easton are working out and we're hanging around."

Today is a day off. No game, no practice. I do have a meeting with team management later, but I came in early and used the gym to do a workout; staying in shape is important to me since I no longer skate hours a day. Now I'm watching video from last night's game. Our video coach, Cal Crider set me up here in the video room before heading out. During games he's in here watching the game on multiple screens along with assistant video coach Clay Forbes, who's in communication with assistant coach Meknikov on the bench through an earpiece. Cal is a master of the software used to edit video and has been a huge help to me.

"Sure. I could use a break." We go into the deserted players' lounge and get coffees.

"So what were you doing in there?" Lilly asks. "Tell us everything about your job. I'm so curious!"

"I was watching video from last night's game." I tell them what I'm looking for and the kinds of things I work on with the players. They have questions about my background and figure skating. And I learn more about them. Lilly runs a dog walking business that she absolutely loves after working in the hospitality industry, and it turns out I know Sara's podcast. She still uses her maiden name for her podcast and influencer work so I never made the connection.

"I'm having coffee with a celebrity," I say to her.

She laughs. "I think you have experience with celebrities, with your family. Your brothers all play hockey, right?"

"And my dad used to."

Then we get into discussion about our families. They're super easy to talk to, engaging and bright, and it's fun having girl talk with women my age.

I glance at the clock on the wall and see I need to get going. "I better go." I stand and pick up all three mugs and carry them over to the counter. "I have a meeting with the big bosses at the Apex Center."

"Oooh." Sara grins. "Is one of them my father-in-law?"

"As a matter of fact, yes." I make a face. "Wish me luck."

"I think you're doing great," she assures me. "And Tag is awesome."

"This was fun," Lilly says. "We should hang out again sometime."

"That would be great."

Josh and Easton show up then, finished with their workouts, so I head back to my office.

I'm ready for my meeting.

I've trained with everyone on the team a few times. I've gone over all my notes and video that Clay, the video assistant, did with me on the ice. I've narrowed down my list of players who need more intensive coaching.

Some of the guys are tentatively accepting of it. Others are neutral. A couple of guys are still resistant. One of them is Logan.

But his resistance is more subtle than it was at first. He's not making smartass remarks to his teammates or laughing at what I want them to do. He does what I ask him, but I still sense he doesn't want to be here. Well, I don't want anything to do with him either, but I'm swallowing my antipathy to do my job. I guess he's basically doing the same. But it's still uncomfortable.

I'm nervous that the guys who aren't particularly amenable to this whole idea may have made their feelings known to management, which could reflect badly on me.

I make my way to Coach Shipton's office. As I enter the room, I'm almost knocked backward by a wall of testosterone. I'm greeted by a whole bunch of former athletes—all men. I'm used to this, though. And I've practiced my assertive communication skills in my head in case of more manterrupting or mansplaining.

Of the Hellers, Jase is here, but not Tag. Then there's Brad, Gary, Viktor, and assistant GM Dale Townsend. I greet them all and take a seat at the table, surreptitiously wiping my palms on my black trousers.

"Thanks for meeting with us today," Brad begins. "We know it's early in the season but we wanted to check in with you and see how things are going."

"I'm happy to update you." I open my folder. Then, looking at each one of them in turn, I go through my notes on the players and my goals for each of them. "There's not much I can teach Jay Bobak. He apparently took figure skating lessons as a kid and he's got a really great foundation of skills."

"He's a great skater," Gary agrees.

"Are the guys cooperating?" Brad asks. "I've heard rumblings that some of them aren't impressed about having to 'learn to skate.'"

"They're all cooperating. Yes, some of them are still skeptical. But I've encountered this before, and once we make some progress and they see the benefits to their game, they'll be on board."

"I've seen the change in attitude already," Gary notes. "With some of them anyway. I give you a lot of credit for knowing how to deal with the resistance. I've watched you out there and you're confident and knowledgeable. You also know how to make it fun."

"Thanks."

"We've seen the players impressed with your own skating abilities," Viktor notes. "That goes a long way to help convince them you know what you're doing."

I nod.

"We're really pleased so far," Brad adds.

Whew. I try not to show my relief. And pride. "Thank you. I'm glad. I'm enjoying it. It's very rewarding when I see the results."

"I'm glad we listened to you on Jack Wasylyk," Jase says to me. "So far he's really fitting in."

Warmth spreads through my chest. "Good."

We talk a bit more about the forward lines and defense pairings and discuss a couple of players who've been healthy scratches lately only because there haven't been injuries or other issues taking players out. "I think Adam would benefit with playing with the Corsairs." The team's AHL affiliate.

"They all would," Gary says. "Rather than riding the pine."

Okay. My comment was superfluous. My cheeks heat.

"Good reminder, though," Brad says. "When we're making roster decisions for both teams. We have to think long term as well as what's needed right now."

Okay, he got it.

We chat a bit more and then the meeting ends and I return to the video room.

Okay. That went well. Whew.

After an hour, I take a break, stand and stretch. I step out of my office to go grab a drink from the machine in the players' lounge. It's quiet here, with only a few other people around; the equipment manager is doing laundry and checking equipment; one of the trainers is working with Kevin Beaven, who strained something last night. I hear skates on the ice. Curious, I change direction and walk down the tunnel.

Not all the lights are on, which gives the ice a different feel—calmer, more laid back. There's one person on the ice, wearing hockey gear, but he's not shooting the puck or doing drills—he's skating.

Logan.

I hang back, watching him. He's clearly working on his edges, like we did the other day, but he hasn't quite got the moves down. My chest fills with a softness and I bite my lip. Should I leave?

Then he spots me. He stops.

My feet move me forward to the boards. "Hey."

"Hey." He doesn't move and even across the ice I can see his displeasure.

I've tried to ignore his rancor during our lessons, chalking it up to pride. He doesn't think he needs to improve his skating. It's not personal.

But I have to admit, sometimes it feels personal. Right now, it feels personal. And I don't know why that bugs me, because the feeling is mutual.

He glides toward me. "Look, Coach, I'm doing my homework."

"I see that. Gold star."

"What are you doing here?"

"Watching video."

His chin gives a slight dip. "You do that a lot."

"It helps me do my job."

Another small nod. "I guess." He pins me with a look. "Watching video of me?"

"Of course." I smile, but it's stiff. "Of everyone. What are you working on?" I ask the question even though I know.

"Edges."

"Want some help?" I tense as I await his response, sure he's going to say no.

After a couple of beats, he says, "Sure."

Surprise floods my veins with heat. I look down at my feet. "Let me go put on my skates."

With a nod he glides backward away from me.

I hurry to my office and grab my skates and a hoodie, then return to the ice. Sitting on the bench, I switch my trainers out for blades. Then I pull the big sweatshirt over my head and step onto the ice.

I skate over to Logan. "Start with a two-foot slalom." I do it to show him.

He follows me.

"Down on the curve...up on the straight to change edges." I nod. "Okay, now one foot slalom."

This is harder.

"Press into the ice with your knee and ankle to keep your momentum up. Bend...rise up...bend...rise up...hold on, you're swinging your free leg too much. And..." I move closer to him and put my hands on his shoulders. "Left shoulder back, right shoulder back..."

He's so big. And sweaty. For some reason, that amuses me.

"That's better. Okay, now keep your free leg back. You can't use it, you have to really work hard with *this* leg." Again, I show him, and we skate side by side.

"This is harder."

"Yeah, for sure." We go around the ice once, then I make him change legs.

He groans. "I hate doing it on my left leg."

I grin. "I know. Me too. We all have a dominant leg. But you have to be strong on both."

"Ugh."

"This'll get you used to really sinking down and lowering your center of gravity to the ice."

And he goes lower still.

"Rotate your shoulders and hips. Yeah...sink down in the knees. Really feel the edge, leaning into the side..."

He leans in, his blade carving into the ice.

"Hockey players often have trouble with outside edges," I say. "Inside edges are more natural for most skaters. Bring that leg all the way around and twist the outside edge every time you change feet." I demonstrate again.

We keep doing it, over and over, and even as I watch it gets easier for him. More natural.

"I know you're skeptical, but it will help," I say as we come to a stop. My heart's pumping faster from the exertion and I feel a little sweaty, too. "The deeper your edge, the sharper your turns and curves are."

He meets my eyes and I'm struck by the clearness of his eyes and the lean angles of his face that are so attractive. He's even bigger and more imposing in his gear.

"Try it," I say. "I'll play defense."

His lips twitch. "You need a stick."

"I'll go grab one."

With a borrowed stick in my hands, the shortest one I could find but still too long, I face him. He's playing with a puck on his blade and looks up and grins at me.

Oh hell. That grin is devastating.

"Don't laugh at me," I say easily. "I can play a little defense."

"Uh huh. I'd crush you in a game, Mini Bang."

"You'd have to catch me first. Come on."

He picks up the puck on his blade and skates away from me, circles, then starts back toward me, picking up speed. As he gets closer, he curls right. I move right. He goes left, curves behind me and shoots the puck in the net. He thrusts a fist in the air.

"There. Those were some sick edges. You're ready for some other drills."

His eyebrows shoot up, but he follows my lead again and I get him doing some even tougher moves, jumping from foot to foot, doing tight turns with one hand on the ice, and more.

Finally we both stop. He shakes off a glove and swipes a hand over his forehead. "You're trying to kill me, aren't you."

I tug at the neckline of my hoodie. "Nah. I may not like you much, but I don't want you dead."

He goes still, his eyes on my face. "So you admit it."

I work to keep my face expressionless. *Shit.* "Don't worry, I don't let it affect my work."

His eyes tighten at the corners. "It's because of what happened with Jensen, isn't it?'

I tilt my head. "What do you think?"

"You didn't hate me before that happened."

We look at each other, the air around us going electric. We're both thinking of Pyeongchang.

No. I didn't hate him then.

Propping his hands on the butt end of his stick, he lifts his chin. His mouth is beautiful, distracting me from this awkward conversation. "Will you let me buy you a coffee?"

I almost flinch at the unexpected words. "What?"

"Coffee. Let's go have a coffee."

"I...don't..."

"I want to apologize."

My eyes fly open wide. "Uh..."

He gives me another look, eyebrows raised, lips pursed, waiting. I'm picking up what he's putting down—I'd be a bitch to turn down an apology.

"Okay," I finally say, a little grudgingly. "We can grab a coffee here..."

He shakes his head. "Too many people around."

"There's no one here."

"Yeah, there is. This is between you and me."

It's my turn to push my lips out. "Okay."

"There's a little place across the street, on the corner. Betty's. I'll meet you there. I need a shower." He wrinkles his nose.

"Okay."

I could probably use a shower, too, my unexpected activity testing the performance of my Lady Speed Stick. Not as much as him, though—wow, he's drenched.

He heads to the locker room, and I return to my office, where I ditch the sweaty hoodie and spritz my favorite Ambré Vanilla from the small bottle in my purse onto my throat, brush my hair and redo the ponytail, and slap on some lip gloss.

I step outside the facility into sunshine and pleasant mid-October temperatures. The leaves of the trees in the land-scaped area out front are starting to turn and even though the temperature is mild, the air holds crisp hints of autumn. I stroll across the visitor parking area. Being Sunday afternoon, there aren't many cars here.

This area is quiet, on the outside edge of town in a mostly industrial area, and it's not busy at Betty's. I request a table for two and the hostess shows me to a booth at the window from where I can see Logan approaching.

Wearing soft, worn jeans and a blue plaid shirt, his long-legged gait is recognizable, his body rangy and tightly muscled, with easy movements. His usual ball cap is on backwards and sunglasses hide his eyes.

God, he's beautiful.

I sigh. I may dislike him but I have to admit that objective fact.

He enters the diner and slides off the sunnies with a cheeky grin at the hostess, gesturing at me, then strides to the booth. He coasts into the seat, tosses his sunglasses down onto the table, and says, "Hi."

"Hi."

A waitress appears immediately. "Can I get you something to drink?"

He looks at me.

"Coffee please. With cream."

"Same," Logan adds.

With a lingering look at Logan's face, she turns away.

I'm only here because I want to hear the apology. "So..."

The corners of his mouth quirk up. "So."

My mouth twists against a smile.

He picks up a spoon and turns it in his fingers. "So. I said I want to apologize."

"Oh, right!"

His side eye look nearly makes me laugh.

"About your attitude, I assume."

After a beat, he says, "If you think my attitude stinks, you should smell my hockey bag."

An unexpected laugh bursts from my lips. "Oh, I've smelled enough hockey bags, believe me. There's nothing worse."

"I'm sorry I haven't had the best attitude about working with you."

I nod.

"I admit I'm skeptical about you making me a better skater."

"Still?" I ask quietly.

"Well." He turns the spoon again. "You do seem to know how to skate."

"Gee, thanks."

"It's just different. Figure skating."

I'm annoyed. "Our very first session, I told you to forget that. It's just *skating*."

He opens his mouth. I can see he forgot that. I feel my blood pressure rising. "You must have a little bit of faith. You were practicing."

The waitress arrives with our coffee, setting the cups in front of us along with a small pitcher of cream. "Anything else I can get you?"

We haven't even glanced at the menus, but Logan looks at me and says, "I'm starving. I'm gonna get a pastrami on rye."

The waitress nods.

I'm flustered. But also hungry. I grab a menu and peer at it. "A tuna melt, please."

"You bet!" She takes the menus and disappears again.

I pour cream into my coffee, taking a breath. "Look. Neither of us is happy about this. You don't think you need to learn anything. I don't want to have anything to do with you. But I need to do my job or get fired. And I want this job."

He meets my eyes. "That."

I frown. "What?"

"You don't want anything to do with me. I know you hate me because I hurt your brother."

"You put him in the hospital. He had surgery. He was out for months."

I'm not prepared for the way his face tightens and his eyes shadow. He gives a stiff nod. "Yeah. I did. But I've said numerous times that I'm sorry that happened. It wasn't my intention to hurt him."

"You're known as an aggressive player."

His mouth tightens and he drops his gaze to the utensil in his hands again. "Yeah. But I've never intentionally hurt someone. I swear." He lifts his eyes and the misery there takes me aback. "After it happened, I said over and over again that I didn't even intend to hit him. I was trying to stop and it was more like I fell on him. It was an accident, but I take responsibility for it. I served my suspension. I took the shit from fans online for months about it. I deserved it."

"Yeah, fans can be brutal."

"It's great to be passionate about your team, but I think sometimes they forget we're all real people." He makes a face. "I got called so many names, threatened, you name it."

My stomach contracts. Oh shit. Do I actually feel sympathy for him? Forget that!

"Anyway, I apologize for that, too. I get that you'd be angry that your brother got hurt. But..." He pauses as if searching for words. "I'm not a monster."

I keep my face neutral. I feel like crying. This is fucked up. I pick up my coffee and sip it, trying to ease the tightness in my throat. Am I being a sucker, charmed by a charming charmer? Or is this for real? I don't know. I don't know him well enough. He seems sincere. "I'm sorry I acted like you were."

He nods, too. Our eyes meet. There's a shift. A connection. A sense of recognition.

Then he says, "I haven't been playing the way I want to."

Oh. I blink and wait for him to say more.

"I want to be better," he continues in a low voice. "A better player. And you're right. We need to work together on this."

My chest tightens. I want to keep hating him, but can I at least accept his apology to smooth out our working relationship? Not to make *him* feel better. To help *me* with my job.

SEVEN

Logan

I can't look away from Annie's face, no matter how uncomfortable this whole thing is. The smooth curve of her cheek, her small nose, her slightly pointy chin...and big blue eyes that a guy could lose himself in. She's an appealing package, no doubt about it.

Her mouth is soft, but those blue eyes are wary. I don't think I've totally convinced her. But I guess I deserve this, too. I swallow a sigh and take a mouthful of coffee.

"Okay, good." She gives a businesslike nod. "I'm glad you agree. Also..." She hesitates. "Thank you for talking to Jake." After my first day when Jake called me "little coach," Logan apparently had a word with him.

"Idiot." He rolls his eyes. "Let me know if he's a problem."

"I can handle it myself, if he is."

"Yeah, I saw that." My lips quirk.

She makes a face. "Too much?"

"It got the message across. You shouldn't have to deal with shit like that."

"No, I shouldn't. But *I* live in the real world." The corners of her mouth lift. "It's happened before. It'll happen again. I'll deal with it."

I'm starting to suspect there's more to this woman than sequined costumes, pink hair bows, and polished nails. I study her across the table, and then the waitress arrives with our sandwiches. She sets them in front of us along with a bottle of ketchup, refills our coffee cups, and chirps, "Anything else I can get you?"

I lift an eyebrow at Annie. She shakes her head.

"We're good, thanks," I tell the waitress with a smile, then look back at Annie.

Okay...what now? We've sort of made our peace.

Except I don't think there can ever be *peace* between us. There's still that humming tension sizzling around us.

We gaze at each other across the table, neither of us moving to eat our lunch. Then I say, "Why didn't you play hockey? Since your whole family does."

"I can't play hockey. Look at me." She dips her chin.

I look at her. God help me, I look. She's fully clothed, but I've seen her naked. And seeing her out of her baggy sweatsuits today, in a pair of dress pants and snug sweater, shows me that tight and toned body. Petite, yes. She definitely doesn't have big hooters, which I admit I'm a fan of, but I discovered that night years ago that firm and small could be sexy as fuck.

"I mean, I'm small," she adds hurriedly, as if sensing my dirty thoughts. "Small girls can play hockey—I did, for a while, and with my brothers—but it's hard to win puck battles. And anyway, I didn't want to try to compete with my brothers. I wanted to do something totally different. I'm much more suited to figure skating."

I nod and tear my gaze away from her. I swallow. "Why do you want this job so much?" I ask, referring back to her earlier statement.

She drops her gaze to her plate and picks up a knife and fork. "That should be obvious. It's a job in the NHL. All my brothers play in the NHL."

I pick up a French fry. "So it's your way of keeping up with your brothers?"

One corner of her mouth lifts wryly. "Wow. Why do you think I have to keep up with my brothers?"

"You're competitive."

She sighs. "Okay, yes. Obviously I couldn't compete with them playing hockey. I was doing pretty well at figure skating and then...well, that ended."

"Why?"

"I got hurt." Her forehead creases and her eyes shadow.

"I'm sorry."

She lifts one shoulder. "Shit happens."

I nod slowly. "Yeah. Still sucks, though."

"It was hard," she admits, looking down. "But I survived and I'm building a new career."

"What happened? How did you get hurt?"

She pops a bite of sandwich into her mouth, chews, and swallows. "It wasn't just one thing. I had a few concussions."

My mouth drops open. "Oh. Wow. That's not good."

"Tell me about it." She looks up and her eyes are full of such heartbreak, I feel my lungs squeeze. "The first couple I recovered pretty quickly. The last one took longer." She pauses, fighting emotion. "I had killer headaches and felt sick all the time. I was exhausted and I couldn't focus, and then I got depressed." Emotion makes her voice quiver.

"I'm sorry."

She gives a quick nod. "Thanks. It was a deep, black hole for a long time. I ended up dropping out of school."

"University of Michigan."

"You remember that?"

"Yeah." She told me that night years ago she got a skating scholarship there and was studying sport management.

"I never did finish my degree. I had a hard time focusing. Things got better, but it scared me. I had long talks with doctors and therapists and my family, and everyone seemed to think I should quit skating. Everyone was worried about more brain injuries and long-term effects."

"CTE," I say quietly, referring to chronic traumatic encephalopathy, which is a kind of dementia. "Yeah, I've heard that talk, too."

"You've had concussions?"

"One or two. I'm a hockey player." I give her a rueful smile. "Luckily they've been mild. But the risk of developing a neurodegenerative disease later in life is still scary."

She eyes me searchingly. "Do you worry about it?"

I don't answer right away. I deny it to most people, but she's been honest and vulnerable with me, telling me about that. "Sometimes," I admit. "It's been a while since I've had a head injury." I play differently now than I did when I was a kid, when my dad was constantly urging me to get out there and fight. "How did they happen? Falling on the ice?"

"Yeah. I've had so many injuries. Broken arm. Meniscus tear. Cut by a skate blade."

I wince. I've seen that in hockey and it's brutal.

"I got stitched up and went back on the ice," she continues matter-of-factly.

I'm holding my sandwich in two hands, staring at her.

"And I've had so many sprains, strains, and bruises you

couldn't keep track of them all." She pauses, then adds, "I'm...I *was* a pairs skater."

I nod slowly. I don't know a lot about figure skating, but I've seen couples skate.

"It's probably the most dangerous of the four skating disciplines because the girls go so high in the air. Like, we get thrown three times as high as singles girls jump, and we're still expected to land on one foot." She smiles wistfully. "I loved it."

My jaw goes slack. "Three times as high...you get thrown in the air," I repeat.

"Oh yeah. I love that flying feeling. Also held upside down, tossed in the air—"

"Jesus Christ." I stare at her. "You love being tossed in the air."

She grins. "Yeah. Have you ever seen a death spiral?"

"Um...maybe?"

"The guy pivots on one foot while the girl holds his hand and stretches out almost parallel to the ice and circles around him with one skate on the ice."

"Okay."

She grins. "You need to see it, I guess. Then there's the headbanger. It's not legal in competitions, but we learned to do it anyway. Ivan—my partner—would pick me up by the ankles and spin me around, going up and down, with my head coming close to the ice."

"Holy fuck." I set down my sandwich, my gut clenching.

"It's not as scary as it sounds." She waves a hand. "I wasn't fully facing the ice, so if I ended up touching the ice it would be with my shoulder."

"Oh. Okay then."

She laughs at my sarcasm. "You definitely have to trust your partner."

"Obviously. Holy shit."

"Once we did a twist where he throws me up and I turn three times and then he catches me. He caught me and pushed me out and I fell straight backward and hit my head."

My mouth drops open and my stomach twists.

"There was blood all over the ice."

"I think...we might have to change the subject." I swallow an accumulation of saliva in my mouth.

Her eyes widen. "What? Oh...sorry! Okay, yeah. Hockey players get injured a lot, too, though. You must be used to it."

"I've been hurt, yeah." But not by doing crazy, reckless shit like that. That's *asking* to get hurt. Also, I wear a lot of protective gear. Figure skaters are out there throwing themselves around basically naked. Jesus. "When it happens to me, it's fine, when someone else gets hurt I get a little squeamish."

She gives me a long look across the table. I can't read her expression. Then she drops her gaze again. "Yeah. Let's change the subject."

I cast about for a different topic. "How's your sandwich?"

"Good! Yours?"

"Yeah, it's good." I look down at the pastrami. "I need a minute."

"The weather's great for this time of year, isn't it?"

I laugh. "I guess."

"Do you have any pets?"

"Yeah. I have a dog."

Her eyes brighten. "Oh, what kind?"

"We think he's a foodle."

She blinks.

"Probably fox terrier and poodle."

"Oh! That sounds cute."

"He's very cute. Although he always looks kind of a mess. Just the way his fur is."

"What's his name?"

"Teemu."

She chokes on her laughter. "Aw! That's adorable."

I pull my phone out and open my photo gallery. "It's not hard to find a picture of him. My whole camera roll is pics of Teemu." I hold out the phone to show her one.

She beams with delight. "I love him!"

Anyone who loves my dog is definitely in my good books. I set down my phone and resume my eating, now that she's distracted me from blood and gore. In particular, Annie's blood.

"He's fun," I say. "Lots of energy, but he's okay being alone."

Her forehead creases. "What do you do when you travel?"

"I have a dog sitter. Millsy's wife runs a dog walking and grooming business."

"Right! I just met her earlier."

"The guy who comes and helps is great. Teemu loves him."

"That's great then."

"You like dogs?"

"I do. Maybe one day I'll be able to have one. I haven't really felt settled in one place long enough." She flashes a nonchalant smile.

"Where were you before this? Oh, Bayard University, right."

"Right. Before that I was coaching figure skaters at home in St. Paul, but I knew I wasn't going to be there forever."

"Bigger and better things," I say.

"Right."

"So you can compete with your brothers."

She sighs. "Why do you keep saying that? It's really not like that."

"Okay." I don't believe her, but whatever.

"So, both our dads played hockey. Remember, we wondered if they played against each other?"

"Yeah." Christ. I hope my dad didn't fight her dad. That would be another reason to hate me.

"Did your dad pressure you to play hockey?"

"Oh yeah."

"Really?"

"I wanted to play hockey. It's not like he forced me to. But he definitely had strong opinions about hockey and how I should play."

She tilts her head. "How so?"

"My dad's kind of old school. He thinks hockey should be rough and tough, mixing it up."

"Aaaah." She purses her lips and nods.

"He thinks hockey's gotten too 'soft.'"

"Too reliant on skill and speed," she says knowingly. "Yeah, I've heard that. Not from *my* dad," she adds hastily. "But others."

I nod.

She sinks her teeth into her bottom lip, biting back a smile. "I'm guessing your father wouldn't approve of a figure skater teaching the boys how to skate better."

My jaw loosens. Then I bark out a laugh. "Yeah. You're probably right. I haven't talked to him about this."

"Like father, like son."

Now I wince. I don't want to be like my dad. But I have been, looking down on figure skating, skeptical of Annie's ability to make us better skaters. And I *know* that the game is faster and more skillful these days. That season opener where I fucked up, turned over the puck and couldn't catch the guy showed me that. "Shit," I mutter, rubbing my beard.

She gives me a curious, look, then says, "Hockey hasn't changed *enough*. There's still so much wrong with it."

I'm instantly defensive of the sport I love. "If you don't like it, why are you working in it?"

She eyes me placidly. "I never said I don't like it. I love the sport. But I can love it and see there are problems with it."

"Like what?"

Her eyebrows elevate. "Racism. Abuse. Sexism. Xenophobia. Autocratic coaching methods—"

I hold up a hand. "Okay. I get it."

"Do you?"

I sigh. "Yeah. I've seen all those things. And I hate them, too."

Her gaze is steady on my face. "Well, figure skating also has those issues."

"Ignoring them isn't a good strategy, huh?"

She smiles wryly.

"I've always hated the things my dad stood for—the old boys club, that whole hockey code. He always told me never to question anything the coach says. The coach is the boss, and if you question him you're not a team player. You get labelled a 'whiner' or a 'locker-room cancer' and so much for your career. But that kind of thing is what led to one of my college coaches getting fired, because he was such a dickhead to a Black player the guy ended up quitting hockey. He couldn't complain about it. To anyone." I shake my head, regret like a rock in my gut. I meet her eyes. "A few years ago we had a problem here, with our coach. I don't know if you heard about it."

She shakes her head slowly. "No. I haven't followed the Bears that closely."

"Our coach was an asshole. He was abusive. When he was ranting and yelling, it was one thing. But he started singling out a couple of guys and he called one of them a homophobic slur. He benched players out of spite. He reamed guys out for a mistake in front of the whole team. He freaked out if anyone tried to question him. Millsy tried to talk to him, and he got scratched. Then he called Jammer stupid and used the N-word—"

She gasps.

"Yeah. And he kicked him."

"Oh my God." Her eyes widen.

He nods. "Millsy, Jammer, and J-Bo ended up going to talk to the GM about it. They were taking a big risk. But in the end, Simmons got fired. That's how we ended up with Gary. He's tough, but he's not a dictator. He listens to us."

"That's good. I wouldn't be working here if I thought he was an asshole."

"Was there sexism at Bayard?"

"Oh yeah. I was their first skating coach. I worked with the women and the men's teams, but some of the men thought I should only be working with the women. I overheard one of them say to another that I was only there for the dick."

I jerk in shock. "Jesus."

She shrugs. "I got called a puck bunny, which is so stupid it's laughable. And there was more." She drops her gaze. "It was hard, but I can stand up for myself."

I fucking hate that for her. But like she said...that's the real world. And I'm ashamed of some of my dickish behavior that first day she had us on the ice. "Why hockey coaching? You said you coached figure skaters...why'd you move to hockey?"

She tilts her head. "I've always loved hockey. When I used to watch my brothers' games and I'd see one guy skating funny, and I'd think, oh if he just did 'this,' he'd be better. I didn't know why they didn't work on their skating as much as other things, since it's such a big part of hockey. It would make their game so much better. I could see the things they could improve."

"Cool. So now you have a chance to make that happen."

"Yeah."

We've both been finished our sandwiches for a while now. But talking to her is easy. And fun. Even if it's opening my eyes about some shit I'd rather not see. But I want to be better than that. It's my whole goal this year.

The waitress brings the bill and I hand her a credit card, waving aside Annie's objections. "I invited you."

She accepts graciously. "Thank you. And thanks for the apology."

"I'm not a total dick," I say ruefully. "But I may have stuff to learn."

She smiles. "Don't we all?"

Our eyes meet again with a flare of heat and awareness. Shit.

I'm in fucking awe of this woman. And...I like her.

EIGHT

Annie

"I need sex."

Ivan holds his arms out at his sides. "Hey. I've told you—any time."

I snort. "We both know that's not happening."

"We could try again."

I know he's talking shit by the curve of his lips as he dishes instant pot Mediterranean chicken onto a plate.

We became skating partners at twelve years old. He knew intimate details about me, like when I was having my period and felt bloated and grouchy, when I needed to wax my bikini line due to a skimpy costume, and the fact that I wore padded bras off the ice to make up for my non-existent boobs. I told him when his nose hairs needed trimming and showed him how to tame his unibrow.

At one point, teenage hormones and curiosity overcame us and we considered dating. We tried making out but ended up both collapsed in laughter. That put an end to any romantic ideas and we continued popping each other's zits and giving dating advice about other people.

"Sure," I say casually, taking the plate he offers. "I could use a good laugh."

He grins. "Me, too."

"I need stress relief." I pick up my fork, sitting at the counter on a stool. "Sex is good for that."

"Nothing better," he agrees. "Is it the job?"

"I guess so? Things are going okay." I tell him about my meeting with management. "It sounded positive. And... I had coffee, er lunch, with Logan today." I poke at a black olive. "We sort of came to a truce."

He lifts an eyebrow. "That's good."

"I still hate him."

Ivan laughs.

"What?" I scowl at him.

"That didn't sound very forceful."

I nod slowly. "I know. He's actually not so bad. I mean, he still did a terrible thing." I'm having a hard time reconciling the monster that hurt my brother with the handsome charmer sitting across from me in the diner, making me laugh, disarming me with his apologies. "He apologized."

"Wow."

"He apologized for what happened with Jensen but also for being a dick to me about the skating." I shake my head. "I don't exactly know how to deal with that."

"Do you think he was sincere?"

I purse my lips. "I do," I answer reluctantly. "And he has paid for what happened."

"Did he learn from it?"

I eat a piece of chicken while I consider that. "He says he's never intended to hurt someone." After a pause, I add, "He actually got kind of squeamish when I was talking about my injuries, like that time I fell backwards on the ice and hit my head."

"Jesus. Don't remind me of that. I lost ten years off my life that day."

I smile. "And he told me about his dad. He played hockey, too. Dennis Coates. Also known as Dennis the Menace."

"Never heard of him."

"You aren't into hockey." I wave a hand. "He was a famous goon, years ago. Apparently he thinks his son should follow in his footsteps."

"Ohhhh."

"I got the feeling Logan doesn't want to do that." When I made that comment, *like father, like son,* he'd seemed really uncomfortable.

Ivan shrugs. "And yet..."

I sigh. "I know. Anyway. It sounds like he's at least going to be more cooperative. Not sure about some of the other guys, though. Jake Colman is kind of a jerk. Although, Logan said he talked to him and told him to cut out the sexist bullshit."

Ivan fixes his gaze on me. "Logan did that."

"Yeah." I pop an olive into my mouth and shrug.

"Interesting." He nods slowly and forks up rice.

"I told him I can handle him myself. I've done it before. There was this guy at Bayard who told me he'd love to serve a five-minute penalty in my box."

Ivan chokes. "Jesus. What did you say?"

"I pretended I didn't understand what he meant." I grin, "I was like, 'What does that mean?' And he said, 'It's a joke.' And I said, 'I don't get it. Can you explain it to me?' And he started sputtering and backtracking and got all red in the face."

"Ha. That's good."

"Sometimes that works. If it's a guy who gets that it's sexist and harmful. But some guys double down on the joke." I roll my eyes.

"You're a tough cookie."

I straighten. "I am."

"So, back to needing sex..."

I give him a look.

"I mean, do you want me to fix you up with someone? I know! Come out with us this weekend. Some of my friends are going to check out a new club in the Meatpacking District. You need some fun."

"Ooooh. A dance club?"

"Yeah."

I love dancing. Dance lessons were part of my figure skating training and I love, love, love moving to music, which totally makes sense. "Okay! That sounds fun."

WE'RE GREETED by pumping music that I feel right in my heart and I instantly want to boogie. I take in the surroundings of Club Crystal. The name obviously comes from the multitude of chandeliers hanging from the high, dark ceiling, all different shapes, sizes, and styles, all dripping with crystals. The bar stretches out in front of us, surrounded by party spaces also lit by chandeliers, and we're led to a small private room with red velvet banquettes and silky curtains tied back. From here we can see the high booth where DJ Phunk is spinning tunes. The dance floor isn't full, but it's early yet.

Excitement ripples through my blood. "This is so cool!"

Ivan has introduced me to his friends Inaya, Maya, Ellen, Khaza, Mateo, and Jack. Ellen and Khaza are a couple; the others are all single. I've met Inaya and Maya briefly and they seem nice. We arrange ourselves in the booth and order drinks.

Maya and Inaya order cocktails, so I do, too, but the guys order a bottle of Tito's vodka, which I know is Ivan's favorite.

My Crystal Rum Punch is delicious and disappears much too quickly as we chat. Inaya and I compare notes on our drinks, and I next order what she had, something called a Flower Power. Also delicious!

The music gets to me and I beg Ivan to come dance. He's my favorite dance partner, and together again we move in a rhythm that's instinctive and familiar. A funky mix of Pump Up the Jam has us grooving to the beat and grinning at each other.

We worked with various choreographers over the years, learning dance moves in the studio that we translated onto the ice. When the tune "We Will" comes on, a hip hop song we used as one of our numbers years ago, we immediately do our choreographed moves. I laugh out loud at how good it feels as I spin.

I'm aware of other dancers watching us. I know we're good dancers and I'm used to being watched. Performing was part of the fun of figure skating.

After a few songs, I grab Ivan's arm. "I need another drink!" I call over the loud beats.

We head off the dance floor, me hanging on his arm, and I stop short when I see Logan Coates standing at a high-top table, staring at us.

"What?" Ivan glances down at me.

"Um." My gaze moves over Logan's companions—Evan Russell, Luke Burrows, and Jay Bobak. "Some of the Bears players are here." I gesture toward them.

Ivan looks that way. "Oh, cool. You going to say hi?"

"I guess I should." I release his arm. "Can you order me a pineapple martini?"

He makes a face. "If I must."

I turn back to the hockey players and walk toward their table. All four guys gape at me as if I'm walking toward them naked. My smile falters but I lift a hand in a wave as I approach.

"Hi!" I greet them. "Imagine meeting you guys here!"

They continue to stare at me, open-mouthed.

Logan looks away first, greeting me with a terse, "Hey," then takes a big pull of the beer he's holding.

My gaze goes back and forth among them. "What's wrong? You all look weird."

"You look...uh..." Jay waves a hand at me, then closes his mouth.

"You look different." Luke blinks at me.

"Oh." I look down at my black dress and heels. "Yeah, I guess this is different than at work."

"Different," Logan mutters. "Yeah."

After an uncomfortable pause, I ask, "Have you been here before?"

"No," they all say at once

"It's new," Jay says. "We had to check it out. We heard it was good."

"Great DJ!" I reply.

"You were burning up the dance floor." Luke rubs a hand over his forehead. "Who knew you had moves like that."

"I knew." Evan elbows Luke. "Haven't you seen her figure skate?"

"No."

"Lots of videos out there," Evan says.

"Oh boy." I shake my head. "You don't need to be watching those."

"Hey, you were good," Evan says.

"Aw, thank you."

Logan drinks more beer.

"Was that your boyfriend you were dancing with?" Jay asks.

"Just a friend." I wave over at the booth. "We're here with some other friends." Inaya and Maya are watching with avid interest. Actually, they all are. The tall, good-looking guys I'm talking to are attracting as much interest as Ivan and I were on the dance floor. Especially from women. I sigh. Hockey players. I've seen it all my life. Even my stupid brothers had girls chasing them all the time. I don't get it.

Then Maya slides out of the booth and trips over to us in her heels. "Hi! Ivan says you work with these guys." She beams at them all.

"I do." I bite back a smile and introduce everyone.

"You should come join us!" she says. "We have lots of room!"

The guys exchange looks, then nod. Well, all but Logan. His face is still frozen in a slightly unhappy grimace.

"Okay, sure," Jay says.

They all pick up their drinks and follow Maya back to our room. My pineapple martini has arrived and I grab it gratefully as I'm crowded in between Logan and Evan.

"You two are such good dancers!" Maya says to Ivan and me. "We were watching you out there."

"Thanks!"

Awareness of two big, warm, male bodies on either side of me has my skin prickling all over.

Dammit. I still need sex.

I inhale and breathe in a scent of herbs and citrus, fresh and clean. It's Logan. I got a whiff of it the other day at the diner. The erotic scent makes me want to press my nose to his throat and gulp it in.

I make more introductions and give Ivan a tiny shrug when he shoots me a questioning look across the table.

"And you guys play hockey!" Maya says. "That's so cool!"

They start talking about hockey and the Bears. Mateo and Jack are hockey fans, and apparently so is Maya. I let the players handle the conversation and sip my drink. This one goes down way too fast also. Maybe I need to switch to Tito's. It tastes like pure alcohol to me so there's no fear of me downing it. I reach for the bottle and pour myself a glass.

Ivan lifts a brow.

I give him a tight smile.

"Would you guys like some vodka?" I hold up the bottle to Evan and Logan on either side of me.

Logan purses his lips and studies my face, close enough for me to see lighter-colored flecks in his brown eyes and his thick eyelashes. The way he looks at me makes heat flow in my veins. "Sure," he drawls. "We should order another bottle."

The party is just getting started.

Jay looks at me. "So tell us how a figure skater ends up coaching hockey."

His question seems sincere, but I'm never sure. I give him a condensed version of my resume.

Jay nods. "Figure skating is totally different, though."

"Well, hockey players don't glide like figure skaters do. Hockey has more quick changes of direction and stop-start motion."

"Yeah."

"Figure skaters need to do clean edges and turns. That's why figure skating blades are longer and flatter, with more ice contact," Ivan puts in.

"Huh." Luke contemplates that. "Figure skating's a whole different sport, though."

"Yes."

"Is it really even a sport?" Jay asks.

I choke and meet Ivan's eyes. We've been through this discussion before. "Oh, here we go."

"Well, most sports are determined by a score," Evan says.

"There *is* scoring in figure skating."

"But it's done by judges, right?" Jay says.

"Yeah."

"So it's subjective. Not like in hockey where things are black and white."

"Yeah," Evan says. "The puck's either in the net or it's not. A goal or no goal. That's how you win."

"I don't even know where to start with that. First of all, hockey's *not* black and white. Refs make calls and they make mistakes."

"True." Jay and Evan nod.

I glance at Logan and see his amusement at this discussion.

"And the scoring for figure skating is very prescriptive," I add.

"Okay.'"

"It is! Every element a skater performs has a technical point value. If you hit the element perfectly you get most or all of the points. If you mess up or fall, there are automatic deductions."

"I thought whoever has the most sequins wins." Jay grins.

I gasp in outrage.

"But isn't there also an artistic part to it?" Evan says. "Isn't *that* subjective?"

"Okay, yeah, there is a Program Component Score. It's based on skating skills," I tick off my fingers as I list the components. "Transitions, performance, composition, and interpretation of the music. But only three of those are subjective."

"There," Jay says. "So it *is* subjective."

"I don't know...figure skating seems more like entertainment than a sport," Evan adds.

I press my lips together briefly. "And hockey's *not* entertainment?"

"Hmmm. You have a point there," Evan says.

"You think hockey's entertaining?" Logan asks.

I turn to him. "Of course it is. I was forced to watch enough of it." I roll my eyes. "I would have died if it wasn't a little fun to watch."

"I think if you look in the dictionary and find the definition of a sport, figure skating meets all the criteria," Logan says casually.

Sticking up for me.

Whoa.

"I don't know," Jay says.

I've had enough of this. My eyes fly open wide and I can feel steam coming out my ears.

"Because it's considered a sport for girls?" I demand. "Women athletes in figure skating aren't only judged on their athletic ability, but on their *performance*. So not only do we have to be strong and skilled, we have to have 'style' and 'grace.'" We have to be *feminine*, which here in the U.S. means white and decorous, and *effortless*. We can't look like we're trying hard. Other athletes, like hockey players, get sweaty and bruised and banged up, but *we* have to stay pretty and elegant. And *that* is why people don't take us seriously. We look like we're not trying hard. And how can it be hard? It's for *girls*."

"Uh..." Logan looks at me like I'm holding up an explosive device, ready to toss it.

Jay grins. "Okay, okay, I've been teasing you. You make a good case for it being a real sport."

I sigh and relax. "Sorry about the rant. You pushed a button. I get a little defensive about it when people criticize figure skating."

After a round of Tito's, Inaya drags Ivan out to the dance

floor, Maya asks Evan to dance, and Jack, Mateo and Luke disappear somewhere.

"You seem to like dancing," Logan says, lightly holding his glass in his fingers.

"I love dancing. Almost as much as skating."

"Let's go."

I blink at him, not sure what he means.

"Dance." He nudges me with his shoulder.

"Oh. Really?" It's probably not a good idea, but the music is pulsing its rhythm into my soul and I need to move. "Okay."

I shimmy my way over to the now-crowded floor with Logan following me. I turn to face him, swinging my hips, smiling. He looks so good—so tall, his beard and hair neat, dressed in narrow dark pants, a thin gray sweater, and a black leather moto jacket He's still watching me with that intense, unsmiling expression and my belly flutters.

"What is wrong?" I ask, leaning and going on my toes to speak into his ear over the noise in the club. "You don't seem in a very good mood."

He sets his hands on my hips to steady me as I wobble. "I'm good."

I tip my head back and give him a look that conveys my disbelief. The corners of his mouth twitch.

"Are you mad that Maya invited you to join us?"

"No."

"Are you mad that you ran into me?"

He sighs. "No."

"Just a bad mood, then?"

He scowls.

"Apparently eating chocolate can improve your mood. Have you tried that?"

His forehead creases, one corner of his mouth deepening. "No."

"You don't like chocolate?"

"I love chocolate. I don't eat it very often though."

"The scent of orange or lavender can also help. Maybe you should invest in some scented candles."

"What the fuck."

I laugh. "Meditation? Oh, wait, you have a dog! You could cuddle with Teemu."

"Jesus." He can't stop the smile tugging at his mouth. "But you know what's really good for a bad mood?" I pause. "Sex."

His smile disappears and his eyes darken, fixed on me. The air around us shifts, becoming hot and close, pressing in on us. We're both remembering how good the sex was.

"Forget I said that," I mumble. "Oh my God."

He surprises me with a low laugh. "No takesie backsies. It's the rule."

I peek up at him. With his hands still on my hips, we move together in an easy rhythm. He's not as good a dancer as Ivan, but then who is? Logan has rhythm, though. We could be alone on the dance floor, I'm so caught up in his energy—the snare of his gaze, the grip of his hands, his scent. "I know," I agree. "It's the rule. Also it's impossible to put toothpaste back in the tube."

His smile reveals white teeth, and it's such an attractive smile I feel like I'm being reeled in by it. "True."

"I didn't mean anything by it. I was just trying to help. And hey—I think it worked! Look, you're smiling now."

He slowly moves his head from side to side, his smile going crooked as if he's perplexed. "Yeah. I am." He pauses. "Are we gonna talk about it?"

"A-about what?"

He gives me a level look. "Pyeongchang."

"Oh. That."

"Only the best night of my life."

I snort. "Oh, come on, it was not."

He gives me a steady look.

My belly does a flip flop. It *was* hot. "I think we should agree that never happened," I say, striving for composure.

"Mmm. Don't think I can do that, Mini Bang."

"Let's pretend."

The song changes, and I step away from him to lift my arms in the air and dig my hips into the tempo of "Naughty Girl," by Beyoncé, letting my hair swing around my shoulders. The lyrics are steamy and I'm acutely aware of Logan watching me, but I'm most confident when I'm skating or dancing, so I let myself feel the rhythm of the music deep down inside me. The lights of the club flash and flare around us in the darkness along with the thump of the bass, adding to the sexy ambience.

It's just dancing.

The song slides into another, a slower beat, Calum Scott's "You Are The Reason" and I lower my arms and look at Logan. Others on the dance floor are moving together, pairing off, and Logan reaches for my hand and tugs me closer again. With his other hand on my waist and mine on his shoulder, our bodies shift together in slower, smoother movements.

"I love Calum Scott," I say.

"Who?"

I grin. "This singer."

"Ah."

"What kind of music do you like?"

"Mostly country, I guess."

"Hmm."

"What does that mean?"

"Country music's not my favorite. Too much twang."

"I like the twang."

I nod and we move to the music, swaying, gazing at each other as the romantic lyrics play and the melody builds.

"Do you have a girlfriend?" I blurt out.

"No."

"I'm not...I'm just asking because of the sex remark I made about sex being good for a bad mood, because if you had a girlfriend sex probably wouldn't be a problem." *Jesus. Say the word sex again, Annie.*

"A lack of sex?"

"Uh. Yes."

"No, if I had a girlfriend, it would not be a problem."

"*Is* it a problem?" Clearly I've had way too much to drink.

He gives me a long look. "It might be."

I don't know what that means and I don't want to go there. "Did you know that Harry Styles has four nipples?"

After a startled beat, he barks out a laugh. "Jesus Christ, you're cute."

I blink a few times.

"No, I did not know that."

"It's a medical condition called...I forget what it's called. But it's true. I read that today."

"That's fascinating."

"Not really, but I wanted to change the subject."

He laughs again. "My teammates and I once had an in-depth discussion about why men have nipples."

I laugh, too. "Did you figure it out?"

"Yeah, it has something to do with the way embryos develop in the womb. They don't know if they're male or female until after the nipples develop."

"Oh. Well, that's interesting." Now I'm acutely aware of my nipples, so close to his chest. Our bodies are touching, swaying together, his hand splayed on the small of my back, fingertips brushing the upper curve of my butt. I have an intense urge to press myself even closer, as if his hand is impelling me, and my muscles tighten as I try to resist. His fingers slip lower and my body is dissolving, liquid heat gathering low inside me.

"So Ivan's not your boyfriend," he says.

"No. He's my roommate."

His eyes narrow. "Roommate?" he barks.

"Yeah. I needed a place to stay when I moved here to take this job."

"Christ."

"It's not a big deal."

"You have a male roommate."

"We're friends. He was my skating partner."

"Is he gay?"

"No. Geez. Not every male figure skater is gay. That's a stereotype."

"Yeah. I know it is." He sighs. "Just checking."

The slow song ends and I force myself to step away. "I think I need another drink."

Hands on my shoulders, he turns me and steers me through the crowd and back to the table. "I don't know about that."

"It's fine. I'm fine."

I feel his breath on my hair and shivers slither down the back of my neck as he leans close to my ear and says, "Yeah, you are."

NINE

Logan

At the table, Annie regards her empty glass sadly, then reaches for the bottle and tips it over the glass.

I sigh and hold out my glass, too.

When we had lunch that day at Betty's and I learned new things about her I realized that not only am I still (again?) insanely attracted to her, I actually like her. But holy shit, when I spotted her on the dance floor I wasn't even sure it was her. She looks so different tonight. At the arena, she wears sweats, with her hair in a ponytail and not much makeup. Tonight, she's dressed in a short, tight, black strapless dress and killer heels that are begging to be tossed over my shoulders. Her blond hair is long and loose and messy and her eyes are all dark and shadowy. She looks absolutely, stunningly fuckable.

There's a whole shitload of chemistry between us and I know she feels it, too. We were practically combusting on the dance floor. After she snapped me out of my jealous funk.

Jealous. Jesus. I rub my forehead and drink my vodka. I

don't know how I can be jealous, but I was. Seeing her with that guy practically having sex on the dance floor had my insides being sliced up by sharpened skate blades.

And then finding out they live together had those blades slashing at me again. I'm a fucking mess right now.

I toss back another mouthful of vodka. I don't really like vodka. I've gotten to like good whiskey but I'm basically a beer guy. And I need another beer.

I look around and spot a waitress. I catch her eye and she hurries over, smiling. Everyone's ready for more drinks, and even though I'm pretty sure Annie's a little drunk and I feel like I should take care of her, it's not my place to babysit her. Christ. She's no baby, despite her small size. She is all sexy woman.

I shift slightly so I can watch Annie as she talks and laughs with her friends. Her face is so expressive, her smiles wide and genuine, her eyes bright. I watch the curve of her full bottom lip and the flick of her long eyelashes. A couple of times she glances at me and our eyes meet with a punch of heat.

I try to focus on the conversation going on around me and participate so I'm not sitting here like an obsessed lump.

"But really, how many French fries is it okay for someone to steal before you tell them to order their own?" Jack says.

"And why do girls do that?" Mateo demands. "Why don't they order their own?"

"I just want a *few* fries," Annie says with a beguiling look up from beneath her lashes that has my groin tightening. "Not a whole order."

"Exactly!" Ellen agrees.

"I miss having a boyfriend I can steal fries from," Maya says with a sad droop of her lips.

"You can steal my fries any time," Russ replies. The two exchange a long look.

I guess he's getting over Hannah.

"I thought it was because other people's food tastes better than your own," Mateo says.

"It does!" Inaya says. "Why is that?"

"I had a girlfriend who always stole my fries," I say. "I broke up with her because of it."

"Shut up!" Annie gapes at me, as do the others.

I grin. "Yeah. But it was because I realized if I really loved her I wouldn't *mind* sharing my fries with her. Therefore, she wasn't the one."

"Awww." Annie's outrage dissipates. "Okay, that's actually kind of sweet."

Again, I watch her face, the way her mouth softens and her eyes go hazy. And then her gaze drops to my mouth...and lingers.

Christ. I feel another tug of desire in my groin.

"I love fries," she murmurs.

I think she just said she loves sex. I'm sure that's what I heard.

The conversation moves on and then people move on, heading to the dance floor or the restrooms or the bar, I don't know, but suddenly Annie and I are alone. Heat crackles around us and every nerve ending in my body tightens. I slowly reach out to brush her hair off her face. She doesn't stop me. Her eyelids grow heavy.

That ache in my groin turns painful as my cock hardens even more.

I don't know who moves first and I don't care because our mouths are crushed together. The kiss is hungry and burning, desperate and uncontrolled and...inevitable. I draw back and stare into her eyes. "Oh, fuck." And I go back in for more, angling my head, opening my mouth on hers, sliding my tongue against hers.

She makes a needy sound in her throat, opening wider to

me. I taste vanilla on her lips and breathe in the scent of her—more vanilla mixed with sugar and something warm and sexy. It sends a flood of heat to my balls, and also to my brain, drugging me. I curl my fingers around her upper arm, then slowly slide them up over her bare shoulder, my thumb brushing over the edge of her strapless dress, then I cup her face and this kiss turns softly exploring. Dangerously sweet.

We're in a night club surrounded by pulsing lights, thumping music, and people. Lots of people. We can't do this here. "We need to go."

She drags her eyelids open. "Go where?"

"I don't care. But we can't do this here." I brush my mouth over hers. "And I want to do this." I let my question show in my eyes.

Those blue eyes are dark and hazy as she gazes back at me. Her lips part. My breath stalls in my chest as I wait for her response.

She smiles. "Let's go."

Thank fuck.

She picks up a little purse and slides out. We stop at the coat check, and I help her into a pink trench coat. Her hand slides under her hair to flip it out from the collar in a seductive sweep that makes my groin tighten. I take her arm and hustle her out onto the dark street.

"I really hate to say this." I pause us on the sidewalk as I reach for my phone. "But...your place or mine?"

She grins. "Do you live alone?"

"Yeah."

"Then your place. Although my roommate is still back in there." She gestures. "Oh shit. I better let him know I'm leaving. He'll freak out." She pulls out her phone and sends a text message.

"Mine, then." I thumb open the app and request a car. "Five minutes away."

"Too long." She slides her phone back into her purse, takes my arm, and presses against me.

"Yeah." I maneuver us out of the path of people walking by, closer to the brick building. "And it'll take another half hour to get to my place." I pull her around and against me, looping my arms around her waist. "I might die."

"Me, too." Her reply is breathy. "We probably shouldn't be doing this."

"Oh, I know." I close my eyes briefly. "But I honestly don't care right now. My dick has taken over my brain."

"I hear that's a problem with men."

I huff out a laugh. "It definitely is."

"Well, if it makes you feel any better, my vag has taken over mine." She goes on her toes and presses against me. As much as I'm pulling her against me, she's trying to get closer, too. Her tits are small but I can feel them through her dress and coat and Christ, she's so fucking sweet and funny and, praise Jesus, horny.

"Are you sure it's not the booze?" I kiss her again.

"I'm a little drunk. But not that drunk." She meets my eyes. "Really."

Yeah, she's not that drunk, just soft and loose and happy. I like seeing her happy—glowing, smiling, eyes twinkling eyes. I nod.

She kisses my chin and I lean back against the wall, pulling her with me, uncaring about the cars driving past on the street or the people walking by us. It's New York. I bend my knees to find her mouth again, delving inside, tasting her sweetness. Her tongue is small and soft.

"Your dress is a goddamn sin," I mutter. "I wanted to run my tongue over your shoulder...your collarbone."

"Do it later," she gasps.

"I will."

A car pulls up at the curb. I check my app and confirm it's ours and then hustle Annie into the back seat. We're kissing again before Ravi has pulled out into traffic.

We make out pretty much all the way up Tenth Avenue. As we approach West 50th, Annie waves a hand. "That's where I live. Down there."

"Huh. Really?"

"Yes." Her head falls back as I slide my lips down her neck. "This neighborhood is called Hell's Kitchen and I thought it was scary but it's actually not bad and close to Central Park."

"My place is close to here."

She lifts her head. "Cool."

We cruise past the Lincoln Center and make a couple more turns to get onto Riverside. The Uber driver stops in front of my building. I add a hefty tip and say, "Thank you, Ravi."

"Thank you!" Annie echoes, jumping onto the sidewalk. She looks up. "Nice building."

"Thanks. A bunch of the guys live here, too."

She checks out the park across the street that almost hides the 9A, the river just beyond that in the dark, then follows me through brass doors and into the lobby with its gleaming stone floor and columns. "Wow. This is way nicer than my building. I mean, Ivan's. I'm staying there until I can get my own place."

Another couple in the lobby is already waiting for the elevator and we get in with them. Exchanging heated glances, we stay apart until we arrive at the eleventh floor where my apartment is. A soon as I open the door, a rapid clicking and scrabbling sound greets us. Then Teemu flings himself at me, bouncing and yipping.

Jesus, I love my dog, but it's one delay after another. I bend and pick him up, letting him lick my chin. "Hi, buddy. Hi. Hi. You're okay. I'm home."

He whines and licks more.

I catch Annie's amused look. "He's cute," she says.

I turn so he can see her and she extends a hand for him to sniff the back of it. He does so, going quiet, then ignores her and attacks me again with his tongue.

Annie laughs.

"I need to take him out," I say apologetically. "Sorry."

"That's okay. Should I come with you?"

"Whatever you want. You can wait here. Make yourself at home."

"Okay." She removes her coat as I fasten Teemu's leash to his harness.

"Closet's right there." I gesture. "Snoop around, if you want."

She laughs.

I take Teemu down and out onto the boulevard where he immediately pees, thankfully. That's all he needs to do, but I let him sniff around for a minute since he's been alone inside for a while, but only a minute because there's a hot, willing woman inside waiting for me.

I find Annie in my dark living room at the big windows, looking at the view of the sparkling lights of Union City across the river.

"Your place is nice," she says.

"Thanks." I grab a dog treat from a package in a cupboard and give it to Teemu. "Good boy. Go lie down."

Hopefully he'll leave us alone.

I walk up to Annie, take her hands in mine, and pull her closer to kiss her.

"Mmmm."

Heat instantly explodes all over again as she leans against

me. Our mouths grind together. I release her hands to hoist her up by her ass and she wraps her legs around me, clutching my shoulders. Her dress hikes up so high I've got my hands on silky bare skin and I turn and stride down to my bedroom.

"Don't I even get a drink?" she asks against my mouth.

I stop and lean back to peer at her face.

"I'm kidding."

"Oh good. Now you made me feel like an animal."

She grins up at me. "I like animals."

"Yeah?"

"Yeah."

I carry her into the bedroom and drop her on the bed.

"This bed is huge!"

"Yeah." I glance at it with satisfaction. "I love my bed."

"It's nice." She pushes at the mattress.

I peel off my leather jacket and drop it onto the chair, then toe out of my boots. "How do you like to be fucked, Annie Bang?"

Her lips part and her breath catches. "Um..."

"Oh, wait. I remember." I undo my belt, then my fly. "You like it physical. Fast and rough."

She exhales on one word. "Yes."

I reach behind my neck to pull my sweater off. When I look at her, she's biting her bottom lip and her eyes are alight. We share a smile that slows things down a little. I pull my sweater off and toss it, too, then saunter to the bed.

"You have something, right? Protection?"

"Yeah." I move to the nightstand and yank open the door to grab condoms. I toss them onto the bed. "Now let's get you out of this little black dress." I draw a finger along her shoulder. "This sexy little black dress."

Going onto her knees, she gives me her back, and I find the

hidden zipper and tug it down. Skin. Lots of smooth golden skin. All the way to her waist. No bra.

The dress loosens and falls around her hips. Then, still facing away from me, she pushes it down to the bed. I'm staring at her back, all slender curves and glowy skin, and her ass— perfect firm globes with only the strings of thong panties stretched over her hips. "Jesus," I groan. I reach out and trace fingers over delicate swirls of ink on her ribs. "You didn't have this before."

"Mmm...no."

"What is it?"

"It's a figure." Her voice is wispy.

"Okay."

"A figure that you do in skating. Years ago, figure skaters had to do figures on the ice in competitions." She peers at me over her shoulder, her long hair sliding over bare skin, and our eyes meet. She's half-smiling, eyes heavy-lidded, and I've never seen anything as exciting and erotic in my life. "This one is figure one eleven. I like doing it."

"Huh. That's cool. Sometime you can show me on the ice." I bend and kiss the tattoo. "I remember you had a skate tattoo."

"Yes." She touches her ribs on the other side at the front. "And I have this one on my arm." She shows me the script that says MAKE EVERY DAY YOUR MASTERPIECE.

"I like that." I kiss that one, too. "Turn around."

She does so, slowly, pulling the dress out from under her. I reach out and take it from her as I check out this new view and it's just as spectacular. Holding her dress in two hands, I take my time studying her. I feel like my bedroom is on fire, flames licking around us, burning my skin.

She's small and slight, but perfectly proportioned. I remember thinking she was delicate, and she is, in a graceful, elegant way. But she's not fragile or weak. Beneath that sleek skin are toned muscles everywhere—curving deltoids, firm abs, taut thighs.

She's surveying me, too, her gaze moving over my shoulders, chest, and abs. And the bulge at my groin. Then she meets my eyes directly, confidently. Patiently.

"You're gorgeous," I say roughly. "So fucking beautiful."

Her lips curve upward. "I think you're gorgeous, too. Come here." She crooks a finger.

I toss her dress to the chair and step forward, and she reaches out to open my pants, parting the opening and slowly pushing them down my hips. Her fingers on my skin send electric sparks skittering down the backs of my thighs. I step out of my pants, now wearing a pair of black boxer briefs, and join her on the bed, also kneeling. We face each other and I can't stop myself from touching her.

"I want my mouth on you everywhere." I press a kiss to her shoulder, trail my lips and tongue over soft skin toward her throat.

Her chin lifts. "I like your mouth."

"You like coming on it." Another reminder of last time we were together, years ago.

"Oh God. Yes..."

I kiss her again, my hands sliding down her back to grip her ass, and she holds onto my shoulders. Then she sets her ass on her heels and runs her palms over my pecs, pressing kisses to my collarbone, my chest, my stomach. Her mouth is hot and her tongue drags over me in wet little licks. Jesus.

The fire in my belly burns hotter.

"Gonna take these off." I hook a finger into the side of her thong. As I drag it down, I turn her with my other hand, bending her over so her ass is in the air. "Fuck yeah. This ass is beautiful." I lean down and kiss her there, open-mouthed kisses, my hands caressing her hips and butt cheeks.

She gasps and pants, her hand in my hair, then shifts onto her butt and I drag the tiny panties down her legs. Her hair's a tousled mess around her face.

I reach for her hips and haul her toward me, tipping her onto her back. She smiles. I kneel between her legs and bend for one more quick kiss to her mouth, then I shift my knees back as I kiss my way down her torso. "I have to play with these pretty tits." I lick all around one, then over the tight little nipple, then take it into my mouth in a gentle pull. She draws in a breath, and I suck harder.

"Oh God...yes..."

I watch her responses as I linger there, cupping the sweet mounds, sucking and nibbling, Lust pumps through my veins and my dick throbs.

"Need to taste more of you." My tongue traces a trail down the groove between her abs. I tease her bellybutton, then lick lower still. My hands go to her inner thighs and push them wider, opening her to me. She's completely bare here, and I brush my lips over the softest skin.

"Look at you," I say roughly, drinking in the sight of her pink plumpness. "Gorgeous."

I lick and kiss her there, then open my mouth wide over her pussy to devour her. She's making erotic little noises, moans and gasps, writhing on the bed. I hook an arm around her thigh and press a hand to her belly to hold her still as I eat her. "Fuck, you taste good." I slide my tongue between wet pussy lips. "I could eat you forever."

She makes another wordless sound.

"Wanna make you come," I mutter, slipping a finger inside her. "So wet here. Are you aching, sweet girl?"

"God yes."

She slides a hand into my hair and I open my eyes and gaze

up along her body at her face. She watches with smoky eyes and parted lips, her cheeks flushed.

"Mmm. Good." I slide my tongue over her again.

I feel her body tensing, her abs contracting, her breath quickening, and I find her swollen clit with my tongue and rub it. Over it. Around it. Over it again. She grabs my hand that's on her belly and squeezes it so tight I'm afraid my bones might break, but I fucking love it as she comes so hard, contracting on my fingers inside her, making noises of pleasure that fill the room and make my cock hurt.

I keep licking, drawing it out, but she reaches for me and grabs my jaw and my neck and tows me up over her. "Too much," she pants. "Oh God."

I kiss her with lots of tongue, wet and sloppy, and her hands fumble at the band of my boxer briefs.

"Need these off," she gasps. "I want to see you. I want to feel you inside me."

"Oh yeah."

I roll onto my back, head on the pillows, and stretch out. Smiling, she crawls over me and lowers her mouth to the stiff outline of my dick through the cotton. She rubs her mouth and her cheek over my erection, sighing with happiness, glancing up at me a few times to see me watching her with an avid gaze. Her pale hair falls all around her face and tickles my thighs as she mouths me, then slips her fingers lower to cup the fullness of my balls.

"Mmmm." She tugs my briefs off, sliding them down my thighs, watching my cock spring up eagerly. "Ohhhh my God."

My lips part as my breath becomes choppy, my body tightening everywhere. The veins in my cock pulse and the swollen head aches.

"Beautiful," she murmurs, closing her fingers around my

shaft. She kisses the tip, licks all around the head, getting me wet, then opens her mouth on me.

Christ. Sensation burns and twists inside me, pressure building at the base of my spine.

I slide both hands into her hair and hold her head, not to push her down, just to hold her as she glides the tight circle of her mouth up and down, swirling her tongue in a dirty little tempo.

My heart is a drumbeat, heavy and pounding all through my body, my balls tightening at the base of my cock. "Okay," I gasp. "I'm so close. Come up here. I want to be inside you."

I slap a hand out to find one of the small packets I threw down earlier. Annie plucks it from me, opens it, and carefully rolls it down over my throbbing dick. That nearly does it for me. Sweat breaks out on my forehead.

Watching my face, she moves over me, rising onto her knees, gripping my cock then lowering herself onto me. At the touch of the head to her hot pussy, a groan rumbles up from my chest. Pleasure burns through me, making me crazy for more.

She bites her lip and eases herself down, slowly. I watch her eyes smolder. She's flushed pink everywhere—her cheeks, her nose, her chest and throat. So fucking perfect.

"Come on, sweetheart. You can take all of me."

She throws her head back as she finally fully takes me. My cock throbs inside her tight channel and she pauses, her pussy contracting, like she's still orgasming.

"Can you come again?" I ask.

Her tongue slides over her bottom lip. "I think so. I want to." She slips a hand down between her legs and rubs her clit.

"Oh yeah." I lift my hips, pushing up into her, not too hard because she's small. But she likes is hard.

She meets my thrust, and then we do it again, finding a rhythm together, picking up speed. She rolls her hips and rides me, moving her arms behind her to brace her hands on my thighs, giving me the most exquisite view. Then she covers my hands on her waist and urges them up to her breasts. I happily squeeze and fondle them, tweak the nipples, making her contract around me.

"I love that," she pants. "More."

I tug at the tender tips as she fucks me, fingering her clit again until she's quivering and whimpering. With a wail, she stretches down over me and kisses me, hard and desperate. I keep moving inside, her orgasm so close. Our mouths part but stay a breath apart, her hair all around our faces, her hand on my jaw. My head drops back and I wrap my arms around her shoulders as my body seizes with sensation exploding, rippling through me, heat burning over my skin. I make unintelligible guttural noises as I hold her so tightly and I'm wrenched with painful spasms.

When we've both gone still, but my body is still pulsating, she pushes up and rolls off me, collapsing on the bed beside me, her tits rising and falling with her quick respirations. "Holy hell."

Yeah. I'd agree if I could form words.

TEN

Annie

I'm stretched out prone in Logan's bed, my body deliciously languorous and replete. "That was amazing. I needed that."

"Why? Were you in a bad mood?" Logan's next to me, partially on me, one thick thigh over my legs, his arm across my back, reminding me of my teasing him earlier.

A smile tugs my lips. "No. Maybe? I was stressed." I let out a long breath. "And this bed is amazing."

He trails his fingers down my back. "Right? I spend a lot of time here."

I lift my head to peer at him through my hair. "That's kind of rude."

"What?" His hand stills.

"Talking about how much sex you have with other people."

He laughs. "That wasn't about sex. That was about how much I love sleeping."

"Oh." I draw a finger down his chest. "You're sweaty."

"Ugh." He makes a face. "I sweat a lot."

"That's okay! I like it. I like sweaty sex."

He stares at me. "You are fucking perfect." He lifts a hand to my face and rubs his thumb along my bottom lip. My belly flutters. "Why were you stressed?"

I dip my chin. "Why do you think?"

His fingertips trail over my jaw and down to my neck. Heat flickers low inside me again. "Your job? Things seem to be going okay."

"I need to do better than okay."

"Ah." The corners of his mouth lift. He doesn't push me, just waits patiently, and the words flood out of me.

"I have to do well at this. I failed at figure skating. I could never play hockey very well, so that was out. This is a way for me to stand out in my family. Everyone's always been more interested in my brothers than me. I have to be good at *some-thing*. And I want to be good at this."

His fingers move gently on my face and he studies me with warm eyes. "You weren't a failure at figure skating. I watched videos of you. You were amazing."

I blink. "You did?"

One corner of his mouth hooks up. "Yeah. Not that I know anything about figure skating, but other people seem to think you were pretty good. And you looked amazing to me. It's not your fault that you had to quit because of injuries. That's not failing."

"It felt like failing." But his words warm something inside me. "I guess I'm afraid I'm not good enough for this job." Saying it out loud feels risky, but the way Logan regards me, the tenderness of his gaze and his touch, make me feel safe. "I worry that my name got me in the door here, rather than my skills."

"I don't think so." He shakes his head. "The team wouldn't

hire you if they didn't think you'd make a difference." He pauses. "But I get that. I worry I'm not good enough, too. That all I'm good for is hitting people."

"You've been working hard."

He doesn't reply.

"Why do you think that?" I ask softly.

He doesn't answer right away. "Let's just say, you think *you're* stressed. Wait until the dads trip."

Every year the team invites family members to come on a road trip. This year the dads or other mentors are going on their road trip with them in a couple of weeks.

"The dads are stressful?"

"*My* dad is."

"So he's coming?"

"Yeah." His mouth twists. "Couldn't leave Dad out. He'd lose his shit."

"Don't you want him to come? It sounds fun."

"I know he's gonna criticize everyone. Mostly me. He'll probably tell us all we we're pussies."

My eyebrows shoot up. "But that's a compliment, right?"

He doesn't get my joke at first, then huffs a laugh. "Pussies *are* amazing." He leans over and kisses me. "Especially yours. In fact..." His hand slides down between my thighs. I swallow a gasp, my inner muscles tightening. "I might need to refresh my memory of how incredible yours is..." His mouth opens on mine.

Well, damn. I was kind of interested in pursuing that conversation, a little disturbed and a lot curious about his dad. Is that why he worries he's not good enough? But his mouth on mine and his hand between my legs and his gravelly voice talking about my pussy has my bones softening and liquid heat pooling in my center.

He moves over me, pressing me into the mattress and God,

I love how he feels on top of me, so heavy and strong. I love that he doesn't treat me like I'm delicate because I'm smaller than him, because I love sex that's active and physical.

I love that he remembered that.

Right now, I'm reveling in Logan moving on me, his mouth open on mine, his tongue stroking mine, his cock heavy on my thigh. I shift my weight, open my legs, and wrap my arms around his neck...

I end up staying all night at Logan's. We have a practice in the morning, though, so I have to go home and change. Showing up at the arena in my black dress and heels would attract a little attention.

I'd walk home but for the heels. I was going to call an Uber, but Logan insists on driving me. He brings Teemu and we make a quick stop on the ground floor for Teemu to take care of business, then we take the elevator down to the underground parking garage. Logan leads me to a shiny new Range Rover and opens the door for me.

When I'm in, Teemu jumps in and wants to ride on my lap. I'm a little startled but okay with it.

"He can ride in the back," Logan says, settling into the driver's seat. "Teemu! Go in the back."

"It's fine." I hold the pup with both hands. "I don't mind."

"He doesn't shed."

"You think I'm worried about dog hair?" I slant him an amused glance.

"I don't know. Lots of people are."

Meaning other women? "The girl who stole your fries?"

"What?"

"Were you serious about her? Until the French fry issue?"

"No. Jesus. I've never really been serious about anyone."

"Really?" I tilt my head.

"Yeah." He frowns. "Relationships never last for me."

Oh. There's a red flag.

"You're wearing a nice dress," he says, losing me for a second.

Oh right. Dog hair.

"I am." I sigh. "At eight in the morning."

Now he grins.

"Drive of shame," I add.

"Nah. Nothing to be ashamed of."

"You are right." I give a firm nod. "Walk of *no* shame. My girlfriends and I used to remind ourselves of that. No judging! It's shaming sexually active women to say we should be ashamed. Men don't get shamed for it."

"Well, I once did a walk of shame in the morning, but it wasn't because of sex, it was because I couldn't remember where I'd been the night before and my knuckles were all scraped up."

"Ohhhh." I press a hand to my mouth to stop my laugh. "Did you ever find out? Did you get in trouble?"

"The guys all told me I got in a fight with a priest and punched him in the mouth. They made it sounded entirely plausible. Turns out I didn't punch anything, just fell against a brick wall."

I can't stifle my laugh. "When did this happen?"

"Last week."

Another laugh bursts out of me.

"Kidding," he says, turning onto Eleventh Avenue. "I was nineteen."

It only takes a few minutes to arrive at my place and he pulls up in front of the building. "Cute."

The cream and taupe brick building is nothing fancy, but it's well maintained, with a blue awning over the door.

"C'mere, Teemu." Logan reaches over to take his dog from me. Before I let him go, I kiss the top of his head.

Ooops. That was way too familiar for a dog I may never see again. But I love dogs. And Teemu is super cute.

"I'll see you in a while," Logan says to me.

Our eyes meet. The air in the vehicle shifts into a sticky silence. I don't know what to say.

"Thanks for a great night!" I finally chirp. Then I drop my face into my hands. "Oh my God."

He chuckles. "This is fucked up."

"I know. We shouldn't have done that."

"We both needed it," he adds easily. "And you weren't wrong." He leans over as if he's going to kiss me but he stops and says softly, "It *was* a great night."

I swallow. "Th-thanks." I grab the door handle and jump out. "Thanks for the ride!"

Then heat floods my face at the double entendre. I hear him laughing as I close the door and dart toward the building.

In the elevator I slump against the wall and close my eyes. "Gah."

What the hell was I thinking? Sleeping with a player! I know better than that. A, he's a hockey player, which I do not get involved with after growing up with five stinky hockey boys, and B, I'm his coach.

I could get fired for that. Maybe? Was there anything in the employment contract about having sex with coworkers? Jesus. Maybe I better check the HR manual.

I rush into the apartment, now fueled by anxiety adrenaline. Ivan's coming out of the bathroom, wearing plaid pajama bottoms and rumpling his thick hair.

"I'm home!" I say brightly.

He folds his arms and nods. "I see that. Did you have a good night?"

"Oh God." I blow out a long breath. "I did."

"Well, good. You said you needed sex."

I gaze at him, my thoughts jumbled. "Um. Yeah." Do I tell him? No. I should tell no one. Absolutely no one can know about this. "I slept with Logan Coates."

"I know."

"How'd you know?" I demand, straightening.

"You two were practically singeing each other the way you looked at each other." He shrugs. "Plus you left at the same time."

I press a hand over my eyes. "Shit." I inhale a big breath. "There's something I never told you."

"What?" He tilts his head.

"Remember that last day in Pyeongchang?"

"Yeah. You went out partying and spent the night with some dude."

"It was Logan."

His head jerks back. "Huh?"

"He was there playing hockey for the U.S. team. We met up and hit it off. We were having so much fun, we hung out all day and I...went back to his room."

"Shut the front door."

I huff out a tiny laugh. "Truth. Everyone was pairing up there. Well, not just pairs. Ha. I heard there was an orgy in the whirlpool. Several countries were involved. Remember all the condoms they gave us?"

He grins. "Yeah. Apparently it was the most condoms given out in the history of winter sports. Also packets of lube."

"Yes."

"I got laid more often in those two and a half weeks than my whole life before that," Ivan says.

"Well, my one night doesn't seem so shocking now."

He laughs. "It was all those pent-up endorphins and adrenaline, plus the physical performance. Everyone was horny as hell."

"Yeah." I sigh. "We were." *Oh boy, were we.* "I shouldn't have slept with him again. Now I have to go to work and face him every day."

"Yeah, that's awkward."

"Also possibly career limiting. Ivan! I just got this job! They're going to fire me!"

"Ugh." I look up and see him wince. "It's not great. But you probably won't get fired. Oh hell, what do I know."

"I have to get to the practice facility. I need a shower. And coffee. And food." I enter my bedroom and close the door. "I'm an idiot."

As I shampoo and scrub my skin, I discover a couple of small love bites and a tenderness between my legs that weirdly make me horny all over again. My tired brain floods with erotic images and my body re-experiences a myriad of dirty sensations. I've never been with a man I'm so physically compatible with. Now I remember why that night in Pyeongchang was so incredible. It seemed like Logan took so much pleasure in figuring how to please me. It was...world altering.

I have to block out those thoughts and be a professional.

When I get to Westchester County, I go through a drive through and get a coffee and a muffin that I scarf down in my office. Then I get my skates on and hit the ice, praying the caffeine kicks in soon.

Of course my gaze goes straight to Logan, already out here, looking fit and energetic. Asshole. I feel like a bag of dirty diapers. *Focus, Annie.*

Today I'm working with four guys after practice. I keep my face neutral as I greet Evan.

"Hey, Annie," he says easily. "Have fun last night?"

"Yeah, that club is awesome." I smile, but I'm hyper aware of his facial expressions and any underlying messages, waiting for a knowing smirk. But no, he skates off and I slowly exhale.

"Okay, today we're doing something new!" I call to them. "Freeze tag. Evan and Garret, you pair up. Adam and Owen, you're together." I outline what we're doing, basically one skating forward, one skating backward (the Dmen), with their sticks, trying to tag each other. They start moving. "Faster!" I yell.

Okay, I'm getting some energy back.

They actually look like they're having fun out here. When one guy manages to tag the other they switch, deking and ducking and cutting with sharp edges. I watch them closely to see who needs more edge work.

At one point I turn and nearly fall off my skates when I see Logan in the stands. He has a cardboard cup of coffee in his hand, wearing his usual backwards ball cap, lounging back, watching. Is he watching me? What the hell? But I have to ignore him.

When we finish up and leave the ice, he comes down the steps. "Hurry up, Cookie, I'm tired of waiting around for you."

Our eyes meet. "We drove here together," he adds.

Oh. Okay, he wasn't watching me. Except, he was.

I tramp down the tunnel and sit on a bench in the hall to change out of my skates. The coaching staff has a locker room but it's all men, and I'm not willing to go in there and risk seeing my boss naked. Then I head to my office to watch video.

This is when I start freaking out.

All the alcohol has truly worn off. The feel-good sex hormones have disappeared. I have a knot in my stomach, and thinking about anyone finding out what happened last night is making every nerve ending in my body twitch.

I need to talk to Logan. Nobody can ever know about it! We have to agree on that! I stand from my desk, then sit down again. What am I going to do? I could probably get his phone number from someone, but I'd rather lick a freshly sharpened skate blade than approach someone else on the team for that.

I'm going to have to go see him.

ELEVEN

Logan

It's Saturday afternoon. Some of the guys went to a movie. I decided to stay home. And spend more time than I'd like to admit watching Annie Bang skate on YouTube.

She hasn't skated for a while, but there are plenty of videos of her and Ivan at various championship events. In some of the earlier ones, they're kids. But then they get older. And their routines turn...very adult.

Christ. I find a video with Annie wearing a bright red little number and red lipstick, her hair in a high ponytail. The song is 'Beggin' by Måneskin.

I watch with a slack jaw and heavy feeling in my gut as she and Ivan skate hand in hand facing each other. Then out of nowhere, gripping her hands, Ivan lifts her up in the air. How the fuck does he do that? Of course, she weighs about a buck ten, if that.

Holding her high over his head, his arms straight, Ivan spins. Then my heart leaps into my throat as Annie falls upside down behind his head. Jesus Christ! Then she's sideways across the back of his shoulders, holding her own ankle in a position that should not be humanly possible. Ivan's carrying her with *one arm* and keeps spinning. Then he *drops her!* But catches her in his arms. Her legs cartwheel above his head then her blades land smoothly and gracefully on the ice.

I exhale a sharp breath and slouch into my chair. Sweating profusely, I swipe at my forehead.

I click to another video. This one's different. The song is a Sam Smith one, full of angst. Annie's dress is white with silver sequins sparkling in the arena lights, a sheer skirt fluttering around her thighs. Ivan's wearing black pants and a white shirt. On top of death-defying moves, they spend a lot of time gazing into each other's eyes and touching each other's faces. At one point, Ivan's spinning, holding her against him, their arms wrapped around each other, noses touching, looking achingly in love. My eyes burn as I stare without blinking.

Jesus. She's beautiful. Graceful and elegant, from the tips of her pointed toes to her dainty fingertips.

They jump, side by side, doing I don't know how many rotations in the air, but it looks like a lot, and they're perfectly in sync, which honestly should not be possible given their height difference. When Ivan tosses her in the air, catches her as she lands, and pushes her away from him, I wince, remembering the story she told me about falling and hitting her head. When he picks her up and throws her across the ice twirling in the air, my skin goes cold and I want to close my eyes. But I keep watching. And she lands fluidly, like it's nothing. How the hell?

She must be insane to let someone do that to her! What if he was holding her over his head and his hand slipped or what if he caught an edge or...Christ. My stomach is in knots.

Then she falls. My heart lurches and I lean forward. Obviously, she's okay, but...it looks bad. But she jumps up and keeps going, barely missing a beat.

Wow. That's not just physical toughness. It takes mental strength to keep going like nothing happened.

Holy shit, Ivan's got his hand right between her legs! My mouth is a huge gaping hole in my face.

Now they live together. And dance together. I tug at the neckline of my hoodie. I'm having trouble breathing.

I need air. Time to take Teemu for a walk.

Yeah. A nice long walk along the river. I get his leash and we head out.

It's into November now. The leaves are falling and a lot of the tall grasses and plants have turned golden brown. The sun shines in the clear blue sky but its warmth is weak.

We stroll down to the riverbank because I like being near the water. I miss the ocean. Teemu takes care of business and I let him stop a lot to sniff as we head toward Pier 1, because that's fun for him

Of course I'm thinking about Annie Bang. Of *course*.

Last night was super fucking hot. My memories of that night in Pyeongchang have always been scorching hot, kind of like a fever dream, and I've wondered if my recollection is accurate or I've just built it into something incredible in my mind. But...wow. Annie's sexy. A little dirty. And fun. I couldn't get enough of her.

Was fucking her a bad idea? Oh hell yeah. We work together. She's my *coach*. Not like any other coach I've ever had, though. She's a tiny little badass in bed and I love it.

She's a tiny little badass *out* of bed, too, now that I think of it.

That thought makes me smile.

We pass Pier 1 and continue to the park where there's a dog run. Teemu loves to be let off the leash there. All kinds of dogs run freely and he quickly makes friends with a Corgi and a Bichon wearing a tiger striped sweater. I take a seat on a bench beneath a tree and watch the dogs play.

I kept things casual this morning when I took Annie home. I didn't want to turn it into a huge deal. It happened, we'll move on. It's not the first time I've had a one nighter, and probably not for her either. We're adults.

Except I keep thinking about her lush mouth, her hands on me, her tight, hot pussy... Reliving last night's events is like a porn movie in my head. It's making me hard. I swallow a groan and try to focus on the dog park again. A couple of big dogs are play wrestling and Teemu starts barking at them.

"C'mon, Teemu! It's okay, they're just having fun." I stand and stroll toward him.

"Your dog's named Teemu?" A girl near me speaks up.

I glance at her. Cute redhead. "Yeah."

She smiles. "You must be a hockey fan."

I bite back my own smile. "Yeah, you could say that."

"He's really cute." She's totally flirting with me.

"Thanks. Which dog is yours?"

She points at smallish dog of indeterminate breed in a blue sweater.

"I think Teemu needs a sweater," I say. "He's feeling left out now the weather's getting cooler."

"He definitely should have one before winter."

I could easily stay and chat with this pretty girl and maybe invite her for coffee or something...but I'm not interested. "Okay, Teemu, let's rock 'n roll! We gotta go!" I hold up his leash as the signal.

He obediently trots over to me and I clip him up. I give the woman and her dog a smile before turning away and leaving the enclosure. Instead of following the path back to the riverbank, we go out onto Riverside and stroll the sidewalk the few blocks to my building. As we approach the building entrance, a small figure shrouded in black walks out.

My eyebrows lift. It's not very often you see a nun in a full habit these days. In her black headdress with white covering her head, neck, and sides of her face, she pauses on the sidewalk in the shade of the building. She touches the cross she's wearing around her neck and appears to sigh.

"Hello, sister," I say as I approach. Teemu strains on the leash to get closer to her; I don't know why. I haul him in.

Her head snaps around. She's wearing sunglasses. And pink lip gloss. Those shiny lips part, and she says, "There you are!"

What the...wait a minute...

I've loosened my grip on Teemu and he's jumping joyfully at the nun's full skirt. She bends down to pet him. "Hi, Teemu! Who's a good boy? You're a good boy!"

"Annie?"

She looks up, slides the sunglasses down her little nose and meets my eyes. "Yep."

My jaw nearly smacks the concrete sidewalk. "What the fuck are you doing?"

"I didn't want anyone to recognize me. You said some of the other players live here, too." She gestures at the building. "I need to talk to you."

The last time a woman said that to me after a one-night stand, she thought she was pregnant.

Turns out she wasn't. Nonetheless, my stomach turns to stone. "Uh..."

"Inside," she hisses, poking her hand at the door. "Come on."

Okay, she can't know if she's pregnant already. *Get a grip, Loco.*

I let us inside the locked building and greet Juan, the doorman, then stride toward the elevator. His gaze shifts to the nun beside me, to me, back to her, then down to his desk. I almost laugh out loud.

When the elevator doors close, I stare at Annie and slowly move my head from side to side. "You are nuttier than squirrel shit."

She looks down at herself. "Possibly, yes."

"Where did you get that?"

"It's a Halloween costume. I wore it to a party a couple of weeks ago."

"Oh."

"Did you go out for Halloween?"

"Yeah, Barbie had a party."

"What did you dress up as?"

"Marty McFly."

Her eyes light up. "Oh! From Back to the Future!"

"Yeah. Why are we talking about this?"

She bites her lip. "Just making conversation." She pauses. "Why did the nun cross the road?"

I stare at her.

"To pray on the other side."

I roll my lips inward on a smile.

"What did the priest say to the nun at the salad bar?" She pauses. "Lettuce pray."

"Jesus."

"Well, that too."

I bark out a laugh.

"I'm a fun nun."

The doors slide open on my floor and I step out.

Annie pokes her head out and gives a look each way down the hall like she's in a spy movie before following me and Teemu.

"Nobody else lives on this floor."

"Just being careful."

Once inside, she rips off the wimple. "Oh God, I'm sweating."

"Come in." I lead her into the living room. "Okay, what is up?"

She sits on my sofa, looking ridiculous. And cute. And hot. Which is a little disturbing, considering her attire.

"We didn't talk. After last night. We need to uh, be on the same page."

I sit too, a short distance away from her. The habit scares me.

"Obviously, we shouldn't have done that," she continues.

I make a face of reluctant agreement.

"I am nun too happy about it." Then she cracks up. "Get it? Nun too happy?"

I slump down into the couch and cover my eyes.

"Sorry. Seriously. Nobody can know about what happened. Right?"

"What happened last night is between us."

"And your teammates who were at the club last night."

"They don't know. When Murph texted asking where I disappeared to, I didn't tell him I was with you. They won't hear it from me." I meet her eyes steadily. "Okay?"

She nods slowly. "We have to work together."

"I promise I'll be as much of an asshole as I was before."

"Really?"

"No."

She tilts her head with a "come on" look.

"I said I'll try to do better in the attitude department."

"Okay. I'm worried I'll be fired."

"Phhht. They won't fire you."

"How do you know that?" She's practically wringing her hands. "They could!"

I reach out and take her hands in mine, separating them and curling my fingers around hers. "Relax. You're not really in a position of authority over me."

She wrinkles her nose. "I suppose."

"It's not like I can get anything from sleeping with you."

She stares back at me.

"I mean, professionally."

"Right."

"No one will ever know."

"And it can't happen again."

I clear my throat. "Definitely not."

She clasps my fingers and stares into my eyes. Her hair's damp and frizzy at the temples. She's not wearing makeup other than her lips and she looks as innocent and chaste as a nun.

But I know she's not.

Heat slides down my spine and my balls throb. Ah, fuck.

The moment stretches out. The air crackles around us. Her gaze drops to my mouth. The heat in my groin builds. Her pretty lips part and her eyes flick up to mine.

I'm holding her hands and I can't stop myself from dragging her across the couch and onto my lap and crushing my mouth to hers.

"Have to get this off," I mumble, tugging at the costume. "I'm so fucking turned on by you, but it feels dirty."

She chokes on a laugh and turns her back to me. "Can you untie me? And unzip me?"

There are two parts to the costume, and I quickly undo them and help her drag the voluminous dress over her head. Beneath, she's wearing flowered pink leggings and a matching sports bra. "Whoa. What a difference." I run my hands all over the smooth, stretchy fabric that hugs her hips, thighs, ass. "But need you out of this, too." I try to work the sports bra up. "Shit, this thing's tight."

"I know." Still facing away from me, she crosses her arms and slips her fingers beneath it., then wriggles out of it.

Then I peel her leggings down over her hips, taking a pair of thong panties with them. I pull her down onto my lap, and her ass presses into my throbbing dick. She lets out a low moan and I reach around her to cup her tits. "Perfect." I squeeze and mold them, then pinch her nipples. Her ass cheeks tighten against me and her breathing quickens.

"Not fair," she gasps. "You're still dressed and I'm naked."

"I can fix that." I straighten, reach behind my neck, and yank off my hoodie. Then I grip her hips and shift her forward on my lap so I can undo the zipper of my jeans. My cock is hard and leaking, poking up beneath the waistband of my boxer briefs, and I shove them and my jeans down my thighs. "Wait."

"What?" she pants.

I thrust a hand into the pocket of my jeans and pull out a condom.

"Ohhhh." She stands briefly and starts to turn, but I keep her facing away from me, kicking off my clothes, then guiding her back to my lap. I admire the view as I do so—the sweep of her waist and hips, the groove of her spine, the perfect smooth roundness of her ass. "I'm on birth control. Just so you know."

What is she saying?

"But condoms are good. For now."

"Yeah." I'm good with it, too. Whatever she wants. And I appreciate her telling me that.

I resume playing with her tits and she falls black against my chest. I slide a hand down over her abs and between her legs and she accommodates by spreading her legs. My fingers brush over velvety skin and she shivers. Then I explore deeper and find a bounty of slick, wet flesh. "Wet. So wet. What a drenched little pussy."

She moans again when I stroke her there, her head rolling on my chest. I flick her nipple, pinch her pussy lips, then pet her clit. Her body jolts against me. My brain is flooded with lust.

"Gotta suit up," I mutter, reaching for the condom. I get it on in a flash, then grip Annie's hips and lift her over me. She curls her fingers around my shaft and together we line ourselves up so I can enter her. "Ah, fuck. You feel so fucking good, babe."

"Yessss." She hisses out the word, squeezing around me as I press upward, clenching my ass and thighs. "Oh God, yes. So good. Filling me up."

I'm there. All the way in, her ass on my groin, my cock buried deep inside her. I pinch her clit and she shudders hard. "I'm so fucking close," I mumble into her vanilla-scented hair. "Gonna go off fast."

"M-me too. God."

I circle a wet fingertip over her clit and Jesus, in seconds she's tensing, tightening, wailing. The squeeze on my dick is excruciating and I thrust up harder. She sits up and, with my hands on her hips, I hold her in place as I fuck up into her in savage, mindless strokes, lost in black bliss. Pressure builds at the base of my spine. My abs tighten, my heart pounds and then pleasure crashes through me, blinding me. "Jesus Christ!" I shout, shuddering.

Her hands push into my knees as she gasps and quivers, then we both collapse back into the couch cushions, a heap of damp skin, messy hair, and sticky fingers. Holy Mother of God in a raincoat.

OF COURSE we end up in my bed for another round. Her endurance and appetite match mine, and I could weep at the perfection of it. I'm almost asleep, drifting pleasantly.

"Three nuns die in a car crash and end up before the gates of St Peter."

My eyes pop open. "What?"

Annie's spread out over my chest, our legs tangled. She rubs one foot up my hairy calf and grins, propping her chin on her hand flat on my chest. "It's a joke. St Peter says to the nuns, 'Given you are nuns and have devoted your life to good works, you only have to answer one question each to enter Heaven.' He looks at the first nun and asks, 'Where did the first woman live?' She says, 'The garden of Eden.'"

I press my lips together, not sure where this is going, although I appreciate the nun humor.

She continues. "St. Peter nods approval and looks at the second nun. 'What was the name of the first woman?' The second nun pauses for a second and then replies, 'Eve.'"

I nod, my smile breaking free.

"'Well done!' says St. Peter. He turns to the third nun. 'As the Mother Superior you should be able to answer this—what did Eve say to Adam when she first saw him?'" Annie pauses. "The Mother Superior furrows her brow and says, 'Oh, that's a hard one.'" The furrow in Annie's forehead matches the one in the story. "'Correct!' says St. Peter. 'You may enter.'"

Yeah, I laugh. "That is terrible." I give one ass cheek a little tap.

"It's funny!" She's laughing. "Come on!"

"Okay, maybe a little funny." My eyes drift closed again.

"Hey, are you going to sleep?"

"Yes."

"Oh."

"Have I told you how much I love sleeping?"

"But it's the middle of the afternoon."

"Doesn't matter," I mumble. "It's my superpower. I can sleep anywhere. Anytime. Especially after sex. Or food. I love sleeping."

She snuggles in closer. "Okay."

"Even better with you here," I say, shifting her into a more comfortable position. "Let's have a lil nap. Sleep with me, Mini."

TWELVE

Annie

"I'm hungry."

"Me too. Do you want to go out?"

We've just been awakened from our nap by Teemu. He's on the bed, staring at us, doing funny little bounces on his front legs. Logan was right. This bed is amazing, he's amazing, and I crashed hard. "Mmm. In my nun costume?"

"Oh, right. Okay, let's Door Dash. What would you like?"

"I have a craving for tacos."

"I love tacos." He reaches for his phone. "We can order, then I'll take Teemu out."

"Is that what he wants?"

"Yeah." Logan grins at his dog. "Right buddy? It's walk time." He looks back at me. "So...tacos? There's a good place in Hell's Kitchen."

"Golden Bottle," I reply immediately.

"Yeah." He looks up and grins. "That's it."

"Ivan took me there one night. Great margaritas."

He frowns. "Ivan."

I tilt my head. "My roommate. Friend. Partner."

"Yeah, I got that last night. When you were practically banging on the dance floor."

"Ohhhhhh no. Come on."

He rolls his eyes and mutters, "Well, it was pretty sexy." He pauses. "I watched more of your skating routines this afternoon."

My eyebrows shoot up and I smile with delight. "Did you?"

"Yeah. Also very sexy. You two looked like you were ready to do each other on the ice."

I sigh happily. "Yeah. That's what we wanted it to look like."

He scowls. "Because he's gay."

I laugh. "No! He's not gay."

"Lots of people wanted you to be a couple. There were all kinds of comments about it on those videos. Like the one that said you two are beautiful and should have a million babies for the good of humanity."

"Oh my God!" More laughter bursts out of me. "Now you sound like my mom."

He frowns. "What?"

"Never mind." I roll my eyes.

"You say you're just friends, but were you ever more than friends?"

I purse my lips and regard him for a few seconds. I'd almost think he's jealous. "We tried to kiss once. It didn't go well. We both ended up cackling with laughter. We never tried it again."

"Huh."

"We *are* friends," I assure him. "He's like a brother. Although I have enough of those. And we do have chemistry on the ice." For a moment, sorrow aches in my chest at what could have been. I blow out a breath and shake it off. "But in real life, there's never been any romantic chemistry."

"Does he see you naked?"

A laugh pops from my lips. "No."

"So, no sexual chemistry?"

"No." I lean forward. "Not like this..." And I slowly kiss his mouth.

Yeah, there's chemistry all right. Just that kiss has heat rising around us.

We draw back, only a breath apart, and stare into each other's eyes. "Yeah. That's...chemistry."

Teemu lets out a sharp bark and we both swivel our heads to look at him.

A smile flickers on Logan's lips and he turns his attention back to his phone to pull up the menu. With our heads together we look it over. We both want beef birria tacos, and he adds on a guacamole and salsa combo with chips, and also some of the butter poached corn. Also margaritas.

"I'm excited!" I say when the order's place, clapping my hands. "That sounds so good."

"Okay, Teemu. Let's go." He glances up at me.

I bite my lip. "You go ahead and take him."

He meets my eyes, knowing I won't go with them in case someone sees us. "Okay. It'll be quick. Be right back."

I stay snuggled in his beautiful bed. The mattress is firm but soft, the sheets the perfect combination of crisp and silky, the duvet like a cloud.

Wow.

How did this happen? I came here to tell him we couldn't sleep together again and I ended up naked within minutes.

There's something about him I can't resist. I kind of don't like it, because I like to think I'm in control of myself, always, but...I also do like it because...ohhhh I'm melting again thinking about it. I think this sensation is called swooning. Entering a state of rapture. I love thinking about him...about his smile, his teasing, his big...stick. How he feels inside me. How his hands feel on me.

I roll myself into the bed covers and press my face into a pillow.

Yes, that fluttering in my belly is desire. And I can't stop smiling.

Swoon.

When Logan returns, Teemu runs to the bed and leaps up onto it to smile at me. "Did you have a good walk?" I ask, sitting up to arrange pillows behind me.

"He did." Logan strolls in behind him. He joins me on the bed, dressed in a pair of gray sweatpants that cling to his hockey butt and thick thighs, a navy Henley, and a backward ball cap. "Get lost, dog."

"Hey. That's not nice."

"We don't need an audience."

"Audience for what?" I bat my eyelashes. "We just ordered food, remember?"

"Right."

"Tell me about why you don't want your dad to come on the dads trip."

His face shutters. "Eh. I told you. He's super critical. Old school tough guy."

I trace my fingers over the soft shirt stretched across his shoulders. "Will he really criticize you?"

"One hundred percent."

"He must be proud of you, though. You made it into the NHL."

"If he's proud, he's never told me."

My stomach twists. "That's terrible." I regard him unhappily. "My parents had their plates full with six of us, and a lot of sibling rivalry, but we knew they loved us. Even when I failed."

"You didn't fail. You were injured."

I hitch my shoulder dismissively. "Whatever. It's still a failure. I failed at hockey, too."

He frowns. "Look what you accomplished. I saw those videos this afternoon. You're talented. Absolutely beautiful on the ice."

My throat squeezes. "Thank you."

"It must have been hard to give that up, when you were so good."

I nod somberly. "It was." I stare at the buttons on his shirt. "I was in a pretty deep depression for about a year. Everyone was worried about me. I didn't know what to do with my life, and I didn't actually care. I just wanted to sleep a lot." I make a face. "Thankfully my parents were on top of me and made sure I got help."

"I'm sorry." He kisses my forehead. "I wish that never happened to you."

My heart squeezes. "Yeah. But it did. I dealt with it."

"You've made the best of what happened. No more getting thrown up in the air seems like a good thing, to me."

My reluctant smile pushes at my lips.

"Now you're using those talents to help others," he adds.

My face softens. "You actually admit I might be helping?"

"Maybe."

My heart turns over in my chest. My fingers move to his beard and stroke it, following the hard line of his jaw. "I'll take a maybe."

We share a slow smile that has heat burgeoning low in my belly. Again.

I sink my teeth into my bottom lip. "This wasn't what was supposed to happen when I came over here," I say quietly.

"Oh sure. I know you wore that nun costume just to seduce me."

I swat his shoulder. "I'm serious! We can't be doing this."

"I know." He runs a gentle hand over my tangled hair. "But here we are."

"Here we are." I'm not exactly dashing out.

"You're not what I thought, Annie Bang."

I press my lips together briefly then admit, "You're not what I thought, either."

"Since you hated my guts, I'm going to take that as a good thing."

I want to protest that I didn't hate his guts, but actually I did, so I say, "It confuses me." Because right now I'm in his bed, remembering the feel of his hair-roughened legs, the heat of his body, the touch of his hands. And his mouth. And I'm sinking into red-hot arousal again.

"Don't look at me like that," he growls. "We have food coming in a few minutes."

My smile is probably a little smug. Because I love the fact that I can affect him like that.

Our food does arrive. Logan pulls a T-shirt out of a drawer and hands it to me. I gratefully slide it over my head, breathing in the scent of the soft cotton. It hangs nearly to my knees and I look ridiculous but I don't care. I find my clothes and slip on my panties under the shirt as Logan goes down to get the food.

We eat at the small breakfast bar between Logan's kitchen and living room. He pulls plates out of a cupboard and points to the cutlery drawer and together we arrange the food then dig in. I study the galley-style kitchen—sparkling all white other than the dark wood floor. In fact, the whole apartment is white on white on white. "Is the all-white décor a choice?"

He glances around. "It's how the apartment came. But I kinda like it. And my stuff all works with it."

I nod. His furniture is minimal—a big gray sectional, a black coffee table topped with pale marble, a couple of squarish charcoal upholstered chairs all sitting on a rug patterned in pale shades of blue and silver. His bedroom is also white, with dark furniture, the huge platform bed with dark gray upholstery and silvery-blue bedding.

I return my attention to the kitchen and the accessories displayed—a fancy coffee machine, a white ceramic pot containing what appear to be well-used utensils, a garlic keeper, and an knife block holding a set of expensive-looking knives. "Do you cook?"

"Yeah. I like cooking."

"Cool. Me too. What's your specialty?"

"I don't know if I have one, but I make pretty good spaghetti and meatballs. Also beer cheese soup."

"Yum."

"What about you?"

"I've been trying a lot of Asian recipes lately. Last week I made sesame beef with gochujang udon noodles."

His eyes light up. "That sounds fantastic."

"I'll make it for you sometime."

What am I saying?

"I once made gochujang sloppy Joes," he says. "So good."

"Ooooh I like that idea."

Crap. Something in common. Other than sex. This is terrible.

I dip my taco into the sauce. "Did you start playing hockey young?"

"I think as soon as I could walk. Dad was pretty determined I was going to play."

"But you like it, don't you?"

"Yeah, of course. But if I'd hated it, I'd probably have been put up for adoption." He grimaces.

I wrinkle my nose. "No."

He shrugs and scoops up guacamole with a chip. "It's not that much of an exaggeration. My whole life I knew the way to make Dad happy was hockey."

His dad sounds...interesting. "Maybe I'll get to meet him when he comes for the dads trip."

"Ugh."

"But first we have to get through the team building retreat," I say.

"Right."

We're going to a resort in the Poconos for three days for a teambuilding retreat. The team wanted to do it before the season started but couldn't make it happen then, so we're taking advantage of a short break in the schedule to do it now. "I'll be the only woman there."

"Lucky you."

I laugh. "Oh God. I'm scared."

"Bullshit. You're not scared of men."

I bite back my smile, pleased at his observation. "True."

"More like we're all scared of *you*."

"Phhhht." I change the subject. "I saw that you're from California."

"Yeah. Born and raised in Redondo Beach."

"Do you miss it?"

"At times, yeah. When it's four hundred degrees below zero here."

I laugh. "I'm from Minnesota. We call that January."

He grins. "Mom and Dad moved there from Buffalo when he got traded. I was born soon after that. I missed being born in Buffalo by a few months. Dad ended his career in California and they stayed."

"My parents did the same. Dad played in St. Paul and

decided to stay there when he retired from hockey." I pause. "You have no brothers or sisters?"

"Nope. I used to ask for a brother all the time. I didn't know until I was older that they tried, but it never happened."

I'm picturing little Logan playing alone, pleading for a brother, and goddammit, my throat tightens. I look down at my food. Finally, I say, "Well, I would have been happy to give you one of my brothers."

He chuckles. "Somehow I doubt that."

"Why do you say that?"

"Because you hate me for what I did to your brother. Obviously you're very loyal."

I pick up my margarita. He's right. I talk shit about my brothers all the time, but I was genuinely terrified when Jensen got hurt and was absolutely willing to hold a grudge against the guy who did it for the rest of my life.

Logan never had that.

It's not that I feel sorry for him. But he had a different childhood than I did, I'm learning, in many ways. And that's made him who he is. Hard-working. Honorable. Kind.

When we're done eating, he feeds Teemu and I help him put away the leftovers and load the dishwasher. "That was so good. Thank you."

Drying his hands on a towel, he moves closer to me in the small space and backs me against the counter. He tosses the towel aside and reaches for the hem of the T-shirt, sliding his hands up my thighs. "You look smokin' hot in my shirt."

I drape my arms over his shoulders, enjoying the flipflop in my low belly. He finds my bare butt and hoists me up easily, setting me on the counter. I open my thighs so he can move between them and he bends his head to kiss me. And here we are again, falling right into it, into a hot dream, mouths sliding, tongues licking. It's crazy and aggravating and wonderful.

That sweet ache between my legs spreads through my pelvis and heat washes through me. I drag my fingertips through his silky hair, over the soft skin at the nape of his neck, and let my head fall back as his mouth glides down to my neck, my throat, gently sucking. I can't stop the needy little moans that fall from my lips and I hook my heels behind him.

He tastes so good. Feels so good. I want to feel more of him, all his hard muscles and warm skin and his thick, beautiful cock. I want to submerge myself in every sensation, breathe him in, lick him all over.

He tugs at the loose neckline of the T-shirt I'm wearing, pulling it down below one breast then bends his head to pull my nipple into his mouth. Pleasure courses from his mouth to my pussy, intensifying that ache. "Oh God." I let go of him and brace my hands on the counter behind me, leaning back to give him access.

He licks all over my breast, suckles hard on the tip again, and I nearly collapse.

"Fucking perfect." He opens his mouth wider and sucks more of me, eliciting a luscious pain, making me shudder.

I sit up to grab at the shirt he's wearing, shoving it up under his armpits, and he releases me long enough to lift his arms and tug it off. My hands slide over his back, delighting in the feel of his skin, the play of muscle beneath. My hips are lifting against him. The ridge of his erection presses against the cotton triangle of my panties, and I shift to get the pressure right where I need it.

"Hot for it, aren't you," he mumbles, moving to my other breast.

"Yes. I want you." I press against him, the faint stirrings of an orgasm gathering low inside me. "I need to come."

"I can tell. Rubbing that hot little kitty all over me like

that." He groans and lifts his head, looking down into my face. "Jesus, you're fire."

I can't stop the wave barrelling down on me, it's out of control and enormous, surge after surge of pure, intense pleasure. I shudder and gasp through it.

"Jesus." He watches me, letting me take my pleasure, his mouth wet and his eyes hazy. "Beautiful girl. That is so sexy."

I can't breathe. I hang onto him again, pressing my forehead to his shoulder, dragging air into my straining lungs. "I'm sorry."

"What?" He caresses my hair. "Why sorry?"

"I came too soon. I wanted you inside me." I suck in another breath. "I want you to come, too."

"Oh, babe. I will." And he lifts me off the counter and carries me to his bedroom.

THIRTEEN

Logan

"This time I'll give you my number."

It's Sunday morning, and Annie's preparing to do another walk of shame, except dressed as a nun I don't think people will be assuming she just got laid. Multiple times.

"Okay." She sighs. "But we still never really sorted out what's going on here."

She's not wrong.

I don't know what to say. The smart thing would be to agree this can't happen again. But I don't want to agree to that. Because I don't even want her to go home right now.

I could totally get addicted to her. To the way she looks at me, like I'm actually worth something. To the way she gets me and my need to do better. To prove myself. To the lack of judgment when I talked about my dad. The way she's forgiven me (I think?) and looked past who I am on the outside. I don't let many people do that and it's fucking terrifying but also...not.

I admire her desire to be successful, to be respected for herself, because I want that too.

And her hot little body doesn't help with that addiction. All I have to do is think about her pussy squeezing me and I get hard all over again.

I settle on honesty, because I can be a cynical asshole but I'm not a liar. "I don't know what to say."

Our eyes meet.

"I know." She sighs again. "I want to be responsible and smart and do the right thing. Doing the right thing is important."

I nod.

"But we're not hurting anyone," she adds softly. "We just need to keep it on the down low."

I settle my hands on her hips. "I think it's riskier for you."

She purses her lips. "Yeah."

"I hate that. I promise you no one will find out from me."

Her eyes soften. "I trust you."

Why? I want to ask her why she trusts me. The fact that she trusts me nearly sends me to my knees, a swelling sensation rising in my chest. I don't know if I've ever felt this before. "Thank you."

She nods, smiling faintly.

I give her a last kiss at my door and, after making sure the coast is clear, she slips out.

I rub the back of my neck as I wander to the living room window and gaze out. Wow.

This is really...something.

The sky is overcast and gloomy. It looks like it might rain. I should have insisted on driving Annie home, but she didn't want to take a chance on us being seen together.

My phone buzzes and I grab it. It's a text.

ANNIE: OMG I ran into Hunter and Easton on my way out

There's a shocked face emoji.
I actually laugh.

LOGAN: Did they recognize you?

ANNIE: I don't think so! They were walking a dog. He's so cute!

LOGAN: Not as cute as Teemu

ANNIE: Of course not

LOGAN: That's Otis. Millsy's dog

ANNIE: I miss Teemu already

LOGAN: What about me

Her response is a laugh emoji.

ANNIE: It might take a wee bit longer to miss you

LOGAN: Jesus. I'm second to my dog

Now I get a kiss emoji. And I grin.

Our text convo stops there, but I keep my phone in my hand. Just in case.

Speaking of walking the dog, I should do that.

"OKAY, let's get this show on the road!" Mike calls, standing in front of the big tour bus parked outside the practice facility. He's the manager of team services and is the guy that herds us onto buses, planes, and trains, and into and out of hotels so we get to our games and practices.

We're heading off for three days of fun in the "sun." We've never done a teambuilding retreat like this, but I guess it shows how seriously team management is taking this "we want to win" stance. I'm honestly not sure what to expect, other than I know we'll be golfing this afternoon, having a couple of practices at a nearby rink, and doing some mysterious teambuilding exercises.

I bound up the steps of the bus and come face to face with Annie, sitting in the second row. She looks up and our eyes meet in what feels like a physical jolt. It's all I can do not to break out in a huge smile and reach for her.

She gives me a polite greeting and I force my feet to keep moving down the aisle of the bus and then I drop into the seat next to J-Bo. "Hey."

"Hey, man. All set for some wild times?"

"I don't think that's what this is about."

He sighs. "I know. But at least we get to golf."

"Yeah, that'll be good. It's supposedly one of the best courses in the country."

"Amazing. The lodge looks really nice, too."

We've got a two-hour ride ahead of us. The bus fills up and the noise level escalates, everyone in high spirits as we take off to do some fun stuff.

It's a good way to get to know each other better. Some of us have been around for a while, but there are a lot of new guys here. Being away from all distractions, just us on the road, is cool, and it's not even a road trip with the pressure of a game.

I listen to a podcast about health and wellness, then one by a comedian that has me chuckling to the point where J-Bo beside me is giving me dirty looks.

I pop out an earbud. "What?"

"What are you laughing at?"

"A podcast."

"It's rude to laugh in front of someone." He frowns.

I give him a what-the-fuck look. "I'm not laughing at *you*."

"How do I know that?" He shakes his head. "It's disturbing."

My jaw dangles open. "You have got to be kidding me."

"How would you like it if I sat here and laughed? You don't think you'd feel self-conscious?"

I stare at him. "Jesus. I don't know. No. Get a grip, man. Also, I have to listen to something entertaining or I'll fall asleep."

He huffs and I have to swallow another laugh. Shaking my head, I resume listening, but this time I cover my mouth with my hand to hide my amusement.

As we near the resort, the scenery is gorgeous. Autumn tints the leaves gold and orange, the foliage dense and lush, the sky a clear blue overhead. We turn off the interstate onto a narrower road and I catch glimpses of sparkling water between some of the trees before we slow and then stop in front of an immense building, three stories tall, all brick and stone and rustic wood.

Nice.

I get settled into my room on the third floor with an amazing view. Before we hit the links we have lunch in a big private room, and the food is fantastic—an impressive salad bar, butternut squash soup, and a choice between meatball bahn mi or a turkey panini. There are even chocolate chip cookies for dessert. I grab an extra one and munch on it as we head over to the golf clubhouse.

Our clubs have been unloaded by team staff and are waiting for us. I change into my golf shoes as Mike goes around telling us who's in our foursomes. My head jerks back when I hear I'm golfing with Annie. Oh hell, who made *that* decision?

Not just her of course; also TK (Tyler Kadny, our backup goalie) and Hellsy (Josh Heller). How did they pick these foursomes? It seems random but cynical me is suspicious.

Annie rolls up with her bag as we climb into carts. She's dressed in a shorts-skirt combo thing and a pink sleeveless collared top, and is wearing light makeup with shiny pink lips. Multi-shades of blond hair are sleeked back into a high ponytail that curves into a perky comma shape and diamond studs glint in her tiny earlobes.

I eye her golf clubs. "Are those children's clubs?"

She rolls her lips in on a smile and gives me a look, her chin lowered. "No."

I catch Hellsy's perturbed look. No doubt he's worried she's going to bust my balls like she did Jake's that time. "Kidding," I say with a smile. "Just a joke."

Hellsy moves to lift her bag into the car. Oh hell to the nah. I step forward, but Annie waves us both away. "I got it, thanks." She hoists it onto the back of the cart, belying her delicate appearance. The bag's nearly as big as she is but she can handle it.

Hellsy hops into the cart with TK leaving me and Annie. Fine.

We get in our cart and cruise over the first hole to wait to tee off.

"I didn't know we'd end up on the same foursome," she says.

"Me either."

"We'll have to be careful."

I nod. "Hopefully I can keep my hands off you."

She smirks. "Touch me and die."

I choke on a laugh. "Got it."

"This is a nice place." She looks around. "I've never been to the Poconos."

"Me either."

As we wait our turn to tee off, I say to Hellsy, "Are your dad and uncles coming to the retreat?"

His dad and three uncles own the team. Yeah, it's a little weird. It's our first season with the new owners, so who knows how involved they're going to be. It has to be weird for Hellsy, too.

"They're coming for dinner on Saturday night," he says.

"I'm impressed with this," I tell him, gesturing. "Nice place. But are they going to make us do weird team building things? Like...two truths and a lie? A scavenger hunt?"

"Build an egg cart," TK adds. "That'll protect an egg when we drop it. I did that once at a teambuilding thing."

Hellsy snorts. "I have no fucking clue what we're going to do." He slides a glance at Annie. "Uh...sorry—"

She waves a hand and cuts him off, grinning. "Don't apologize. You guys have heard me swear." She makes a face. "I swear like a sailor. Much to my mom's disappointment."

"You have five brothers," I say.

"Thank you, Captain Obvious," she replies. "And yeah, they swear like sailors, too. Or should I say, like hockey players. My mom never stood a chance."

"I played with Jakob years ago," TK tells her with a smile. "Great guy."

She smiles back at him. Damn, she's pretty and I can tell TK notices that too. "He's okay."

When I get up to the box to tee off, I'm conscious of her behind me. I want to look at her so badly, to see if she is watching me, what the expression on her face is, but I force myself to stare down at the small white ball as I adjust my stance and my grip. I take my swing and with a perfect ping I send the ball flying a good two hundred yards, nice and straight.

I exhale, straighten and turn. "You're up," I say to her.

How self-conscious does *she* feel, surrounded by guys? Actually, she seems pretty relaxed.

My gaze lingers on her hands gripping the club—her nails are a pearly pink, perfect oval shape—then drops to her legs, slender and toned. She may be dressed appropriately for a golf course, but she doesn't look like a golfer. She looks like five feet two of pure sex.

I swipe my forehead.

She glances down the fairway then swings, and holy shit, her ball goes nearly as far as mine. Well, about hundred sixty yards, maybe. Pretty good for a little thing.

I exchange a glance with TK, both of us lifting our eyebrows.

I want to grin. She's fucking awesome.

"Was that just lucky, or do we actually have a chance of winning today?" I ask her.

She purses her lips and gives me a saucy look. "Totally luck."

"It's not a tournament," Hellsy reminds us.

"Everything's a competition," Annie and I say at the exact same time.

Our eyes meet.

Electricity dances over my bare arms, and I laugh. "Glad we're on the same page."

Our eyes meet and hold and it's like pulling two magnets apart for us to disengage.

We watch TK tee off.

"Try choking down on the shaft!" I call to him.

He straightens and turns to face me.

Hellsy cracks up and Annie hides a laugh.

"Are you serious?" TK calls.

I bite back my grin. "Yeah. Also, spread your legs a little more."

Hellsy nearly falls down onto the grass and TK sags over his club, laughing too. "Fuck," he mutters. "Shut up, man."

I catch Annie's dancing eyes and we share our amusement.

Look away.

We can't be eye fucking on the golf course all afternoon.

Things get easier when TK jumps into my cart with me at one point, leaving Annie and Hellsy together. Hellsy's all married off, so I don't need to worry about him flirting with her.

At the eighth hole as we watch Hellsy tee off, I'm looking at the map of the course and the dogleg at this hole, and I call out to him, "It bends a little to the left."

I hear a choked laugh and look up at Annie.

"That's what she said," she says.

Hellsy drops his head forward, and TK snickers.

I guess we don't have to worry about her complaining to management about us making her feel uncomfortable.

I manage to finish the game with a respectable score of ninety-nine. Annie ends up with a hundred five.

"So, not luck," I say to her dryly back at the clubhouse. "You know how to golf."

She tosses her ponytail and smiles. "I golfed with my brothers a lot in the summers. My parents are both good golfers, too."

"Your dad had a great hockey career. What's he doing now?"

"He coaches. He and Mom still live in St. Paul."

I nod. "Nice."

LIGHT 'EM UP   149

Things get awkward again, but Axe and J-Bo stroll up to us. "How'd you play?" J-Bo asks me.

"Decent." I shrug. "Okay, ninety-five. How about you?"

"Didn't break a hundred." J-Bo frowns. "I hear Nate shot ninety-one."

"Damn."

"We told you it's not a tournament," Hellsy says with a laugh and a slap on my back. "Let's go get beers."

We start moving toward the clubhouse and I sense Annie hanging back. I turn. "Coming?" I ask casually.

"Yep." Her reply is equally as casual and she follows along.

That's pretty much our itinerary for tonight. We have dinner in the private room, a three-course meal where we choose our starter, salad, and main course. I enjoy a delicious char broiled pork chop. Annie and I manage to take seats far apart, but I can't stop myself from looking over at her, time after time.

After dinner, she disappears and I hang out for a while with the guys, bragging about our golf games and basically shooting the shit, then we head up to our rooms. We have practice in the morning.

In my room, though, I can spy the outdoor hot tub glowing steamy turquoise blue through the trees. Man, I'd love to sink myself into that and let the jets pummel my muscles. Why not? I did pack a pair of swim shorts knowing there's a pool and hot tub here, so I quickly change into them and grab a towel from the bathroom to sling around my neck. I head back downstairs and find the exit to the hot tub.

Crap. It's chilly out here. My sandals slap softly on the wooden deck as I stride toward the pool nestled among trees and some big, rugged rocks. The pool lights illuminate the steam rising from the water, giving the space an eerie kind of vibe. I pause at the steps down into the water and drop my towel onto the deck, then descend into the wet warmth. Aaaah.

"Um. Hi."

I miss a step and pitch forward, nearly going face first into the pool. With some blundering splashes I manage to save myself from falling in, and when I finally get my feet firmly beneath me, I focus on the other person in the hot tub—a small blonde I didn't notice in all the vapor.

FOURTEEN

Annie

"Whoa. Easy there." I didn't mean to startle him into falling in the pool.

"Hi." His gaze circles the pool, clearly checking to see if anyone else is here. "I didn't see you there."

I nod. "I figured that. Sorry."

He's standing right in front of me, all carved muscles, broad shoulders, and lean hips. Jesus. I am up close and personal with thick thighs beneath clinging wet board shorts not to mention the bulge at his crotch.

I've spent my whole life around athletes. Sure, they have great bodies. But this man is freakin' Greek god perfection from head to toe.

The air around us is already steamy and now goes thicker and hotter. As our gazes lock on each other, I can feel the pull between us.

"Uh...okay if I join you?"

Oh God. Please do. Please... My lips pucker up on a smile. "It seems inappropriate."

"I want it to be inappropriate," he says with a low groan. He takes a couple of steps away from me and sits on the bench below the water surface, submerging that perfection up to his shoulders. My gaze lift to his face. He lifts a wet hand and shoves it into his thick dark gold hair.

Now I'm tingling in my pleasure place.

"It feels amazing." He leans his head back, eyes closed. "I love hot tubs."

I've only been here a few minutes and the water *is* decadently warm and soothing. "Me too. I came here for some peace and quiet."

He opens one eye. "Are you saying you want me to be quiet?"

I pucker my lips on a smile. "*Can* you be quiet?"

He snorts. "Of course I can be quiet."

The burble of the water surrounds us here at the edge of the woods. I tip my head back to peer up at the inky black sky dotted with pinpricks of brilliance and the glow of the Milky Way. You don't see the sky like this in the city.

Still silent.

I shift so a jet is pushing at my right shoulder blade. I'm feeling the golfing from earlier. I haven't golfed in ages. It's not my favorite thing to do, but I wanted to be a good sport.

More silence.

Jesus. He's really not going to say anything.

I catch one corner of his mouth lifting, as if he knows this is bugging me, as if he knows I want to talk but can't say anything and he's not going to be the one to break.

Competitive. Just like me.

I blow out a sigh.

"You okay?" he asks.

"Yes. Just relaxing."

"You don't seem relaxed."

I roll my lips in and bite my top lip. "How am I supposed to relax when you're..." I gesture at him and his near nakedness. "You're stressing me."

"I'm *stressing* you? I'm sitting here quiet as a one-handed clap."

Yeah, but you're sitting there...

"Maybe you should talk." God, I sound like an idiot.

"We could talk quietly." He rises halfway out of the water, looks around again, then glides over to sit beside me.

I swallow. "I think it was better with you over there."

"Better how?" He rubs his leg against mine.

"Um. Safer," I choke out.

"Yeah. Probably." His hand rests on my thigh. "But I like touching you."

I whimper. I like it too. "We can't do this. Someone could come..."

"I know." He caresses my leg and leans down to brush his lips over my temple.

Arousal sweeps through me like fire. His lips whisper more kisses over my cheek and a throbbing heaviness develops between my legs.

Oh God.

His hand slides over my thigh again, then between my legs...higher. I can't stop my legs from parting or my hips from lifting, and then he cups my pussy through my bathing suit bottom. I pulse against his palm.

"Logan..."

"Mmm. I know." He kisses my jaw.

I suck my bottom lip between my teeth to keep myself quiet. I glance around the wooded space in case there's someone there. But it's quiet and dark. He rubs my pussy and the ache there intensifies.

"We can't do this."

"Shhh." He nudges my face with his to turn my mouth toward him and captures my lips in a soft, clinging kiss. He increases the pressure on my straining clit.

I have to feel him, too...my hand floats through the water to his lap and searches out his erection. "Oh yeah." He's hard. Thick and solid beneath the thin fabric of his shorts. I stroke him and he groans in my ear.

"Fuck yeah. Feel my dick. You made me hard."

My inner muscles clench hard, everything pulling up tight.

"So hard." I grip him tighter.

His other hand presses on my chest, between my breasts. My nipples are hard, tingling points and I shift to brush against his palm. He cups me through the Lycra. "Oh yeah. Hard little nipples." He brushes fingertips over the tight tip. "So fucking hot." He curls his fingers into the top edge of the suit and yanks it down to expose me.

I gasp. "Logan!"

His fingers pinch the tender peak and sensation bolts straight to my pussy.

"You can't do that!"

"As if I can stop," he says on a low groan. "Jesus, Annie."

I look down. Water swirls around my bare breast and his big hand playing there. A moan mounts in my throat and I try to hold it back.

He presses against my clit. "Does it hurt here?" he whispers.

"Y-yes."

He grunts with pleasure. His fingers rub over me. "Do you wanna come now, beautiful?"

"Oh God, yes," I nearly sob.

"You have to be very quiet, though. Can you do that?" He licks my ear and shivers cascade down my spine.

"I don't know." I whimper. I'm so close to coming, I can't think. This is so risky but so goddamn good. I'm helpless. All I can think of, all I want is that sweet, sweet satisfaction. I want that curling heat inside me to swell higher and higher and...

His hand glides up my chest, over my throat, and covers my mouth. My eyes widen and he look at me, our foreheads touching. "I got you," he whispers. "Let go."

I made a strangled noise and my eyes fall closed as I reach that pinnacle, every sensation coalescing into a sharp spike of pleasure that then spreads through my shuddering body. I make noises, but Logan's firm hand on my mouth keeps them muted.

"Fucking gorgeous," he mutters, removing his hand from my mouth. He presses his mouth to mine in a long hard kiss and squeezes my pussy as endless ripples pulsate there.

When I'm cognizant enough, I tug my swimsuit up to cover my breast. My hand went still on his cock when I came and I stroke him again. He captures my hand, though, and moves it away. "Better not," he says hoarsely.

"But..."

"Yeah. I want to come to bad. I need to fuck you...I'll come to your room."

"No." My response is immediate. Instinctive. "We can't do that."

He rests his forehead against mine, his jaw clenched. "I know. Fuck."

I fill my lungs with air and let it out. Then again in a long exhalation. "I better go."

He nods. "Yeah. Get out of here before I lose my goddamn mind totally." He gives me another hard kiss and releases me.

On legs that feel like cooked asparagus, I scramble out of

the hot tub and grab my cover up and towel. I glance back at him. His arms are stretched out along the edge of the pool, his biceps bunched. He watches me with hungry eyes and I fumble my feet into my sandals then make a hasty exit.

I pad down the carpeted hallway, eyes darting around in case someone sees me, and skip the elevator to take the stairs to my second-floor room. The adrenaline beating through my veins has me running up the stairs and when I get to my room and the door is safely shut and locked, I drop into the armchair and stare at the subtly-patterned beige carpet. I exhale a long gust of air.

Gah. I'm still vibrating with arousal. I was almost ready to throw discretion to the breezes and give Logan a hot tub lap dance with a happy ending. He is way too tempting. This day was a test of my fortitude. Watching his amazing butt as he teed off on the golf course. Flirting with him in the cart knowing we couldn't act on it. Trying not to watch him every minute. Our eyes meeting across the room, both knowing we had to ignore each other.

And there's still tomorrow to get through.

FIFTEEN

Logan

After a practice at a nearby arena, we have lunch back at the resort and then it's time for the dreaded teambuilding activities. First we do a game to find out how well we know our teammates. We're given a bingo card with things like "speaks more than one language," and "has the same number of siblings as you." We have to mill around and find someone who meets each of those categories. Some are easy—I head straight to Axe, who obviously speaks Swedish and English. Also, I know Beav is an only child, like me.

"Do you play piano?" I ask Millsy.

"Nope."

"Guitar?"

He shakes his head. "I'm not musical at all."

"Shit." We move around asking questions.

I come face to face with Annie. We've been trying to avoid each other. I immediately remember making her come in the hot tub last night and my blood heats.

"You don't have five siblings," she says in a resigned tone.
"No."

She sighs. "I'm the only one here with five siblings. How am I going to win this?"

I repress a smile. "I don't think it's actually a competition."

Our eyes meet in a flurry of sparks.

Her lips twitch. "Right."

I peer at her paper. "But I do have a unique talent."

"Oh, yeah, what is it?" Then her expression turns wary. "And please don't tell me it's something sexual. One of the guys already tried to tell me he can suck his own, uh..."

I choke. "Jesus." I scowl. "I have a dirty mind but even *I* wouldn't say something like that to you." I look around for Snake, knowing it was him. Do I have to talk to him again? "My talent is juggling."

She brightens. "Okay!" She marks down my name on that square. "What do *you* still need?"

"Have you ever bungee jumped?"

"Oh yeah, I have."

I give her a look, then write her name down. "Wow. Brave girl."

"I guess you haven't seen me skating." With a breezy smile, she moves on.

Oh yeah, I've seen her skating. I know she said that for the benefit of the others around us. And I guess I shouldn't be surprised that she's bungee jumped, after how I saw her being thrown up in the air to spin several times.

After this, Coach gives us a talk about the kind of team we want to be this year. He brings up mental toughness again. And that leads to the next activities, where we work through things we can control and things we can't control and drives home how trying to control the uncontrollable leads to increased stress and frustration, as well as decreased levels of performance. There's a lot of discussion about some of the factors and it's actually pretty cool. The next one makes me want to roll my eyes at first, because we have to act out different "skills"—like reacting to a bad call, taking a cross check, turning over the puck, facing the media after a loss. We're told to think of ourselves as Hollywood actors playing the role of hockey players, and we talk about how we want to act: confident, relaxed, focused.

Some of the guys get right into it, like they're looking for an Academy Award, leading to a lot of laughter, and in the end it does make me realize how much better I can prepare for pressure situations and how acting like I'm calm about getting slashed can stop me from reacting in a bad way and maybe taking a stupid penalty.

After dinner, we all gather in a breakout room where chairs have been arranged in a semi-circle around three seats at the front of the room. Millsy, Hellsy, and Morrie take those three seats and our GM Brad introduces them, telling us they're going to talk about the tragedy that happened in their lives, how they dealt with it, and the things they learned from it.

Most of us know what happened to them. About nine years ago, they were playing major junior hockey in Canada, all on the same team, when their team bus crashed on the way to a game. But they share details most of us don't know or have forgotten.

"Fourteen people died," Millsy says. "Including my brother and my dad. My dad was an assistant coach."

"Our coach also died," Hellsy adds. "Our bus driver died, a guy from the local radio station died, and our athletic therapist died. And nine players died."

"Some of us were injured," Morrie adds. "And not just physically. Hellsy spent months in the hospital and rehab. He wasn't sure he'd ever play again. My injury was psychological. I had PTSD. And that was hard because a lot of people feel like if they can't see your injury, you're fine." He pauses. "I wasn't fine."

The room feels like a funeral, the air dense and silent as they talk. I slide a glance over to the Heller brothers, all sitting in chairs against one wall. They arrived late this afternoon and had dinner with us. Tag Heller is Hellsy's dad. He rubs his mouth as he listens, his eyes red, and his three brothers wear identical expressions of sadness. That must have been hell for that family to go through.

Morrie tells us about his therapy, Hellsy about his rehab. Then they talk about how they let each other down. They were best friends before the accident. They were all supposed to be drafted that spring. But the accident ripped that all apart.

"What was really our downfall was our inability to talk about our feelings," Hellsy says. "Or to even *admit* our feelings. I felt like I'd been abandoned by my friends, but I had no idea what Morrie was going through. Or Millsy. Even though he wasn't injured, his brother and his dad had just died, and his mom checked out. He was trying to hold things together, even though he'd been through hell."

"If only we'd been able to talk to each other about what was going on, we might have recovered a lot quicker," Millsy says. "Not that you ever really recover from something like that."

"That was part of the reason for us starting Play Well," Hellsy says, referring to the organization the three of them started to bring attention to mental health issues. "You guys know about it and we've appreciated your support."

There's a lot of nodding in the room.

"The specific reason we're talking to you about this now is to remind us all how important it is to acknowledge how we're feeling. There are a lot of ups and downs over the season. Shit is going to happen. Guys are gonna get injured, we're gonna lose games, and stuff's gonna happen in our personal lives. As a team, we want to be mentally tough. But what does that mean?" Morrie looks around at us.

"Men are conditioned to think that showing our feelings is weakness," Millsy says. "We're taught that asking for help is weakness. And we just did some role playing where we saw times it's not good to show your feelings. On the ice we need to stay in control. But off the ice...we need to talk about shit. If we screw up, talk about it. If we're pissed, talk about it. If something's going on in your personal life, talk about it. It's not weak. We want men to know that being able to ask for help is a sign of confidence. Masculinity. Strength. Opening up and talking about it is the biggest, bravest step you can take."

"Let's be there for each other," Hellsy adds. "We all need to know that we don't have to handle our shit alone. When someone's struggling, let's help each other out. Sometimes all it means is listening. You don't have to solve the problem. You don't have to make things better. Just listen. Listening without judgment is *huge*."

"Another thing we learned from what we went through is that you have to do the work." Morrie looks around at us. "We can't just play hockey and hope to make the playoffs. Or hope we're going to win the Stanley Cup. You can't just hope. You have to *believe* in it. You have to take the risks, and it's fucking scary. But it's worth it."

My chest is full and fizzy. I look around the room and see the sober expressions on my teammates faces. And then my gaze lands on Annie. Her face is soft, eyes glossy, lips pouty. She's as affected as the rest of us. Did that resonate with her, too? She's not a guy—*definitely* not—but I have a feeling she keeps her emotions pretty tightly wrapped. She seems controlled. Cool. Confident.

But I've seen hints of her vulnerabilities. I've seen her let loose. Come apart. Shatter.

I shift in my seat.

Coach stands up to wrap up the evening and tells us to head to the bar or whatever we want to do as long as we're at the bus at nine o'clock for one more practice before we head back to the city. As we all rise to leave, Tag Heller walks over to his son and wraps his arms around him in a hug.

I swallow, my throat suddenly scratchy.

And then I meet Annie's eyes, glowing blue and full of feeling. As we move with the others toward the door, our steps bring us together. As much as we try to stay apart and not look at each other, it's futile. There's an energy that flows between us, some kind of gravitational pull.

"That was powerful," she says quietly.

"Yeah."

I think about the things they said for a long time after I get to my room later. It all sounds good, but how can I buy into that? That's not how I was raised.

My dad played pro hockey. He wasn't the most talented player, but he was big and strong and physical and he ended up in the role of an enforcer. He played with Joe Bready, a super star back in the day whose records for most goals in a season and most assists in a career still stand. It was Dad's job to protect him, and he did it with zeal.

Dad wasn't that involved in my hockey when I was a little kid because he was still playing, but after he retired because his body basically gave out after playing that hard for years, he turned into a classic hockey parent, at the rink all the time, yelling at the coaches and the refs. People let him get away with it because of who he was, but I hated it.

As I got older, his constant feedback to me was "be tougher." Take the man out. Hit 'em hard. Drop the gloves.

I hated it. But more than that, I hated disappointing him. Because when I didn't play like that, Dad was pissed. Distant. Disapproving. As a kid, that's hard. *Fucking* hard. It's scary. So I tried to do what he wanted.

I sure as hell didn't cry when I got hurt. I didn't complain about cuts and bruises and raw knuckles. I pretended I loved it all. I learned that emotions make you weak. That unless I played "the right way" I didn't deserve to be loved. That I wasn't good enough.

So all this talk about acknowledging our feelings, talking things out...that is not going to happen for me. I have a goal this year. My worth as a player—hell, as a person—is tied to being the best hockey player I can be. My dad will always see me as not good enough, so fuck it, I don't care what he thinks. I'm going to focus on things other than aggressive hits and try to be the best I can be. For me. For the team.

SIXTEEN

Logan

Dad flies into town the day before our road trip. He comes to the rink with me on Tuesday morning for our practice. A bunch of other dads are here, also an uncle, a brother, and a couple of step-dads. Everyone's in high spirits, looking forward to the trip. Tag Heller is also a dad of a player and he's hanging out with them, making jokes and laughing. Coach is here as well, greeting all the dad/mentors as Rick Blackmore, who works in Communications, introduces them.

Dad and I join the group and I introduce him to Rick.

"Heeeey!" One of the fathers slaps Dad on the shoulder. "Dennis the Menace! It's good to meet you!"

Dad's old nickname from playing. He loves it.

I make a bit of small talk but then I have to get dressed and I take off to the locker room.

So far Dad hasn't been on my case about things. We went out for dinner last night at a restaurant he liked last time he was here, and he's pretty pumped about coming on the road trip with us.

When we all jump onto the ice, the dads are in the stands, most of them with coffee cups in hand, and they already seem to be best buddies judging from all the chatter. It is kind of cool, and for my dad I know it's bringing back memories of his playing days.

Our coaches put us through our paces and I work hard because I always do but maybe a little extra hard because Dad's watching.

I get distracted for two seconds when I spot Annie near the boards.

Right. I have a coaching session with her after the regular practice. Me, Adam Wong, and Brick. My competition for that spot on the third line, which gives me extra motivation.

As usual, she looks fresh and pretty in her black Bears sweats, ponytail swinging, smile flashing. She casts an amused glance at the group of men watching us.

I stay on the ice when the other guys leave. I exchange a look with Annie as she comes on and flies around the surface to warm up. That look heats me up more than the workout did.

I gesture at Dad as he's coming down the stairs. "I have to stay for an extra practice," I tell him. "You can watch if you want, or go hang with the other dads."

"Extra practice?" He frowns. "Why?"

"We have a skating coach this year." I gesture at Annie on the far side of the rink. "She's uh, giving us extra, uh, practice."

Dad cocks his head, forehead still creased. "That girl?"

"Yeah. That's Annie Bang." I say it like he should know who it is, but his expression doesn't clear. "One of the Bang family...you know, Lars Bang's kids."

His eyebrows shoot up. "She doesn't look like a hockey player."

"No, she's a figure skater."

After an open-mouthed beat, Dad barks out a laugh and doubles over. "Get the fuck out of here. You're taking figure skating lessons?"

My jaw tightens. I'm aware of Annie gliding toward us. She probably heard that.

She scrapes to a stop near me. "Hi! You must be Logan's dad. It's so nice to meet you. I'm Annie Bang."

Two other dads have gathered next to mine.

"And you're Adam's Dad," Annie says with a warm smile at one of them. "He looks so much like you." She greets Brick's dad as well. "Well guys, let's get started."

She glides backwards and gets us going. "Backward outside edges," she calls, and shows us what she wants us to do.

It looks weird and awkward and slow. I keep my face neutral. I can only imagine what Dad is thinking.

"Stay low!" she calls. "Okay, faster!" She crosses her legs faster. And faster.

And holy shit, I'm skating backward and lucky I'm not tripping on my own blades. Brick does trip and goes sliding across the ice. And yeah, we laugh.

"That's okay," Annie says, smiling. "Try it again. Turn around, everyone, let's go back."

Once I get the rhythm, it feels good. After practicing that, she starts us working on transitions.

"Forward to the center line on your right foot," she calls. "Then transition to backwards. Inside. Out. Inside. Out!" She looks so graceful, and then, on that one foot, she turns elegantly. I'm sure my turn isn't that graceful. I fucking hate looking like an idiot in front of my dad, so I focus hard on my edges as I shift from inside to outside.

"Good work, guys! Okay, we're going to work on some tight cuts around the cones."

She has a couple of orange cones set up and she skates toward them. "Forward cuts first. Get some speed up...lean into the cone and stay close to it..." She curls around it effortlessly then speeds to the next one.

Easy peasy. We take turns and I focus on bending my knees and leaning in. Adam is having more trouble with these and Annie guides him, showing him how to use his shoulders. Then we do backward cuts.

"Sprint forward to the cone, turn backward, and circle around the cone," Annie calls. As she twirls around the cone, arms extended, she's so graceful she looks like she's going to do a figure skating spin. "We'll do right first, then left."

I set my jaw as I race toward the cone, shift my weight and sink down low, and curl around it.

"Yeah, good job!" she calls. "Okay, other side."

I pause. I don't like doing the other side and she knows it. But I press my lips together and do it.

"Again!" she cries. "Really press into those edges! Good!"

We practice it over and over, and I feel my edges getting deeper and surer every time. Then she has us skating in pairs, doing the same kind of transition and cut around each other. After a few more drills, we're done for the day.

I coast up to the boards, sweat dripping off my face. Dad's there to meet me. "Well, that was cute," he says, grinning.

Cute. I give him a slitty eyed look.

"Never thought I'd see the day you'd be figure skating." He shakes his head. "That stuff's a waste of time. You should be working out in the weight room."

"Hockey's not all about strength," Annie says cheerily. "Maybe in your day it was, but the game has changed. Skating's important. Being able to shift your weight efficiently and make use of your edges effectively."

Dad's eyebrows snap together.

"Players are younger and faster," she continues. "Hockey players are much more athletic than they used to be."

Dad's face gets red.

"That's true," Adam's dad replies, unaware of the tension as Dad takes Annie's comment personally.

"These young guys are after my job," I joke, nodding at Adam and Brick. "I have to keep up with them."

They laugh and disappear down the tunnel with their dads.

"You were always a fast skater," Dad says.

"Yeah," I agree. "But these days that's not enough. A game isn't just an end-to-end sprint."

I catch Annie's eye and the curve of her lips.

"That's right," she agrees. "It's those moments between the sprints where you have to rely on agility and mobility. It's more of a transition game, where the action can shift in an instant from one way to the other. Being able to pivot and use your edges is so important."

Dad laughs. "Okay, Kristi Yamaguchi."

Annie's eyes flicker, but she smiles. "That sounded kind of patronizing."

Dad's mouth opens, then closes.

"You're not one of those men who thinks figure skating isn't a real sport, are you?"

I choke on a laugh. "Don't get into that argument with her, Dad. You'll lose."

"I can't believe they're making you do this pussy bullshit," Dad mutters. "I'm gonna have a word with Tag."

Like Tag Heller is his best friend now. Jesus. "No, you're not," I say through a clenched jaw. "I admit I was skeptical of this when we started but if it's something that'll make me a better player, I want to do it."

Annie's eyes shine at me. I fucking love it.

"He *was* resistant," she says to Dad. "But you know what?

It takes a real man to overcome pride and ego and be willing to admit there's something he can do better at. All these guys are pros. Learning something new when you're considered an expert is hard. I give them all credit for it. Anyway. Nice to meet you! I hope you have a great trip!" She holds my gaze for a second, then turns and treks away in her skates.

Dad glares at her back.

"Let's go grab some lunch," I say, hoping he's not going to be a total dick about this. "I'll meet you in the lounge after I shower."

SEVENTEEN

Annie, *Dad's Trip Day 1*

Things are quiet with the team on the road. I've been watching the media coverage and enjoying the posts of Ed Karmeinski, Nate's dad, who is hilarious.

There's a post on Instagram from the team with a video of Ed interviewing the other dads and asking for their best dad jokes.

"This is a good one," says Brandon's dad Jeff. "What do you call a fake dad? A faux pas."

I grin.

"I know you're not a dad," Ed says to Nils' brother Iver. "But what's your best dad joke?"

"Where does the majority of a hockey player's salary come from?" Iver says in his Swedish accent. "The tooth fairy."

I laugh out loud.

Ed next asks Hunter Morrissette's dad, Mike for a contribution. "Last night my wife and I watched two movies back-to-back," he deadpans. "Luckily I was the one facing the TV."

That cracks me up again.

Ed doesn't ask Logan's dad to tell a joke. I hope things are going okay for Logan and him.

I'm doing laundry when I get a text.

> LOGAN: Save me. My dad is picking fights with the other dads.

> ANNIE: LITERAL FIGHTS???

> LOGAN: No! Just stupid arguments.

> ANNIE: About what?

> LOGAN: Burr's dad was talking about too many dirty hits and Dad told him of course you don't like hits because you're only this tall

> ANNIE: Those are fighting words!

> LOGAN: Yeah fuck me

After a few seconds of the dots dancing around another text arrives.

> LOGAN: He also told Coach he needs to bench players more often.

> ANNIE: So it's going well then

I get a laugh emoji in return.

> LOGAN: I hope I don't punch him before we get back.

> ANNIE: You won't punch your own dad

LOGAN: Probably not. But it's all distracting me. I'm supposed to be napping right now.

ANNIE: I thought sleeping is your superpower

LOGAN: It is!

ANNIE: Put down the phone

LOGAN: Okay. Just needed to vent

ANNIE: I'm here anytime

LOGAN: Thanks.

ANNIE: Good luck tonight. Don't let that asshole Meyers get under your skin. Skate around him

LOGAN: Ha

Of course I watch the game. I'm settled on the couch with a big bowl of popcorn when Ivan comes home. He joins me and reaches a hand into the bowl.

I smack it away. "Get your own."

"Jesus. That's a huge bowl! You can share."

"You know I don't share popcorn."

He heaves a sigh. "Yeah."

"I'm a strong woman capable of many things, but sharing my popcorn is not one of them."

"Who's winning? Oh, no score."

"Not yet. The Bears are playing well though." I lean forward as Brandon intercepts a pass between two Condors players and heads to the Condors net. He passes to Easton who fakes a shot and passes it back to Brandon who puts it in the net. "Yesssss!" I throw my arms in the air. "That's it, baby!"

"Hmm. I don't think I've ever seen you this passionate about a hockey game unless one of your brothers is playing."

"I work for the team."

"Okay, yeah." He pauses. "What happens when the Bears play the Icehawks?" My brother Jakob's team. "Or the Bucks?" Tanner's team. "Or...wait for it...the Phantoms." Jensen's team.

I wrinkle my nose. "Logan and Jensen have played against each other since that happened."

"But who will you cheer for?"

I chew on my bottom lip. "Nobody."

He laughs. "Okay."

I shove more popcorn into my mouth and focus on the play. Logan gets the puck and rushes to the net, cuts to the inside around a defenseman, then goes backhand, forehand, shoots the puck...and scores!

I'm so excited popcorn goes everywhere. "Oh my God!" I cry. "Did you see that?"

Ivan shakes his head. "He scored."

"Yeah, but did you see that move? Wait, they'll replay it. Watch, watch." We watch a number of slow-motion replays while the commentators exclaim over Logan undressing the Florida Dman. "Beautiful!"

"You're going to take credit for that, aren't you?"

"Oh hell yeah I am!" I laugh, happiness bubbling up inside me. I clean up the popcorn and settle back down, the Bears now leading two-nothing. I pick up my phone to check what social media has to say about that goal. I laugh when I see Ed Karmeinski's posts with a play-by-play commentary of the game.

DID YOU SEE THAT MOVE! LOCO YOU BEAUTIFUL
BASTARD!

I send Logan the post, even though he won't see it until
later, repeating the "you beautiful bastard" line with a big smile
emoji.

Between the second and third periods Ivan loses interest in
the game and goes to bed. The Bears are leading four-nothing,
with goals from four different players. I'm so glad they're
playing well in front of the dads. So I watch the end of the
game alone, trying not to think about those two little words that
start with S and O. With a couple of minutes left in the third,
Florida pulls their goalie, and then the Bears take a stupid tripping penalty! Gah!

I sit on the edge of the couch, every muscle tense as I watch
Florida keep the puck in the Bears end, cycling it around and
around. Of course they're dominating, with a two man advantage. My eyes follow the action. "Come on, guys! Get it out of
there!"

But Florida's controlling the play. And getting shots on net.

It's not like we're going to lose, if they score one goal. But...
for our goalie Colton's sake, I don't want that to happen. Finally
I can exhale when the horn blares and the game is over.
Everyone mobs Colton to congratulate him on the shut out, and
when he takes off his mask he's wearing a huge, sweaty smile.

I clap my hands even though I'm alone. Yay!

Then I send Logan another message.

ANNIE: Congrats on the win!

I sink back into the couch. I did that without even thinking.
He texted me earlier. So I'm sure he's okay with it. Whatever.

It's way late now, so I turn off the TV and go to bed.

Dad's trip day 2

> LOGAN: Did you see my goal

> ANNIE: No, I missed it sorry. YES I SAW IT THAT WAS AMAZING. Impressive edgework

> LOGAN: I knew you were going to say that

> ANNIE: I'm gonna make sure everyone knows I'm responsible for that

> LOGAN: I knew you were going to say that too

I laugh, a fun, effervescent feeling in my chest.

> LOGAN: We're golfing today. Guess who Dad and I are paired with?

I tap my fingers on the counter in the kitchen where I'm drinking coffee.

> ANNIE: Tag and Josh.

> LOGAN: Yes! Fuck me sideways with a golf club and no lube

I collapse into laughter. When I've recovered enough to type, I message him back:

> What's so bad about that?

LOGAN: BEING FUCKED WITH A GOLF CLUB?

Still dying, I reply,

No, golfing with the Hellers.

LOGAN: Dad's going to have his head so far up Tag Heller's ass I'm gonna be so embarrassed

ANNIE: You're not responsible for your dad.

LOGAN: Okay

ANNIE: Have fun! It's a cool time

LOGAN: I'll try.

I smile at my phone.

LOGAN: What are you doing today?

ANNIE: Watching video from last night

LOGAN: Jesus. Well you have fun too

ANNIE: I will

Still smiling, I finish my coffee and scrambled eggs.

Dads trip day 3

LOGAN: Dad's pissed because I didn't go after Delorme for that hit on Wendy

I'm in bed. The game ended over an hour ago but I'm still awake.

ANNIE: Oh no

LOGAN: Did you see it

ANNIE: Yeah. It was ugly

LOGAN: It was. But Wendy was okay and Delorme got a penalty for it and we got a PP and scored. If I'd fought Delorme, we'd have both ended up in the box.

ANNIE: That goddamn code

LOGAN: That's what Dad said! It's THE CODE. Jesus. You can't fight a guy every time there's a clean hit

ANNIE: Some would say you should

LOGAN: You?

ANNIE: Not me!

> LOGAN: He went on and on about how these days there's no code and you have to protect the guys who are game changers even if it's a clean hit because you don't want guys taking liberties and running star players, you have to have each other's backs and…shit, that all sounds positive.

> ANNIE: I get it. Sometimes a good fight gets the team going

> LOGAN: I know

> ANNIE: But you have to play smart. You also don't want your game changers to be sitting in the box for fighting for no reason

> LOGAN: Yeah. I knew you'd get it. I'm just tired of arguing with my dad.

I stare at my phone. My stomach knots. I want to say I'm sorry, that I hate his dad, that Logan's right about everything. Impulsively, I hit the button to call him.

It barely rings before he answers. "Hey."

"Hey. You okay?"

He sighs heavily. "Yeah."

"Where are you? In your room?"

"Yeah. We went out after the game but I said I was tired and came back here."

"I'm sorry about what your dad said."

"Don't be sorry. It's just the way he is." I hear a rustling noise. "I just wish I didn't care."

My heart clenches. "Of course you care. He's your dad. We all want our parents' approval." I snort. "I might not be the best one to talk about that, though."

"Why not?

I tug the duvet up under my chin. "As I kid, I felt like my brothers got all the attention. All the approval. Especially when I tried playing hockey. So I...acted out. I was never going to live up to them, so why even try? I got an attitude. Started drinking and smoking weed. Once, I took the car without their permission. I didn't even have a license."

He makes a low noise. "I am shocked, Annie Bang. But did you die?"

I choke out a laugh and close my eyes. "No, and neither did anyone else, luckily. Okay, that might not be the worst thing a teenager has ever done to rebel, but it was a lot for me. It was when I almost got suspended by my figure skating club that I got scared."

"Scared straight." Amusement colors his voice.

"Well, yeah. I guess I wasn't too far down a criminal path, but still. Anyway, my point is we all want to make our parents proud. We know our parents have sacrificed for us. Jesus, especially parents of athletes. And I don't think we lose that when we grow up."

After a couple of beats of thick silence, he says, "Yeah."

"Have you had a conversation with him about it? Like, not an argument when he's said something dumb, but at another time, when you're both calm."

"No." His reply comes slowly.

I hitch a shoulder. "Maybe you should do that. Think about it ahead of time and plan what you want to say to him. Tell him how it makes you feel."

"Oh, yeah. Dad looooves talking about feelings."

I smile ruefully at the sarcasm. "I get it. But you could." I pause. "Remember at the start of the season, in the Poconos, when Easton and Josh and Hunter were talking about Play Well?"

More dense silence. Then he says, "Yeah."

"They talked about this. About not being able to talk about their feelings."

"I remember." His voice is low and rough.

"They could probably help you figure out what you want to say to your dad. Like, part of growing up into an independent adult is forming your own opinions and values, even if they're different than your parents'."

"Uh-huh." He's quiet again for a moment, but I stay quiet, too. "You're killing me, Mini."

One corner of my mouth lifts and I roll my eyes. "How so?"

"Because you're right."

My smile deepens. "I know I am."

"You know what would make me feel better?"

"What?"

"If you show me your boobs."

I cough out a laugh. "Oh my God."

He chuckles.

"They're small," I tell him. Like he doesn't know that.

"I don't care if you have small boobs. I still want to see them."

Is he serious? Because that's kind of hot, but also... "You won't take any screenshots, will you?"

"Fuck, no. In fact, let's do a video call. We can see each other."

"Ohhhh." My heart kicks against my ribs.

My phone rings from a different app. My skin tingles everywhere as I end one call and accept the other. There's his face, a little blurry in the dim light of his hotel room. He's in bed, like I am, white pillows piled behind his head.

He smiles.

That smile gets me every time. His eyes crinkle up and his teeth flash white.

I smile back and tuck my hair behind my ear. "You really want to do this?"

"So damn much." He pauses. "But only if you do, too."

My heart flutters at his thoughtfulness. "I do."

He slowly pushes the white covers down his chest, moving his phone away from him so I see more. My gaze tracks over the ridges of his abs. At the trail of hair beneath his navel.

"Hang on," he says in a husky tone. "Let me get my phone set up."

I do the same, turning on a lamp, finding a good spot, and propping it up. Then I unbutton my pajama top. One. Button. At. A. Time.

He groans. "Watch me jerk off while you play with your pussy." His hand grips his cock. I swallow thickly at the sight, so erotic and dirty. Like my own personal porn movie. But even better, because it's Logan.

Hot desire slides through me and I'm so wet, I can tell without even touching myself.

I part the sides of my shirt, revealing my breasts.

"Fucking perfect," he growls. "Touch yourself."

I cup my tits and give my own nipples a pinch. "It feels better when you do it."

His smile is filthy. "Of course it does. I wish I could suck on those pretty nipples."

God. I'm dissolving. "I wish I could squeeze your cock."

"I wish that, too. Jesus." His hand moves, up and down, the head of his cock glistening in the low light. He rubs his thumb over the moisture. "Are you wet?"

"Oh yeah."

"Are you sure?" He lifts an eyebrow. "You should check."

I slip a hand under the elastic waistband of my shorts. "So wet."

"Christ. I'm gonna come in, like, two seconds."

I let out a muted moan. "I'll try..."

"No. Take your time. I can hold off." His jaw tenses and his hand slows. "Show how me you make yourself come."

I slick up wetness onto my fingers and find my clit, sensitive and aching. Sinking my teeth into my bottom lip, I force myself to keep my eyes open and on the small screen as I rub there. He watches me with an intense, hungry expression and that makes me even more turned on. His body is shadowy but still beautiful. Veins stand out on his forearm and his big hand on his thick shaft is obscene but so, so sexy. I stare at his muscular thighs and the fullness of his balls at the base of his shaft and I want to touch them so bad.

"I wish I was there," I whisper. "I wish I could touch you there. And lick you. And suck you."

"Awwww, damn." His eyelids lower to half-mast. "Same, baby." His breathing is ragged, mixed with groans and curses.

Sweet pleasure gathers low inside me, a thread that I clench down on. It grows and twists and expands and ripples from my center, sensation sliding down my arms and legs and weakening me. I whimper and cry out, my eyes closing, vaguely aware of Logan grunting. "That's it baby, come so hard."

I let out another near-sob, shuddering and contracting, and then I drag my eyes open to watch Logan's hand do the same for him, pumping faster and faster, his abs clenching, his jaw tightening. "Awwww...fuuuuuck..." His thighs move and he grunts again. "Watch me...are you watching me? Watch me empty my balls for you...yeah...uhhhh...aaah..." Thick white semen splashes onto his firm stomach and thigh and slides over his fingers. "Oh fuck." He lets out short breaths as his hand slows and his other hand squeezes the wet glans and more semen drips.

I have never seen anything so hot. I can hardly breathe and

my skin is burning. I press my thighs together and roll to my side, facing the phone. "God, Logan."

"Yeah. Yeah." He's still panting. "That was fucking gorgeous, Annie."

"Mmmm."

His eyes flicker open a moment later and he smiles again and my heart melts down to my toes. I pull the covers up over me and hold my phone on the pillow next to my face. He does the same.

"I feel so much better," he mumbles, smiling.

I grin. "Wow, me too. I bet you'll sleep now."

"Yep."

"Good. You need it." I pause. "Good night, Logan."

"You sleep, too, beautiful. We'll be back tomorrow."

EIGHTEEN

Logan

I think a lot about what Annie said—about having a conversation with my dad. There was no time on the trip, since we headed home the next morning, and Dad flew home that afternoon from Miami. But that's okay because I need to think about what I want to say to him. If I do that.

I also think about talking to one of the guys—maybe Josh. I think he saw my frustration when we were golfing. He saw firsthand how old school Dad is. But holy shit, confiding in one of my teammates how shitty my dad makes me feel, how I want to do better...well, I'd rather take out my own tonsils with a spoon.

So I push all that to the back of my mind and focus on hockey. I played well on the trip and even though Dad was disappointed in me, Coach praised me, so I need to concentrate on that.

I also want to concentrate on Annie.

I fucking missed her on the trip. Which is crazy, but I kept thinking about her. When I was torqued about Dad, I wanted to talk to her. I didn't intend to have phone sex, but that was fucking hot, so I don't regret it. I want more.

We have a home game tonight, then tomorrow is Thanksgiving. We have another home game on Friday afternoon, so we only get the one day off. Fine with me. Gunner and his girlfriend Layla are doing their annual Thanksgiving potluck dinner.

After our morning skate, I'm heading to the player's lounge to grab lunch when I see Gunner talking to Annie.

"Layla said to invite you for Thanksgiving dinner tomorrow," he says.

Every nerve ending in my body goes on alert. Will she come?

"It's a potluck," he adds. "And we'll be watching football."

"Oh, that's so nice of you." Annie smiles at him. "Thank you, and say thanks to Layla. But my parents are in town for Thanksgiving."

"Ah. That's cool." Gunner nods. "We didn't want you to be alone. You're new in town."

"Yeah, I'd totally come if it weren't for them flying in. Thanks again."

Gunner disappears and Annie meets my eyes. I walk closer to her. We're alone in the hall. "Your parents are here?"

"Yes." She widens her eyes dramatically. "My mom's been threatening to come visit since I got here."

I grin. "Threatening?"

"She's on a rampage trying to get her kids married off. She retired last year and she wants grandchildren." She rolls her eyes. "She thinks she's responsible for four of my brothers now having partners, and it's my turn."

"Huh. Does she have anyone in mind?"

"Oh yeah. Ivan."

I scowl, my gut clenching. "Seriously?"

Annie laughs. "She's been shipping us since we partnered up. We were twelve." Another eye roll.

I don't like this. Not one bit. My back molars grind together and I glare at her.

"I told you we're just friends," she says softly.

"Uh huh. Okay."

It's not that I don't believe her. I do. I trust her. It's just hard to imagine that any guy in close proximity to her wouldn't want to be more than friends.

"We're coming to the game tonight."

I gaze at her. "Oh."

She'll be at the game. With her parents. Great. "Well, have fun with your family." I turn and stride to the lounge, my stomach burning.

I'm irritable and I don't feel like eating, but I fill a plate with salad, grilled chicken, and a whole wheat roll, then join J-Bo, Russ, and Murph. "You guys all coming to Gunner's place tomorrow?"

We discuss our various contributions to the potluck dinner. They're not into cooking but I'm planning to make an autumn veggie gratin.

"I don't even know what a gratin is," Murph grumbles.

"And what veggies are autumn veggies?" Russ asks.

"Parsnips, sweet potatoes, carrots, and beets," I list off. "They get all sliced up thin and mixed with cream and cheese and baked."

"Okay." Murph nods. "That sounds decent."

"I'll be stopping at Trader Joe's for something," J-Bo says, not even joking.

"I'm bringing party size bags of chips," Murph says.

I lift my eyebrows.

"Come on, you can't watch football without chips."

"Fair." I nod.

But I'm distracted about Annie's mom trying to fix her up with Ivan. She lives with the guy, for shit's sake. How hard would it be to make a little sexy time happen? Annie keeps saying they're friends, but that's her opinion. I don't know what Ivan thinks. Maybe he's been horngry for her all this time. I saw those videos. He's had his hands all over her body. He had his face in her pussy, for Chrissake! "Shit," I mutter.

"What?" Murph looks at me.

"Nothing." I shake my head. "Gotta go. I need a nap." I stand. "Oh right, I came with Millsy." I look around. He's leaning on the counter talking to Cookie. Who also came with us. I head their way. "Okay, boys, let's go."

"What's the rush?" Millsy straightens.

"I need my beauty sleep."

Cookie grins. "Oh yeah, you do."

I'M ON THE BENCH. It's the third period and there's still no score. Our power play team is out there trying to score while Washington has a penalty. We need this. I watch as Washington gets the puck in their own end and carries it out. Shit! Then my jaw drops as Millsy and J-Bo skate to the bench to change. Meanwhile, two Washington players are going in on our net, two-on-oh. What the fuck! There's nobody there!

Nate chases them but he can't catch them and after a quick back and forth pass, Washington scores.

Coach goes berserk. And I don't blame him.

"What the fuck are you doing?" he yells at Millsy and J-Bo. He jabs his arm into the direction of our net. "They had a fucking two-on-oh while you guys decide you're tired and need a change! Jesus Christ!"

The mood on the bench goes black and murky. None of us know what to say.

"You guys sit!" Coach barks at Millsy and J-Bo. "Logan, you're out. Hunter, you take the faceoff. Brando, on the wing."

We jump over the boards. This is a new line combo. I'm a little shook, but I have to focus. I take my place at the faceoff circle. Morrie lifts his chin at me and I nod.

Morrie wins the faceoff and the puck comes to me. I pass it to Brando who passes tape to tape back to Morrie on his way to the Washington net. Their defense is all over Morrie and I go to the net, my blade on the ice, left all alone. Morrie doesn't even seem to look at me but the puck is coming and with a quick flick of my stick I deflect it into the net behind the goalie's shoulder.

"Fuck yeah!" I laugh as Morrie and Brando throw their arms around me, the crowd cheering, the goal horn blasting.

There. We're back in the game.

I skate over to the bench to bump gloves. Coach is nodding at me, still not looking entirely happy but better than the steam coming out of his ears moments ago.

Millsy and J-Bo warm the bench for the rest of the game, shockingly. They're two of our best players but Coach has got a mad on for their fuck up. He keeps me, Morrie, and Brando together and Morrie scores another goal and I feed one to Barbie on the point for a final score of three-one.

It feels great. I mean, we all feel for Millsy and J-Bo. I don't know what they were thinking. We all screw up, though. I know that only too well.

"Come on, this is basic," Coach rants after the game. "You never change when the puck is in transition from offense to defense and the other team is attacking! If you're gassed, suck it up, buttercup, and stay out there and get the goddamn job done. Then you make your line change!"

I can see how bad Millsy and J-Bo feel. They cost us a goal. In the end, we won, so they didn't cost us the game, but they could have.

But I felt like I was flying out there tonight. Playing with Morrie and Brando was easy, even though it was new. We were clicking. Morrie's a playmaker, reading the puck and where everyone is. Brando knows how to score. And with my physical presence in front of the net, we're a good combo. I loved having all those minutes.

I don't know what'll happen next game, but a sense of excitement heats my blood as I consider the possibility that Coach might keep us together.

And the one I want to talk about this with is Annie.

She was here. I'm sure she's gone by now.

I have to talk to the media—of course they want to talk to me, Morrie, and Brando—then I head to the locker room.

"You coming out tonight?" Russ asks me. "Day off tomorrow."

What the hell. I should celebrate. "Okay, sure."

I shower and dress back in my suit, still lit up after that great game. When I step out of the player's suite, I see Annie in a small group, talking to Gary and Brad, the assistant GM, along with a couple who must be her parents. Annie looks like her mom, who is also petite and pretty, but with her dad's blond hair, although Lars Bang's hair is now more silver than blond. He's still fit-looking, with an imposing presence. And oh yeah, Ivan's with them.

I have to walk past them to get out of the arena. I almost duck back into the locker room.

I don't look at them as I start walking, but Coach sees me. "Hey, Logan. "Great game."

Brad smiles. "Yeah. You were on fire tonight."

I have to stop to talk to them.

Annie's eyes meet mine.

"Hi," she says, her businesslike tone belying the warmth in her eyes as we lock gazes. "Congrats on the win. You played great tonight."

Wearing a black puffer jacket and a big colorful scarf, her blond hair down and waving around her shoulders, she's totally hot and cute at the same time.

"Thanks." I give her what I hope is an equally professional smile back.

"Have you met Logan?" Coach says to Mr. and Mrs. Bang. "Logan Coates, these are Annie's parents Stella and Lars Bang."

The air around us goes heavy.

"Logan Coates." Mr. Bang repeats.

I extend a hand to shake, but he ignores it. Oof. I drop my arm to my side.

"And you've met Ivan," Annie says with a desperate breathiness to her voice.

"Yeah, hi." I try not to scowl at him.

Mr. and Mrs. Bang are scowling at me, though. The air around us feels as thick as gravy.

"No goals in the first and second periods," Annie says with a light laugh, sensing the tension, I'm sure. "I thought it was going to be a really boring game. But then things got interesting."

"Hockey's never boring," Lars Bang chides her.

She scrunches up her face. "If you say so."

I shift my weight from foot to foot, my neck and jaw stiff.

"Well, enjoy your stay in New York," Coach says to Mr. and Mrs. Bang. "We'll talk Friday, Logan."

We will? I nod, keeping my smile in place.

"Happy Thanksgiving everyone." He and Brad leave.

"Are you on your way somewhere?" Annie asks casually.

"Yeah. A bunch of us are going out."

She nods, smiling. Our eyes meet again. I want to talk to her so bad I'm vibrating with it. I think she knows it.

"We're going to take Mom and Dad back to their hotel," she says. "Then going home after that."

Ivan smirks.

"You two should go out," Mrs. Bang says to Ivan and Annie. Tossing her dark brown hair, she gives me a hostile glance and turns her back on me.

Ooookay.

"Happy Thanksgiving, everyone." I make my escape.

Fuck. Fuck. Fuck. I stride down the hall and exit the arena onto Sixth Avenue. I pull the collar of my black coat up against the chilly wind. There are still a few autograph hunters hanging around, so I take a deep breath and stop to sign my name a bunch of times. I get lots of congratulations on my goal and my assist. So much for the buzz I had after the game. Now I'm testy.

I zigzag through dark streets to the Amber Horse Brewhouse, a hole-in-the-wall pub with a concrete floor, high dark ceiling, and big frosted windows. The space is a typical New York bar, long and narrow. And packed. It's the night before the long weekend so it makes sense. I make my way through the crowd and find a few of the other guys at a table in the back.

I drain my first beer way too fast.

Well, that was fucking awkward. Her parents clearly despise me. And I did not need to hear Annie's mom urging her and Ivan to go out together. I nod to the waitress to bring me another drink.

I got Annie's hint that she'd be home alone after dropping her parents off. I could text her and arrange to go over to her place and see her. I couldn't wait to see her when I was away on the trip. But having just endured her parents' contempt, I don't think that's a great idea.

A giant screw twists into my chest.

When I was away, texting and talking to her was my reprieve from the pressure of being around my dad so much. I was all hot to see her again when we got back. But meeting her parents was a slap of cold water in the face. Or whatever. A wakeup call.

"Dude, what are you scowling at?" Russ asks me. "You should be in a good mood. We won. You played great. You got *the hat*."

"I *am* in a good mood."

He snorts. "Sure, man."

Snap out of it, asshole. I need to get my shit together.

NINETEEN

Annie

I'm sitting in bed with my phone in my hand. I want to text Logan and find out where he is and see if he wants to come by.

Dad fumed about him all the way to the hotel. Mom was going along with it, too.

"How can you work with that guy?" Dad demanded. "He's an asshole. I should have punched him."

A band tightens around my chest, remembering it. I wanted to defend Logan, but I didn't, and then I felt like shit about it because I've gotten to know him better and he is *not* an asshole. But if I defend him, will they wonder why I'm sticking up for him so much? If they knew I'm sleeping with him, they'd flip right the fuck out.

If I thought I came second to my brothers before, I'd probably be expelled from the family if they found out about *that*.

I've gotten myself in a little pickle here.

Not only have I possibly put my job at risk by getting involved with Logan, I could lose my whole family.

Alright, that's dramatic, I know it. Still, after years of never being good enough, the thought of having the wrath of my family directed at me is worrisome.

Now I'm in bed, guilty and angry and sad, and thinking about Logan out in a bar somewhere with women coming on to him and then I remember how he looked at Ivan and I thought he was jealous and I sort of liked it.

I'm a mess.

I throw myself back into my pillows, expel air from my lungs, and stare at the ceiling.

All because I was stressed and horny and Logan has a hot body and a beautiful penis. And a great smile. And...

No. Stop thinking about him. And I certainly can't text him. In fact, we should probably stop whatever it is that we're doing. Sneaking around in a nun costume! I make a strangled noise that almost drowns out the chime of my phone.

A text.

I fumble with the phone to check the message, sure it's from Logan.

It's not

> MOM: Our reservation for lunch is at 1, should we meet you there?

Right. Our Thanksgiving lunch at Tavern on the Green. Glumly I type in my reply.

> Sure.

I'm such an idiot. I'm not going to text him, but I want him to text me. I toss my phone onto the nightstand, turn off the lamp, and pull the covers over my head.

I ENDURE all Mom's comments about what a cute couple Ivan and I are. She praises me to Ivan, and compliments him, and reminisces about our skating past. Ivan's nice enough to put up with it as we partake of mushroom soup, free-range turkey with all the sides, and pecan butterscotch tarts for dessert.

When Ivan goes to the men's room, she leans across the table. "He told me he's been in love with you forever."

"No, he didn't."

Her eyes widen. "You don't believe me?"

"No. He wouldn't say that." I don't think. No. He wouldn't.

"Stella." Dad's tone is quiet but firm. They exchange a look and Mom sits back in her seat. I can see her mind is still working, though.

When Ivan returns, Mom says, "Ivan, did I tell you I learned a little Russian?"

He gazes back at her. "Uh. No."

Ivan moved here from Russia when he was a little kid. He doesn't even have an accent anymore, and rarely speaks Russian. What is Mom doing?

"Well, I have." She looks back and forth between him and me. "Iz vas dvoikh mogli by rodit'sya prekrasnyye deti."

Ivan's mouth drops open, then he laughs and shakes his head. "Oh, Stella."

"What did she say?" I demand.

"Never mind." He flaps a hand.

"No, I want to know."

"I said you two would make beautiful babies." Mom beams at us.

"Oh my God." My chin hits my chest. "Mooooom." I look at Dad. "Please. Stop her."

He snorts. "As if I could do that." But he gives Mom another pointed look.

Since it's a clear, crisp day, we walk back to Ivan's place. As we stroll out of Central Park, I can't help but look down West 66th and think about Logan's apartment at the end of the street. I swallow a sigh.

Mom and Dad link arms and walk in front of us along the wide sidewalk. Ivan and I follow.

"Sorry about all the unsubtle hints from my mom," I say in a low voice.

"It was worth it for a free lunch at Tavern on the Green."

I snort-laugh and bump my shoulder into arm.

"She told me that you said you want to be more than friends."

I stop walking and gape at him. "No!"

He grins. "Yeah."

"I didn't say that."

"I know."

"She told *me* that you said you've been in love with me forever."

He laughs and we walk again. "You didn't believe her."

"Nope. She is shameless. Thanks for being a good friend."

After a moment, he says, "You seem down. What's up?"

"Oh geez. I'm not putting on a game face." I slap my gloved hands to my cheeks. "I'm usually good at that! Must smile more."

Ivan says nothing as we walk another half block and then I blurt out, "I don't think I can see Logan anymore."

"When you say 'see him'...what do you mean by that? Dating? Or bedroom rodeo?"

I let out a strangled laugh. "We haven't exactly been dating. So...yeah, rodeo."

He nods. "It's complicated, huh."

"Yeah." I exhale slowly. "But it's okay, because like I said, it's not like we were in any kind of relationship. We just, uh, did some riding. At the rodeo."

"Hopefully not bareback."

I choke again. "Jesus! No!"

"Good, good. Things would be even more complicated if he knocked you up."

"Shhhh!"

He grins.

Mom turns to look at us at that point and I cringe at what she sees—us close together, heads leaning into each other. Greeeeat.

"What are you two talking about?" she calls playfully.

I hesitate only a beat. "Horses."

She frowns. "Oh. Okay." She turns back and they continue walking.

"Horses!" Ivan chokes out, laughing. "Jesus."

"We also texted a bunch. And talked on the phone." My bottom lip pouts. "The road trip with his dad was rough for him."

Ivan gives me a sideways glance with an arched brow. "That sounds kind of like...more than just bull riding."

"I guess we kind of got to be friends." Sadness squeezes my trachea. "Shit."

Mom and Dad come into Ivan's place to watch football. I don't watch football and I don't know anything about it. Neither does Mom. Or Ivan. Dad's the only one really interested, but it's Thanksgiving and I'm down for some junk food and beer. I change into a pair of soft joggers and a big sweatshirt.

Mom lifts her eyebrows when I come out of my room. "Why did you change? That dress was so pretty."

"I want to be comfy."

"Didn't you like that dress she had on, Ivan?" Mom looks to him. "You looked so nice in it, sweetie."

I can see Ivan trying not to laugh. "I didn't notice."

Mom sighs.

Her meddling is mildly annoying, but deep down inside, I feel bad for her. In the last year, she retired from her job as a teacher, and she lost her best friend to cancer. Dad's still coaching and on the road with the team a lot. I know Mom was feeling adrift and sad. Probably depressed. Then she started on a mission to get all her children paired up. So far she's been successful with three out of six of us. Now it's my turn. It's not going to work with me, though, so I wish I could convince her to let it go.

She means well. She wants her kids to be happy. Doesn't every mom?

⌐══

I'M in my office Saturday morning when I get a visitor after the game day skate.

"Hey, Annie."

I look up to see Hunter Morrissette, still in his practice jersey. "Hi, Hunter. What's up?"

"I was talking to a friend of mine the other day." He takes a step into the office. "He plays for the New Jersey Storm. I was telling him about you and the coaching you're doing here, and he's really interested."

I grin. "Too bad he plays for the wrong team."

"I know." He grimaces. "He's wondering if you do any coaching on the side."

"Oh." I blink. "No. I mean, I haven't, but... I'm not sure if I could do that, working here. But I could check into it."

"Could I give him your number and you could talk to him?"

"Sure."

"His name is Dillon Landry."

"Okay. We can chat."

"Thanks! He'll be happy."

Huh. Okay. That's interesting.

I check the time. I better get going. I'm meeting Mom to go shopping. She decided to stay in New York after Dad went home. I know why, but apparently nobody can stop her.

We start with lunch in a lovely restaurant at Columbus Circle, with a table at the window and a view of the Christopher Columbus monument and Central Park. Then we walk toward Fifth Avenue. Our first stop on the way is Nordstrom. After browsing through handbags and Mom picking up a gorgeous Ferragamo tote, the price of which makes me break out in itchy welts, she wants to go down to the shoe department.

I love shoes, too, so I willingly follow her there and wander around admiring pretty heels and cute booties. I pause to fall in love with a pair of knee-high boots. The black leather is smooth and expensive looking, the heel a nice chunky shape. "I love everything about these," I say to Mom with a sigh. "Except the price."

She peers at the sticker on the sole. "Well, they're quite practical. Boots like that will always be in style."

"I suppose." I run my fingers over the leather.

I don't feel inferior to my brothers because they're rich and I'm not. They're all millionaires, and we grew up well off, although I'm not sure how Mom and Dad never went broke from putting all their kids into expensive sports like hockey and figure skating. But I've never made that kind of money. If my figure skating career had continued, I might have landed lucrative endorsements and maybe been able to make money from touring, but even so, that would never be close to what professional hockey players make. And that didn't happen anyway, so I'm the one in the family pinching pennies, living in New York City on a modest salary, squatting in my best friend's spare bedroom.

There are many reasons to feel inferior to my brothers, but money's the least of them.

I put the boot back on the display table.

"Try them on," Mom says. "What size do you need?"

"Six. But that's okay. I don't need them. Did you find anything?"

"I don't need much either." She makes a face. "Especially since I retired. But you know what, let's go look at the kids' clothes. I want to buy something for Ryder and Rowan."

My brother Jakob has twin boys, six years old. Mom's only grandchildren. She's crazy about them.

"Sure." I trail after her again.

"Oh my God, look at these sweaters!" She picks up cotton cardigans.

"Those are grandpa sweaters."

"But they'd look so cute on the boys!"

She moves from display to display, loading her arms up with designer sweats and shirts. Then she pauses at a display of dresses. "Ohhhh, look at these dresses."

"I don't know if Jakob would let the boys wear those."

She slides me a chiding glance. "I need a granddaughter."

"Ah."

She moves into the baby girls' area and finds a tiny dress covered in pink roses. "I love this!"

It *is* cute. "I would wear that."

"Annie." She looks up at me. "You need to have babies."

"Mom!"

"Just think. Beautiful little Russian babies."

I choke. "Mom!"

She picks up another little dress, red velvet with a tulle skirt. "This would be perfect for Christmas."

"I can't produce a baby that fast."

She sighs. "I know. But for next Christmas...I should buy it!"

"No!" I curl my hands into fists at my sides, my muscles tight. "Mom, please, stop. Fixing me up with Ivan isn't going to happen."

"I don't understand why not! You two are such good friends. And you're both so attractive. I—"

"The truth is, I'm involved with someone else."

Oh no. Did I really just say that?

Mom stares at me. "What? Who? Why didn't you tell me?"

I rummage frantically through my brain to find an answer to those questions. "It's new. I don't want to say who it is."

She pouts. "Why not?"

"I just don't want to. Yet." I cough.

"Oh." She ponders this. "But it could be serious?"

"It's new," I say again. "Let's drop it."

"But I want to meet him while I'm here."

I shake my head.

"Annie! You can't tell me that and then drop it. You know I want you to be happy."

"I am happy."

Her eyes soften. "I want my children to have what your father and I have. Love. Commitment. Trust."

My heart becomes tender. "I know, Mom. You and Dad are couple goals. And I hope I will have that one day. But it will happen when it happens."

She worries her bottom lip for a few seconds, then lifts her chin. "I suppose you're right. You know I just want you to be happy, no matter who it's with."

Really? I try not to let my suspicion show on my face.

"As long as it's not someone like that nasty Logan Coates."

My smile slides right off my face.

"Whoever it is should feel lucky to be dating you." She slides her arm through mine. "Now, let's go buy those boots." She leads me away from the display of baby dresses.

I stumble along after her in a daze. "I don't need those boots."

"I know. But I'll buy them for you anyway because they're beautiful and so are you."

I frown. "Do you think buying me boots will make me tell you more?"

She stops and looks at me with a wounded expression that seems sincere. Guilt pokes me in the chest. "No. Of course not." She pouts. "I said, I'm buying them because I love you."

"I'm sorry." My face softens. "Thank you."

Oh God. She's my mom and I love her and she loves me, but wow, this is a mess.

TWENTY

Logan

Our Saturday night game against Buffalo is a barn burner.

I met with Coach yesterday and he told me he's making changes to the lineups and wants me to play with Morrie and Brando again. He likes how we played the other night against Washington. He wants to use our strengths together.

This is what I've been working for. Second line minutes. A chance to show what I can do.

The bad thing is my buddy J-Bo is down in the dumps about it all. We went for a beer yesterday. He's pissed at himself but he knows we're all on the same team and we have to do what's best for the team.

I was pumped for the game tonight. Nothing like your coach's confidence in you to fire up your own confidence. And it showed. Once again, Morrie and Brando and I were on fire. Five points between the three of us in a game that ended six-two. I made some good hits that caused an uproar on the Buffalo bench. But we stayed disciplined.

I'm still riding the high of it after the game as I shower and dress. Tonight some guys are going out again, this time to a club. Which reminds me of Annie and running into her that night and dancing with her.

We haven't talked or even texted since the night I ran into her and her parents after the game. I had some major second thoughts about us that night and I guess she did, too.

I fucking hate that.

Also, I fucking miss her.

So I'm shook when I pull my phone out of my locker and see a text from her. I swear my chin nearly hits the floor.

> ANNIE: Hey...good game tonight.

I blink, and a slow smile spreads across my face.

> Thanks.

She replies immediately, which tells me she's been waiting for my response.

> Can we talk?

My eyebrows shoot up.

"What are you grinning about?" Morrie asks me. "Some chick send you nudes?"

I frown at him. "No." I look back at my phone.

"Are you coming to Indigo with us?" Russ asks.

"Not sure. You guys go ahead."

"It *is* a chick," Morrie says smugly.

I turn away to text Annie back. *Sure. Want to call me?*

> ANNIE: Maybe we could get together?

> LOGAN: Is this a booty call?

If it is, I'll take it.

> ANNIE: No!

> LOGAN: Because you do have a nice booty.
> Brains, beauty and bootie.

There's a pause while she types in another message. I shove my tie into my jacket pocket, not bothering with it, and slam the locker door shut. "Later, guys." I head out. In the corridor, I pause to look at my phone again.

> ANNIE: My mom's making me crazy. And I did something stupid.

Okay, that's not good. What the hell is her mom doing?

> LOGAN: Your place or mine?

> ANNIE: You can come here. Ivan's out.

Well, thank fuck for that.

> LOGAN: Be there in about 20

> ANNIE: Okay. You remember where?

> LOGAN: Oh yeah

I book it to the subway station, checking train routes on my phone. I get off at 50th Street and then walk a few blocks.

Annie lets me into the building then opens the apartment door.

She's fucking gorgeous.

She's wearing black sweatpants and a long-sleeved pink T-shirt that looks soft and touchable. Fluffy pink socks make me smile. "Cute."

She rolls her eyes but the corners of her mouth lift. "Come in."

I enter the small apartment. The kitchen's on our right and she leads me past it and into a surprisingly spacious living room. There's a big window, now with blinds over it, and a floor lamp glows in the corner. It's very tidy and cozy, with taupe walls and furniture, some cool art, and a soft rug on the pale wood floor.

"What's going on?" I sit on the couch.

She sits there too and shifts to face me. "Remember I told you my mom is on a mission to get her kids all married off?"

"Right. She wants you and Ivan to get married."

She makes a face. "Right. She's still in town. My dad went home after Thanksgiving, but she stayed. She's not giving up."

I immediately grimace. "What the fuck."

"Right?"

I study her. "You don't want that?"

"Gah! I told you, we're just friends! Why don't people believe us?"

"You are pretty close. When I watched your skating videos, I was convinced you two were together. So it's not surprising people think that."

She huffs. "Fine. But people close to us should believe us. We keep telling her it's not going to happen. Anyway, things have kind of changed. I, uh...well, today she took me shopping and somehow we ended up in the baby department and she was looking at cute little girl dresses and practically begging me for a granddaughter."

Annie's daughter would be adorable.

Wait, what?

"I kind of lost my shit." She picks up a textured cushion

and runs her fingers over it. "And I told her I'm involved with someone else."

I stare at her, my mind completely vacant. Then I say blankly, "Who?"

She bites her lip, drops her gaze, swallows, and says, "You."

My mouth opens, then closes. "You told your mom about us?"

"No! I didn't tell her it was you! I told her I couldn't tell her who it is."

"Ah." I'm still befuddled. "Um. Okay. But..."

She looks up and meets my eyes.

"We haven't even talked for almost a week."

Her bottom lip pushes out. "I know. I...after that night we ran into you, I realized how upset my family would be if they knew about you and me. And I thought we shouldn't see each other again."

I nod somberly. "Yeah. That's what I figured. I thought the same." I pause. "Why did you ask me here? Because you didn't need to tell me that...if you're trying to make your mom think you're involved with someone."

"Because..." She stops and meets my eyes. "Because I miss you."

Shit. I stare into those Nordic blue eyes. My chest cavity fills with heat.

"I miss talking to you," she says, her voice quivering ever so slightly. "I wanted to tell you about my mom bugging me, like you told me about your dad. You make me feel better about stuff. And I miss hearing about what's going on with you. You played so well in that game that night and now you're on a new line and it looks great, and I want to know how you're feeling about it and what your dad thinks about it, and..." Her voice trails off. "I just miss you."

My blood is hot in my veins. I clear my throat. "I miss you, too."

We gaze at each other as time bends and stretches in the quiet room.

"I know we shouldn't see each other," she adds. "Practically speaking. But...I want to."

I want that, too. I know exactly what she means, because I feel the same. But holy shit, this is a little terrifying. We've been banging and hanging out and getting to know each other and...I can't be catching feelings for her. I don't know how to love. My dad only loves me when I do what he likes. Love has always felt kind of like a tool that he uses to get what he wants.

I look into Annie's clear eyes and the honesty and vulnerability shining there. I feel like I should be asking myself what she wants from me. And then I feel ashamed of that. Because being with me is a huge fucking problem for her, not a benefit. And yet she still wants to be with me.

That thought sucks all the air out of my lungs.

She gnaws briefly on her bottom lip. "I'm sorry. It's okay if you don't want to." She holds up her hands in a placating gesture. "I understand. I wanted to be honest with you, though."

Honest.

I want to believe her—that she missed me and wants to be with me for no other reason than she...likes me? But I've never taken a chance on getting serious with anyone because I've always been convinced that I don't deserve love unless I do what they want.

Yes, Annie Bang is honest. Determined. A bit of an underdog in her family trying to prove herself. But she's never down. She puts her whole self into coaching us and making us better and cheering us on. She doesn't realize how motivating she is, how much she's impacting the team. And me. Especially me.

I reach out and take her hand. "I do want to be with you." I rub my thumb over her knuckles. "But I don't want to become a problem for you. We both know a relationship with a player isn't a good idea. And your parents...your brothers, too, probably...hate me."

"They don't know you. But I'm not suggesting that we actually tell them about us."

A hard knot forms behind my sternum. "So you want a secret relationship."

"Well." Her long eyelashes flutter. "We agreed to keep things on the down low because of the team."

Right. Right.

The knot in my chest grows bigger. Harder.

I remember how hard it was at the retreat to keep my eyes off her. To stay away from her. I wanted her by my side. I wanted to share amused looks at things people said, to exchange glances, to touch her.

I don't want to sneak around.

She squeezes my hand. "Thank you for your concern. But this isn't about my family. We talked about it...remember? When I told you part of growing up is making your own decisions apart from your parents? Well, I need to do that, too."

If I was standing, that would take me out at the knees. Emotion swells behind my sternum and I have to take a deep breath. "Okay."

And I lift her onto my lap, thread my fingers into her hair to tilt her head, and kiss her.

She makes a small noise in her throat, wraps her arms around my neck and kisses me back, opening to me. I missed her taste, her sweetness, the slide of her tongue on mine. A groan climbs up my windpipe. "Annie."

"Mmmm."

I kiss her cheek, her jaw. I nuzzle her ear. "You're so sweet." Kissing her has my cock thickening with need for her.

She smiles, eyes closed, head angled to give me access to her neck. I slide my tongue over smooth skin.

"I'm not supposed to be sweet."

"What does that mean?" I suck gently.

"I was always told, don't be too sweet or...or..." Her voice goes breathy. "Or they'll eat you."

My lips curve up. "That sounds like a *great* idea."

Her eyes pop open wide and I almost laugh. "That's not what I meant!" Then she smiles. A sexy, smutty smile. "But okay."

I stand with her in my arms. Ivan can hold her up over his head on skates. I could do the same. "Where's your bedroom?"

She gestures and I carry her around the corner to a short hall lined with closets. Her door is straight ahead and I take her in and lower her feet to the floor. It's mostly dark so I can't see much, but all I want to see is her glowing face, pale ivory in the dim light. I have an impression of pale colors, lots of soft cushions on the bed, and the faint vanilla scent of her lingering on the air.

I slip my hand between her legs and cup her pussy. She's warm and damp there. "I want to taste you here."

"Ohhhh God..."

I pull her sweater over her head. Beneath she's wearing a white lace bra, two little triangles of stretchy lace sheer enough to see her nipples through and a gold clasp at the front. I flick it open to bare her sweet tits and bend to press an open-mouthed kiss between them while I hook my thumbs into her leggings to drag them down.

When she's out of them and her panties, I nudge her backward onto the bed. She stretches out sideways across it and I pull off my own sweater, kick off my jeans and kneel between her leg. She parts them further for me and I set my hands on her inner thighs and lower my head to kiss her on one hip then the other. "You smell delicious." I breathe in her earthy sweet scent, an aphrodisiac that makes my dick so fucking hard it hurts.

I kiss and lick her thighs, teasing and tasting her, moving closer and closer to her center.

"Lick me," she begs in a smoky voice. "Please."

"Mmm." I like that. I part her soft lips with my thumbs and her hips lift off the bed.

"Oh, God."

I lick over the softest skin then point my tongue and dig into her opening. She moans as I lap at her, savoring her taste, and I kiss her plump flesh, little suckling kisses, so gentle, so patient. I like this, too. I like her taste. I like the way I can make her quiver and moan.

My dick throbs.

"Sweet, Annie. You taste like honey and peaches."

She arches with pleasure.

"And you're so pretty here."

I pull her swollen flesh into my mouth, gently release it, then moved to the other side and do the same. Then I move my mouth up and suckle my way up to her clit. When I finally take it into my mouth, tugging and nibbling it at, my teeth holding it while I lick over it, she explodes against my mouth.

She cries out, body arching, digging her heels into the mattress, pressing up into my mouth, flooding with wetness.

"Jesus," I mutter against her pussy, still giving her little licks and sucks, drawing out every last quiver of delight until she lies limp.

"Oh my God, you're good at that."

I smile against her lower belly. "I love making you come. Making you feel good."

Her hands slide into my hair and she lifts my head. I peer into her lust-hazed eyes. "I love it, too."

"Wanna make you come again. With my cock inside you."

"Yessss. Please..."

My cock's on fire, my balls full and throbbing. It takes seconds to get rid of my boxer briefs, find a condom, and suit up, and then I'm inside her, I'm in fucking heaven, her pussy still twitching with aftershocks, and that makes me lose my mind. My jaw clenched, my hips thrusting, I fuck her with hard, powerful strokes and she takes it, takes it so good, she fucking loves it, encouraging me with whimpered words of praise and delight. I bury my face in the side of her neck as heat explodes from my core in a white-hot bolt of pleasure and I pour myself into her. And not just physically. I feel like I'm pouring my soul into her. My gratitude. My trust.

This feels different. It feels like...more. And yet, not enough. I want more of her. All of her.

Oh hell.

TWENTY-ONE

Annie

Logan has to go home to Teemu. Neither of us wants to part but we suck it up and make a plan to go out tomorrow since the team has a day off. I'm hesitant but he convinces me it's a big city and no one we know will see us going for a walk in Central Park or having dinner somewhere.

In the morning I get a text from Mom asking about getting together. I sit and look at my phone for a long time before I text her back.

> ANNIE: Sorry Mom I'm going out this afternoon and maybe for dinner

> MOM: With your new man?

> ANNIE: Yes

> MOM: We could all meet up for afternoon tea!

> ANNIE: Mom

> MOM: Fine. I want to go to the Metropolitan Museum. I can do that by myself.

> ANNIE: Okay. We can have dinner tomorrow night. Do you want to go to the game?

> MOM: I'd love to!

This time I'll make sure we don't run into Logan.

Logan picks me up in the afternoon. When I tell him where Mom's going, he drives up Central Park West on the opposite side of the park from the museum. We find a parking garage and then explore the park on foot for a while.

"What do you usually do on a day off?" I ask him as we stroll up to the Stone Arch.

"Sleep."

I laugh. "Besides that."

"Hang out with the guys. Go to a movie. Play video games or ping pong."

"Ping pong?"

"Yeah. There's a game room in the building and we have tournaments."

"Huh. Who knew."

"I'll take you on sometime."

"Oh, no. I can't play ping pong."

"Some days..." He hesitates.

"What?"

"I work with a school in the Bronx. I've donated hockey equipment and money, and sometimes I go get on the ice with the kids."

My heart. I press a hand to the swelling sensation behind my breastbone. "That's awesome."

"I like doing it." He clears his throat. "What do *you* do on a day off?" Our gloved hands are twined together as we walk.

"Well, I'm still new here. I've been working a lot on my days off. And I don't know many people here. So I haven't done much."

"What would you like to do now you're here in the Big Apple?"

"Well, I'd like to go the museum my mom's at today. Don't laugh, but I kind of like museums and art galleries."

"I'm not laughing. There are lots here to see. I haven't been to many. But one I've been to is the Spy Museum."

"I didn't know there was a Spy Museum."

"Yeah, and it's really cool."

"I've done some of the typical stuff—the Empire State Building, the Statue of Liberty. I've been to a few Broadway plays, but I'd love to see more. There's a new one I hear good things about—The Raven."

"Oh yeah, we should totally do that. I'll check into tickets for a night we don't have a game." His fingers tighten briefly on mine.

We're really doing this. Like...dating.

I pull in a long slow breath and let it out.

"Now Christmas is coming, it'll be fun to see all the holiday decorations," I say.

He nods. "Honestly, I haven't paid much attention to that since I've been here."

"We could go skating." I bump his upper arm with my shoulder.

"Ha. *That's* what you want to do on a day off?" He grins down at me.

"Maybe."

"Would you show me a camel toe spin?"

After a beat, I burst into laughter. "Oh my God! That's not what it's called! Not a camel *toe*."

"I don't know! I thought that's what it is."

"It's just a camel spin."

"Can you do it?"

"Of course I can."

"I want you to put on those sissy white figure skates with the toe picks and show me your moves."

"Sissy!"

I catch his eye. He's yanking my chain. And we both smile.

I'm bundled up, but it's cold today and the sky has clouded over. A few icy flakes pelt us from the sky. "My hands are freezing," I complain.

"Aw. Want to warm them up on me?"

"Yes." I take my gloves off and reach for his belt buckle.

"No!" He grabs my hands. We both start laughing.

"I bet it's nice and warm down your pants."

"Oh, it is. But your cold hands aren't getting anywhere near my beefy baloney."

I almost fall down, I'm laughing so hard. I hang onto him. "Beefy baloney! Oh my God!"

"My man-sized manicotti?"

I'm dying.

"Zipper sausage?"

I wipe a tear. "How about love stick? Magic wand?"

"Those are good." He nods. "But I like something that gives a better indication of size. Like Moby Dick."

"Aaaah." I wipe more tears. "Stop!"

"Okay. Let's go warm up in the natural history museum. Since you like museums."

I try to get control of myself. "Is it far?"

"No, right near where we parked."

"Okay." Then I start giggling again.

"I think we have to book ahead." He pulls out his phone. After a moment of swiping and tapping he says, "Okay, we're good."

When we arrive we discover there's an exhibit about elephants.

"Cool," Logan says. "Elephants are kickass."

"I don't know much about elephants."

"Prepare to be amazed."

We wander from exhibit to exhibit, exchanging amused glances about the kids there.

"They are amazing," I say, after learning that an elephant's trunk is strong enough to pull down a tree and yet he can pick up a blade of grass with it. Also they eat five hundred pounds of food a day. "I'm jealous of that." I pat my belly.

Logan scoffs. "I can almost eat that much."

"Sure, Loco."

We also learn how they hear with their feet.

"Excuse me."

We both look down at a little boy wearing a Bears hat.

"Can I have your autograph?" he asks in a near whisper.

Logan smiles. "Sure."

The boy hands him a pen and paper. I notice a couple standing a few feet away, watching, I presume the boy's parents. Ack. Here we are out in public and someone recognized Logan. I take a few steps back, attempting to fade away. Sure enough, the boy's mom pulls out her phone.

"It's Logan Coates," I hear someone else say.

Now he's attracted attention.

"Thank you!" the boy says, beaming. "You're my favorite player!"

"Yeah?" Logan lays his hand on his chest. "I'm honored."

The kid's dad steps closer. "You played great the last couple of games."

"Thanks." Logan nods. "I appreciate that."

"I hope Shipton keeps that line together. You guys have some real chemistry."

Now someone else approaches for an autograph.

Logan looks around for me. I'm across the room learning that elephants are afraid of bees. Keeping my hand at my side, I lift my fingers in subtle acknowledgement. His expression changes, hardening, his eyebrows sloping down. But he quickly smiles at a fan.

A few more admirers crowd around and Logan signs things and makes easy small talk until they disperse. He strides up to me and closes his hand around my upper arm. "Fuck, I'm sorry."

"It's okay! I like seeing you with your fans."

He closes his eyes briefly, his jaw tense. Then in a low voice, he says, "Let's get out of here."

"Okay."

He starts toward an exit and I have to jog to keep up with him. Yikes.

"Want to get something to eat?" he growls.

"Yeah. I can't eat five hundred pounds but I could eat a hamburger the size of my head."

He slows and smiles at me and it's so affectionate and his eyes are so warm, I lose my breath. After a momentary freak out, I smile back.

"I know a place not far from here with good burgers," he says.

He leads me across Columbus Avenue toward Broadway and takes me to Prime Bites. It's a busy casual place and we find a table and take seats.

"I should have a salad," Logan mutters as he looks at the menu. "Sixteen hundred calories in this burger."

"Holy crap." I, too, peruse the menu. "But you want a burger."

"I do. I want this Prime Burger. Two organic grass-fed patties."

"It's healthy!"

"Right. Don't be yelling at me tomorrow if I'm dragging my ass on the ice."

"Are you going to get fries?"

He grins. "So you can steal some?"

"Yes. Hmm. Oooh, they have a bison burger—that's what I want."

We order our sandwiches and both order lemonade.

"I'm sorry about that," he says again. He rubs his face. "I didn't think we'd run into anyone who knew me."

"Everyone knows you."

He snorts. "Yeah, no. But enough do, I guess." He looks unhappily down at the table.

"It's okay," I reassure him again. He seems upset by this.

He looks up at me, his mouth twisted. "I don't want you to have to hide."

Aaaah. I lift my chin, then lower it in a slow nod. "Yeah."

Our eyes meet.

The server brings our drinks.

"Will you go home for Christmas?" I ask him when the server's gone.

"Yeah, I think so. We only have a few days off, so it's a quick trip. What about you?"

I nod. "I hope so. We all try to get home for Christmas, but now Jakob and Kingston and Jensen and Leif all have girl-friends, they might not be able to. Do you like Christmas?"

"Eh. It's okay."

"Just okay?"

"We don't have a big family. I'm an only child, remember?"
He shrugs. "Christmas was never that exciting."

"And I was the opposite. Five brothers. Christmas was insane. Dad travelled a lot and the boys did too, playing hockey, so it was special when everyone could be together."

"I get that. It makes me a little envious."

"I actually used to fantasize about being an only child. Getting all my parents' attention."

"That's great, if your parents *want* to pay attention to you."

I tilt my head curiously. "Your parents didn't pay attention to you?"

"Oh yeah, they did, when they wanted me to be a hockey star. I was one of the best players on my teams as a kid and they loved that. Especially my dad."

"Yeah, I can see that."

"But if I screwed up or didn't play like he wanted me to, I got the silent treatment."

I blink, my lips parting. "Really?"

"Yeah." He shrugs as if making light of it, but I can see it's painful. "I always felt I had to earn their attention. Their love. I felt guilty that I didn't do what they wanted." He grins. "It's why I have such a huge fear of failure."

"Well, I ended up with a huge fear of failure even though my parents weren't like that."

"It's hard when all five of your brothers are so talented."

"Right? Man, it killed me when Mom and Dad couldn't come to one of my competitions because one brother had to be in one place and another had to be somewhere else and Kingston was driving a third brother to another tournament." I look down at my lemonade.

"Aw. That sucks."

"It really did." I look at him. "And then, I looked for attention in the wrong ways. By acting out." I roll my eyes at my teenage self.

"I think we're both our own worst critics."

I nod slowly. "Yeah. I think you're right."

Our food arrives and we dig in. My bison burger is delicious, but messy, dripping bacon jam and blue cheese onto my plate. "I have sauce all over my face, don't I?" I ask Logan.

"Just a little." He reaches over and uses a fingertip to swipe at the corner of my mouth.

I reach for a fry from his plate, then hesitate. Our eyes meet. And hold. His expression is almost...puzzled.

Then he slowly smiles and lifts his chin for me to go ahead.

I pop the fry into my mouth. "Yum. How's your burger?"

"Excellent."

After a moment of eating, I ask, "What's your favorite season?"

"Hockey season."

"That's not a season!"

"Sure it is." He grins.

"Okay, so winter."

"Well, fall is when training camp is, and that's exciting, too. And spring is playoffs, although it's a bummer when you're out."

"You don't like the off season at all?" I eye him curiously.

"It's okay. I go home to California. I have a condo in Venice Beach. Right on the ocean."

"Oh, wow. That must be so nice."

"I love it there. Sometimes it feels disconnected, though. All my buddies disperse all over the place for the summer. But they come visit." He flashes a smile. "Everyone loves the beach."

"I'll bet."

"Okay, your turn."

"My favorite season? Um...you know, I've spent so much of my life in arenas, I've never really thought of it. I think it's summer, though. Winters are cold in Minnesota, but summers are wonderful. But summers were still work for me. Training, and developing new routines, getting ready for competitions starting in the fall."

"It was a lot of work."

"Yeah. But I loved it." I smile wistfully.

"It must have been hard giving it up."

"Hardest decision I've ever made."

"I'm sorry."

"It's okay. I've adjusted. And you know what? I've found something else I'm passionate about. Something I love. So...it's all okay. And you know what they say."

"What?"

"What doesn't kill you makes you stranger."

He looks at me. "Stranger?"

"Ooops, that's supposed to be stronger." I laugh. "Okay, both."

His slow smile tugs at the corners of his mouth and his eyes crinkle up. "Stranger is probably accurate. What doesn't kill you can actually fuck you up. I think it depends on the person."

I cock my head, considering that. "Yes. You're probably right. But I think we've both been through adversity. And I think we're both pretty strong."

We share a moment of understanding. And heat. And... some kind of feels.

Lots of feels.

TWENTY-TWO

Logan

We go back to my place after dinner. The anticipation of getting Annie alone and naked is killing me. Although today was fun, just being with her. I walk into my building with a satisfied, contented feeling that's not from the double patty burger I just ate.

I had a minor melt down inside when she took one of my fries.

Because...*I didn't mind.* I'd give her *all* my fries. Gladly. And, with the force of a Zdeno Chara slapshot, I realized...she's the one.

Honestly? I never thought I'd find "the one." I never thought such a thing existed. For me, anyway.

Teemu greets us excitedly and I clip on his leash to take him outside. "Make yourself at home," I tell Annie. "Help yourself to a drink if you want."

This gives me a few minutes alone to deal with the noise inside my head that's like traffic on 42nd Street with police cars and fire trucks and horns honking. I try to calm the chaos and clear my brain in the elevator.

Realizing I'm falling in love with Annie in that moment scared the shit out of me. Why? Why does that scare me?

I don't have to dig very deep to know. It's because chances are damn fucking good she's not going to love me back.

That's always been my fear. It's why I've never had a real long-term relationship...my feeling that I don't deserve to be loved. That I have to be what they want me to be to deserve love.

But I'm myself with Annie. I've always been just myself. And...she's here. She asked me to come see her, to talk. She told me she wants to keep seeing me.

Holy shit, it's exploding my brain.

I take Teemu over to the park and make a loop. He does his business and I dispose of it and then stroll home, letting him sniff at shrubs and fire hydrants.

It's fine. Everything's fine. I got this.

Back in my apartment I find Annie on the couch, gazing out the window at the night view, a glass of wine in her hand.

I grab myself a beer and join her. "Want to watch a movie?" I pick up the remote for the TV.

"Mmm. I don't know." She turns to me with a smile.

Clearly, she wants *something*.

Heh.

"You know what I'd really like?" She lays a hand on my forearm.

I lean closer. "I bet I do." And I'm so ready.

She laughs softly. "I bet you don't. I'd really like a bath."

I blink. "Uh. What? A bath?"

"Yeah." She bites her lower lip and peers up at me through her eyelashes in a seductive look. "Ivan doesn't have a bathtub. I haven't had a bath in months."

"Hopefully you've showered."

"Yes, I've showered." She pokes my chest. "I'd just like to have a nice, long, hot...bath."

I cough. "You can totally have a bath." I pause. "Do you want to be alone?"

Her mouth curves enticingly. "I don't mind some company."

All righty then! I jump to my feet. "Let's go."

We zip into the bathroom off my bedroom. The bathtub and showers (there are two showerheads) are in a glassed-off wet room which I thought was cool when I moved in. I step into it and start the water running into the tub.

I turn to see Annie pulling her sweater over her head. Her sheer lace bra cups her tits sweetly, and I move toward her to help with her jeans. Together we get them off her and I discard my own jeans and sweater and boxer briefs. I let her unfasten her bra and step out of her panties as steam fills the space.

"I don't have baths very often, but I think I have..." I open a cabinet and peer inside. "Yeah." I hold up a bottle of bubble bath.

"Nice."

I pour some under the faucet, releasing the scent of flowers into the warm air. "You can get in. I'll be right back."

I go retrieve the drinks we abandoned, along with a few condoms and some lube. Just in case.

When I come back, she's reclining in the water, bubbles gathered around her. I hand her the glass of wine.

"Thank you."

My dick is huge and hard and I'm about to blow a load, but I need to slow things down. Even if she wants sex, she deserves to enjoy her bath before I jump her.

I climb into the tub and sit with my back against one end. I reach for her and glide her through the water so her back is to my front and she's sitting between my legs. I turn off the tap and I guide her to gently recline against my chest, the hot water lapping and bubbles mounding around us.

"Am I just supposed to ignore that?" she says, nodding at my erection.

"Yes, please. For now."

"Mmmmkay. This is so nice." She sips her wine and relaxes against me.

I slide my arms around her waist and hold her. "Your hair's getting wet."

"Yeah. That's okay." She rubs a foot along my calf. "There's lots of room for both of us."

"It's not a problem when one of us is miniature."

"Hey. You know dynamite comes in small packages."

I kiss her shoulder. "Yeah. I do know that."

When she finishes her wine, I take the glass and set it on the small stool next to the tub with my empty beer. Then I lay my hands on her shoulders and massage her muscles.

She lets out a low moan. "Oh, God. That's nice."

I keep going, digging my thumbs into tight spots. caressing her bare, wet back and her shoulders, slow and sensuous. I push her wet hair forward over her shoulder, then lean down to kiss her nape. I slide my lips along and kiss and suck on the back of her neck, her shoulders.

"I love touching you. Your skin is so smooth." I sit up straighter and find her tits with both soapy hands. "Wet tits...so slippery...hard little nipples." I squeeze and shape soft flesh and pinch her nipples, kissing her shoulder, drinking in her soft gasps and sighs. I slide a hand down her abdomen to between her legs. She parts them and gives me access and I glide my fingers through her pussy lips, down low all the way to her puckered rear opening and rub there. "Have you ever been fucked back here?" I murmur.

"Noooo."

"Mmmm. Maybe we can try it sometime."

"Y-yes. Oh..."

I return to her clit and stroke over it. She shudders in my arms. My other hand rises to her throat and clasps her there, carefully, holding her in place as I play with her clit, making her gasp and shake.

I think the water's getting hotter. Or maybe that's just us. I lift her and turn her so she's facing me, managing to do it without drowning us or getting splashed in the face. She smiles and we drift together, her legs apart and on either side of my hips, my throbbing cock between us. With my hands on her ass, I pull her closer still and kiss her mouth. I want to consume her. I bite so gently on her lips, suck her tongue, swallow her taste.

"This is so decadent." She sighs against my lips.

We make out for a while in the water, endless, drugging kisses and wet touches. Then she wraps one hand around my dick and strokes. "I want to suck you."

"Aw yeah." I run a hand around the back of her head. "Wanna see that pretty mouth on my cock."

I slosh out of the water and plant my ass on the edge of the tub, and she moves between my thighs, on her knees. I gather her hair in a messy tail and hold it at the back of her head as she grips my cock. "Lick the tip."

Her tongue slides over the swollen head. Sensation sizzles up my spine.

"Aw yeah...suck on the head..." My fingers tighten on her hair as she opens wider and her lips slide lower. Her tongue swirls and she sucks gently. "Oh yeah. So good. Take more."

She hums and looks up at me as I fill her mouth.

I touch her cheek. "I love looking at your beautiful face when you suck on my cock. Oh yeah, take it all."

She gives a tiny shake of her head.

"I know." I fix the ponytail in my hand. "I know. It's okay." Her mouth is small. I can feel the back of her throat. Heat pulses in my balls.

"So hot. Your mouth is like fire on my dick. Suck me, baby."

She sucks greedily, using her tongue, her lips and even the very edges of her teeth to gently scrape me.

"Oh fuuuuck...yeah." I let out a long groan. "I'm fucking your mouth, babe." In and out with short strokes, I fuck her mouth, so carefully, gritting my teeth, my abs and my ass clenched with restraint. "Suck me like that, and you're gonna make me come, huh? Yeah?"

"Mmmm."

"Can I come in your mouth, Annie?" I twist her hair around my hand. "Tell me now."

She flicks her gaze up to me, nods, and keeps sucking and I groan again. Pleasure escalates. I gulp for air, my thighs quaking. "That's it. Take it...swallow it all down. *Christ.*"

It's a gift. A pure, generous, gratifying gift.

White hot electricity bolts through me, almost painfully, up my spine, through my chest, and my cock surges and gushes into the hot, softness of her mouth.

She sits back on her heels, blinking up at me, her eyes damp, and her lips wet with my come. Water and bubbles ripple around her waist. I cup her face with one hand and rub my thumb over her slick bottom lip. "God. Look at you...Jesus. Did you like that?"

"I loved it."

I slide back down into the water, wrapping my arms around her tight enough to squeeze the breath out of her.

"HEY, HELLSY."

Hellsy tosses a bottle into the recycling bin in the players lounge and turns to me. "Hey, Loco. What's up?"

This is worse than the first time I ever asked out a girl. "Could we go, uh, grab a coffee or something, sometime. Uh." I adjust my ball cap on my head. "I have something I could use some advice on."

He regards me thoughtfully for a couple of beats then says, "Yeah. Of course. Any time."

"Whenever works for you."

"How about right now?"

We've finished practice, meetings, video review, and lunch. "Sure. Sounds good."

"Let's head over to Betty's?"

"Works for me."

"Do you have a car here?"

"Yeah." I drove my own car here, hoping this might work out. "I can drive you home after."

"Great."

We walk over to the diner, talking about bullshit stuff. Once we're seated in a booth, me with a coffee and Hellsy with his caffeine fix in the form of a Coke, he says, "So. What's up?"

I stir milk into my coffee and sigh. "It's about my dad."

He nods.

"He called me last night after the game and was on my ass about Crossley avoiding my hit in the third." I make a face and set down my spoon. "Apparently I didn't try hard enough."

Josh shakes his head.

"He's been like that my whole life. I could score a hat trick and he'd be pissed because I didn't chuck knucles when the other team got too close to our goalie."

Hellsy purses his lips. "That's tough."

"It's really getting to me because I've been trying to change my style of play. I'm a physical player, but I've been trying to play smarter."

"I've noticed you've been bringing it."

"Well. Thanks. I got some breaks, too. I mean, not that I wanted that to happen to Millsy and J-Bo, getting benched that game, but it gave me a chance to prove myself and Coach noticed. And...even the fucking skating lessons." I smile ruefully and rub my chin. "I wasn't exactly enthusiastic about that."

"You weren't the only one."

"Yeah. Coach lectured me about it, told me to improve my attitude, so I went along with it even though I was still skeptical. But shit, it's making a difference in my skating."

He smiles. "Yeah."

"I didn't want to be the guy who lays a hard hit on someone and then I'm out of position and we lose possession. Sure, I finished the check, but that doesn't help."

"Not always. There's a time for it, but yeah, I know what you mean."

"I'm trying to be more strategic about using my body to force the puck away from other players. Smarter body checking."

Hellsy nods. "Yeah."

"But every time I talk to my old man, he tells me I'm playing like a pussy." I exhale sharply. "I tell myself I don't care what he thinks. And I know I shouldn't let it get to me, but it does and I don't know what to do about it." I look up at him. "I guess that's where I need advice. I don't mean from you!" I add hastily. "I just wanted to talk to...someone...and get ideas of..."

"You've talked to Dr. Fiorino, yeah?" She's a sports psychologist who works with the team sometimes.

"Long time ago, but yeah."

"You could talk to her again."

"I was afraid you were going to say that."

He grins. "She's a doctor. If you were having trouble with your shoulder, you'd go to a doctor, right?"

"Right."

"It's the same."

I get that it *should* be. "But seriously, I don't think I need a doctor. I really want to know what to say to my dad. Annie—" I stop dead. Oh shit.

He lifts his brows. "You talked to her about it?"

Shit.

"Uh. Yeah. A bit. She's the one who suggested talking to you, or Millsy or Morrie. She asked if I'd talked to my dad about it. And I have...but it's usually when I'm pissed off and I've lost my cool and it's ugly."

"Ugh."

"Yeah. I almost lost it last night when he called, but I don't want to do that anymore."

"He's definitely an old-time player. It was interesting hearing him talking to the other guys on the trip."

"Yeah, he doesn't like the way that hockey's changing. But he needs to deal with it."

"That's a him problem."

"Right."

"I think it's reasonable for you to tell your dad you're an adult and it's your life and he needs to let go."

"Yeah." I nod like a bobble head. "That's what I want to say."

We talk a while longer with him giving me some ideas of how to phrase things.

"And now when do I do this?" I ask, rubbing my jaw.

"Bring them out for a visit. Invite them to a game."

"Hmmm. That's a good idea."

On the drive home, I process it. I don't want to talk to the doc about it.

But why? I know other guys have gotten help that way.

Maybe because...that would make Dad even more sure that I'm a gutless wuss. Real men don't talk about their feelings, especially to a shrink. According to him, anyway. Real men don't ask for help. Asking for help is a sign of weakness. Real men don't learn to skate from figure skaters.

Oh Jesus.

I almost have to pull over at the intense wave of queasiness rising up my esophagus.

I want to be a better player. And yet I resisted the help that could get me there—skating help. I'm still resisting the help that could get me there—talking to someone.

And then words from the teambuilding retreat float through my head. We don't have to handle shit alone. Asking for help isn't weak—it's strong. It shows confidence. *Opening up and talking about it is the biggest, bravest step you can take.*

If I really want to be better—and not just a better hockey player, but a better man—I need to rethink all those ideas Dad pounded into me.

TWENTY-THREE

Annie

"And I know another guy who'd like to hire you. He plays for our farm team in Hartford."

"Oh wow."

I've just told Dillon Landry I can't coach him while I'm working for the Bears. It's kind of a bummer, but I need to focus on doing the best job I can with the team I work for. I've been busting my butt and I think I'm winning over the guys and seeing results. I can't screw that up.

We end the call and I tell him I'll let him know if things change.

Now I have to deal with my mom.

She's still here. And even though I thought I'd managed to get her stop her matchmaking, I underestimated her tenacity. She *is* a hockey mom, after all. There's a saying that the only thing tougher than a hockey player is his mom, and it is *truth*.

"I don't believe you have a boyfriend," she says to me over

dinner at Ellington's Steakhouse. "I think you made that story up to get me to go home and leave you alone."

"Would you blame me?"

She gasps. "Annie! Am I right? How could you lie about something like that?"

"I'm not lying!" Well, at the time I sort of was. But now... Logan and I are actually...a couple. I guess. Even though it's secret. "I just can't tell you who it is."

"Why not?"

"Because...reasons."

She shakes her head and cuts a piece of her steak. "Well. Here's what I think. If a relationship has to be secret, you shouldn't be in it."

I sit back in my chair and blink. Ooof. That hit a little too close to home. "Dammit, Mom," I mutter.

She raises her eyebrows and lifts her fork to her mouth, regarding me provokingly as she eats her steak.

I look down at my plate. My filet mignon was delicious, five minutes ago.

I hate not being honest with my mom. I love her. She loves me. I know that. Even when I screwed up, she was always there for me. I know I always felt overshadowed by my brothers, but I never felt like my parents didn't love me and want the best for me. Guilt lodges like a stone in my gut.

If I tell her the truth, she'll still love me. Right?

I nibble the inside of my bottom lip and play with my food.

But if I tell her the truth, she's not going to be happy. I don't want to make my mom unhappy. Or my dad. Or my brothers.

On the other hand...I really care about Logan. We haven't known each other long—unless you count that night in Pyeongchang, and hey, why not count it, it was one of the best nights of my life and now I know why, because Logan is one of the best men I've ever met—but there's an undeniable chemistry and connection between us that I've never experienced with anyone else.

It's not fair to him, to hide him like a dirty secret. He doesn't deserve that, I know now. I care about him and I want everyone to know that.

My breath catches in my esophagus. I press my fingers there. Oh. My. God.

I'm falling in love with this man.

I close my eyes as the room starts slowly turning around me. I've never really been in love before. I've had a few boyfriends, but my life was so focused on skating that relationships never really had a chance to grow into love.

I can't stop thinking about him. I want to be with him all the time. I hate how his dad makes him feel and I love that he's working so hard on his goal.

How can I keep him a secret?

But I have to.

"Annie. What's going through your mind?" Mom sets down her fork and picks up her glass of cabernet. "Tell me."

I want to tell her. No matter how old a girl gets, she'll always need her mom. I want to tell my mom that I'm in love with the best guy in the world. The lump moves from my stomach to my throat. "I love you, Mom."

Her expression changes, a crease forming between her eyebrows. "Oh, Annie." She closes her eyes. "Is he married?"

"No! It's not that." I sigh.

She pierces me with her gaze again. "Then what is it?"

I swallow. "It's Logan Coates."

Her head jerks minutely but her expression doesn't change. Then the furrow in her forehead reappears. She blinks. "Logan Coates."

I press my lips together and nod.

"The player who broke your brother's ankle and put him in the hospital."

I close my eyes. "Yes."

"Good God."

I straighten my spine and open my eyes. I have to own this. "He's not a bad person, Mom."

Her lips part. "He's a goon!"

"No, he's not. Yes, he's a physical player." I want to tell her everything about Logan's dad and his upbringing and why he's always played so tough, and how he's working on changing that. "But he's not a goon. You know teams don't have 'goons' anymore."

She makes a scoffing noise. "There will always be enforcers."

"Oh God. Now you sound like Logan's dad."

She frowns. "What does that mean?"

"It's a long story. Do you want to hear it, or no?"

She slowly moves her head from side to side. "I really don't think I do. I can't believe this. Why would you get involved with someone like him? You know that's a slap in the face to Jensen."

"I get that it seems like that, but it's not my intention. I wouldn't want to hurt Jensen. But that happened years ago. And it was a mistake. Logan never intended to hurt Jensen."

"But he did."

What can I say? I pull a slow breath in through my nose. "I know."

"Well, you need to end things with him."

My mouth falls open far enough for Mom to see my tonsils. I snap it shut. "No."

She blinks again. "Annie. It can't be serious. How long have you known him? Three months?"

"Six years."

"Whaaaat!" Her hand goes to her throat, her eyes bugging out.

"We met in Pyeongchang. Nothing came of it then, but when we met again here, there was still a connection. Even though I hated him at first."

"Good lord." Mom sits back in her chair. "You never said anything."

"No. I mean..." I wave a hand. "What was I going to say? Anyway, I'm not ending things with Logan. We almost did. Because we both knew this would be an issue. But..." I roll my lips in briefly. "I missed him."

"I can't believe this." Mom pushes her plate away. "You and Ivan make a perfect couple. We all love him."

"But *I* don't love him. Not that like, anyway. I love him as a friend."

"Well." Mom looks across the restaurant. "I think we should go now."

My eyes feel hot. "You haven't finished your steak."

"I know. I'll take care of the check." She gestures to our waiter.

Neither of us talk as she does that and then we walk out of the restaurant onto West 52nd.

"Are you going back to the hotel?" I ask.

"I need to come to your place to get the things I left there. I'm going to fly home tomorrow."

"Okay. Right. We can walk then." We set off toward Ivan's place. It's dark and chilly and I wrap my scarf around my chin and pull on my gloves. "I'm sorry, Mom."

"I'm just so disappointed."

"I know." I sink my teeth into my bottom lip. "Are you going to disown me?"

"Disown you?" She turns wide eyes on me. "What does that even mean?"

"I don't know. People always say that. Like, kick me out of the family."

She snorts softly. "I don't think we can do that." She fills her cheeks with air then blows it out.

She didn't say she doesn't *want* to kick me out of the family. And I know as soon as the others hear about this, I'm going to be in shit up to my shoulders.

We walk into the apartment, and I stop right inside the door when I see Logan sitting in the living room with Ivan. My eyes widen. "Hi."

"Hi." Logan's gaze shifts behind me to see my mom. "Oh...hey."

They both stand.

"Hi," says Ivan.

I move in so Mom can follow me inside and close the door. Then a skunky scent reaches my nose. I lift my chin and my gaze sharpens on the joint in Ivan's hand. "What's going on?"

Logan stands too and gives me a loose smile. "I came over to make friends with Ivan."

I stare at him. "Seriously?"

"Yeah. He's not gay."

I blink rapidly a few times. "I know that, Logan."

"Yeah, I did, too. But I kept hoping. Ah well. We're getting to know each other better."

"Over a joint." I lift an eyebrow.

"Well. Yeah."

Mom goes around me and stops. "Logan Coates."

"Yes, ma'am." He straightens. "You want to punch me, don't you." He looks like he's prepared to take his punishment. For a wild minute, I think she might do it.

Holy laughing grass, what is happening? I rub my forehead.

"I do," she agrees, frowning. "Annie told me about you two."

"Oh." He gulps and looks at me.

I make a "sorry" face and shrug.

"Well, this is great!" He rubs his hands together. "We can get to know each other, too!"

Mom sighs. She takes off her coat, turns, and hands it to me. I hang it on the coat rack near the door, along with mine. Mom walks farther into the room, plucks the joint from Ivan's fingers, places it between her lips, and takes a long puff. Then she sits on the couch and exhales a long stream of smoke. "It's been a day."

I gape at her. I look to Ivan who's trying not to laugh, then Logan who looks like Mom just stripped naked. That's probably how I look, too.

Logan tips his head at me and I walk over to him and lean on him. "Holy hell what is happening."

"You broke my son's ankle," Mom says.

"I know. It was an accident." Logan sits back down on the chair he was in. I perch on the arm of it. "I didn't intend to hit him like that. I apologized to him. I got suspended and fined for it."

"Yeah. Four games." Mom takes another toke.

I cover my eyes.

"The department of player safety assessed that. I accepted it."

Mom hands the joint to me.

"Mom, I don't do that stuff."

She gives me a look. "Annie."

I reach for it and take a drag. Then I hand it to Logan. "Well, if we're getting everything out in the open, Mom's not happy about us."

Logan nods. "I understand."

"I don't know if my opinion counts for anything," Ivan says to Mom. "But I like him."

"Thanks, man," Logan says cheerfully.

Mom gives Ivan a sad look. "It should be you."

"Stella." He puts a hand on her arm. "No. It was never going to be me."

Mom wiggles her fingers for Logan to pass her the doobie, which he does, saying, "Ivan's a good guy, too."

"Thanks, man." Ivan beams at him, then looks at me. "Did you know this guy helps kids learn to play hockey?"

"I did know that." I smile. I love that he does that.

Mom appears unimpressed.

"And he likes Luke Combs."

My mouth twists. "Country music. Ugh."

"Country music is great," Ivan and Logan say at the same time.

I have to laugh.

"And Ivan likes the Spy Museum!" Logan adds. "We're gonna go back there sometime."

I regard my best friend and the man I love with amusement and affection. "That sounds great."

"Well," Mom says. "Annie always has been a rebel."

I frown. "What does that mean?"

"I should have known when you found a man it would be someone we don't approve of."

My mouth drops open and I straighten in outrage. "That is not what happened!"

"I should go." Mom stands.

"You can't go. You're stoned."

Mom laughs. "I am not. I'll Uber to the hotel." She pulls out her phone.

We collect her things and the car arrives quickly. I walk out to the sidewalk with her. "Text me when you get to the hotel."

"How things change. The kids worry about the parents now."

"I just want to know you make it there okay."

"I'll be fine."

"You're going to tell everyone about me and Logan, aren't you?"

"Well, *I'm* not going to keep it a secret."

"We're, um, trying to be discreet. Because we work together."

She regards me somberly. "Like I said earlier... if a relationship has to be secret, you shouldn't be in it. You should have thought of that before you got involved with him."

I did. But I did it anyway. And now I'm going to face the consequences of that. I lift my chin. "You're right."

Her eyes flicker and she swallows. Then she hugs me. "Bye, Annie."

TWENTY-FOUR

Logan

The door opens and Annie comes back in, arms wrapped around herself from the cold. The droop of her lips and shadowed eyes makes my throat ache. I want to hug her and soothe her and make everything right in her world.

"I shouldn't have told her." She sighs and meets my eyes. "I'm sorry."

She walks toward me and sits on the couch.

I glance at Ivan, who's looking at his phone. He looks up at me. Then at Annie. Then he jumps to his feet. "I gotta make a call. I'll do it in my room."

He disappears.

"We both knew this was going to happen." I cough so I can get the words out. "I know how important your family is to you. How loyal you all are to each other." I pause. "We should end things now."

She jumps up. "No!"

I don't know if I have the strength to push it. Because I

don't want that, either, even though it's obviously for the best. "You should think about it. Think about if it's worth it to piss off your family." I already know the answer to that. Obviously they're more important to her than I am.

"I *have* thought about it." She takes a step closer, her hands twisted together, her eyes full of pain. "I have, Logan."

The look on her face rips a hole in my gut. "Let's take some time," I say hoarsely. "To think things through. Your mom has a point. If a relationship has to be secret, we shouldn't be in it."

Bitterness sloshes like acid in my gut. I stand, too, facing her.

I've caught feelings for her. I don't want us to be secret and hiding. I was fine with her telling her mom—but she obviously isn't. And if I make her choose...between me and her family...I know who'll she choose.

"Is this what you do?" She crosses her arms, her stare boring into me.

I stare blankly at her. "What?"

"I know you've never had a real relationship. Do you walk away when things get hard?"

I can only gape at her, totally flabbergasted.

"When you get scared?" she challenges, eyes flashing. "What are you scared of, Logan?"

My heart is pounding in my chest, nearly bursting out, and my legs feel like rubber. "I'm not scared."

I see her disbelief in the flicker of her eyes. She lifts her chin, but her voice is soft. "I get it, you know? I'm afraid, too."

My lungs burn like I'm breathing in fire.

"I'm afraid I'm not good enough for this job. That I'm not as good as my brothers."

I know that's how she feels. I hate it. And there's no fucking way in hell I'll be the one to take that away from her, that chance to show what she can do.

Her eyes are shiny. Fuck. I fucking hate this. "Let's take some time," I repeat, my throat full of sand. I stand there, hands in fists, shoulders up at my ears. We stare at each other.

"Fine." She gives a short nod. "But I'm disappointed that you don't have the guts to be honest with me. Or with yourself."

What the fuck? I'm not a coward. I'm doing this for *her*. And it's fucking *hard*.

Her words are like the butt end of a hockey stick jabbing into my gut. I keep staring at her.

"You're more than just a tough guy hockey player. You need to know that. I want you t-to know that."

I can't stop myself from taking a giant step toward her and wrapping my arms around her. I squeeze her up against me, my face pressed to her hair. Her arms slide around me, too, and we stand like that for a long, vibrating moment, a hollow sensation spreading through my gut.

I know how important this job is to her to, to prove she's as good as her brothers. And it only makes sense that she doesn't want people to know about us.

I don't want to leave. But I use all the courage I have to let go of her. And let her go.

I watch the hope in her eyes fade as I step back and fuck, it hurts like a motherfucker to see that.

My thoughts are a jumbled mess and my insides feel hollow and empty as I leave. I set out up Eleventh Avenue and I'm halfway home before I realize my jacket's not done up and my hands are freezing.

I'm playing the things she said over and over in my mind. Her worry that she'll never accomplish what her brothers have. Maybe not. But that doesn't mean she's not as good as them, and I fucking hate it that she thinks that. She's had a huge impact on the team. All the guys love her. She's made us better, and not just better skaters. By encouraging us to overcome our pride and ego to be willing to learn something new, she made us better people.

She made me want to be better.

Or to deal with your father.

I've been thinking about the things Josh and I talked about, and I've done some reading about conditional love. It's been hard reliving how I felt as a kid when I didn't get Dad's affection or respect. I felt that he didn't really love me. How can it be love when it's only based on getting satisfaction from me doing what he wanted? Like he was living through me or something, wanting me to be the hockey player he was, so his ego would be gratified.

And I think about Annie's comment about me never being in a real relationship with a woman.

I arrive at my apartment building and in the lobby, I run into the guys going to play ping pong.

"Hey, Loco," Hellsy says. "Come on."

"I dunno. I'm kinda baked." My hands are in my jacket pockets, my shoulders hunched.

Hellsy looks at me. "You okay?"

"Fuck." I close my eyes and tip my head back. "I'm not sure."

"Come on. We can talk while we play."

I follow them into the games room. Millsy and Cookie take paddles and start a match. Hellsy and I lean against the wall. "Something happen with your dad?" he asks.

"No. I mean, not recently." I make a face.

"What's up with your dad?" Millsy asks, overhearing.

"Long story." I shake my head. "That's not what this is about."

"Okay. What is it about?" Hellsy asks.

I glance at him. "I didn't tell you about this, but I've been kind of seeing someone, and it's kind of...serious. Even though it's been fast."

"Oh, hey." Hellsy smiles. "Cool."

"Not really. I mean, it's great. But it's complicated." I hesitate. "It's Annie Bang."

I can almost hear their jaws hitting the floor.

"Holy shit," Cookie mutters.

"Ha, I knew it," Millsy says with a smirk. "I've seen you two together on the ice. They have to send the Zamboni out to fix the melted ice after."

I stare at him. Then I exhale sharply. "Shit."

"We won't say anything," Hellsy assures me.

The other guys give him skeptical looks. "You tell Sara everything." Cookie says.

Hellsy narrows his eyes. "So do you guys."

"The WAGs have a way of finding shit out." Millsy sighs.

"Whatever. I don't care. Wait, yes I do. This is a problem for Annie." They all give me a knowing look that makes me frown. "What?"

"Nothing." Hellsy shakes his head.

"Her family hates me," I add.

"Oh. Yeah." They all frown.

"Her mom found out about us tonight. And she is *pissed.* I'm sure the rest of the family is giving Annie hell right now. I could see how upset she was about it. So I told her we should break up."

They all make identical "ohhhhh" sounds.

"Her family is really important to her," I add.

I look at the floor. "She called me a coward."

"Yikes," Millsy mutters.

"We men *are* cowards." Hellsy shrugs.

I look at him.

"When it comes to talking about our feelings? Our fears and insecurities? Oh, hell yeah."

I swallow past the puck lodged behind my Adam's apple. "She asked what I'm afraid of. And I didn't answer her. But I wasn't being a coward. I was trying to do the right thing. I was trying not to come between her and her family."

They all nod thoughtfully.

The silence expands.

Finally, I sigh. "I *was* being a coward."

"Yeah," Hellsy agrees.

"What *are* you afraid of?" Millsy asks. "Go head, let it out."

I bow my head again. "I've fucking fallen for her. She's *the one*. I knew it when she took my fries." I look up at them.

"Uh...okay." They all exchange glances and it nearly makes me laugh.

"I've never felt like this. And fuck yeah, I'm afraid. I'm terrified." My hands curl into tight fists. "I'm terrified that she doesn't feel the same. Of course she'll choose her family and her career over me. I'm not worth it. I don't deserve her."

After a thick pause, Hellsy says slowly, "You wanna talk about your dad?"

Well, this is humiliating, telling everyone how my dad never loved me.

"Hey." Millsy says. "You don't think we've all been through crap?"

He doesn't need to remind me that he was in that bus accident and was sitting there in a snowy ditch when his father and brother died only a few feet away from him.

"Yeah," Hellsy says. "Think of this as therapy. No one's going to judge you."

Cookie nods. "These guys and Morrie did an intervention with me when I was losing my shit. My brother was a drug addict. He overdosed and died a few years ago."

"I'm sorry." I didn't know that about him.

"Obviously it affected me," he says. "I used hockey to escape, only it kind of turned into an escape from too many things. When I was seeing Emerie, I used it to keep things between us from getting serious. It fucked up my game. I injured someone."

I remember that.

"I wouldn't have figured all that shit out without talking to someone about it. So spill your guts."

Like it's that easy.

I tell them the stuff I told Hellsy. They nod. They're not playing ping pong. They're listening. No judgment.

"This year I was determined to play the way I want to play. And I'm doing it. But he's still not happy about it." I drop my head. "If I don't do what he wants..." I shrug. "It doesn't matter."

"Yeah. It does," Hellsy says.

"We all want our parents' approval," Cookie says. "We all want to make them proud. I think it doesn't matter how old we get."

"But there's always going to be differences," Hellsy adds. "I was lucky my parents were always supportive. I guess for some parents it's harder to loosen the grip." HJe pauses. "Maybe for Annie's family, too."

I blow out a breath. "Oh yeah."

"It's okay to want our parents' approval," Cookie says. "But it doesn't mean you have to always do what they want."

"I know. But I don't want to be the problem between Annie and her family."

"Maybe that's her decision to make," Cookie adds.

I blink, a band tightening around my chest. "Yeah," I say slowly. Shit. I haul air into my lungs. "Dad always made me feel like I disappointed him. Like, if I didn't play the way he wanted, I didn't deserve to be loved."

"So that's what you're afraid of," Hellsy says. "You think you don't deserve to be loved."

I already said that, but now it all connects in my head. "Jesus." I swipe a hand across my face. "This is embarrassing."

Nobody laughs.

"I know," Cookie agrees. "Tough it out."

I think back to Hellsy's question—*is it possible you feel that way because of your dad?*

Of course it's because of that. Of *course* it's because I don't trust love. I don't believe someone will love me for myself without some kind of personal gain. I've always ended relationships when they started to get serious because of that.

Annie was right. I *am* a fucking coward.

I meet Hellsy's eyes. "I need to talk to Annie."

"Maybe you should talk to your dad," Hellsy says slowly. "Do the hard work first."

"Ugh."

"It might help you sort shit out. I mean, it's not going to happen overnight, with one conversation. It takes time to change. But you have to start somewhere."

I push away from the wall. "Okay. I gotta go check the schedule and book a flight for my parents." I pause. "Thanks, guys. Good talk."

Okay I've made myself vulnerable and confessed all my weaknesses and fears to a bunch of guys and the world didn't end. In fact, it almost feels...good. I feel lighter. A little.

Now I need to do it with my dad.

TWENTY-FIVE

Annie

The first call is from Jensen. Of course. "What the fuck, Annie?"

I sigh. "You heard from Mom."

"Oh yeah. What are you doing? You can't be serious about Logan Coates."

I choke up and plop my butt down on my bed. I squeeze my eyes shut against hot tears and try to get control of my voice.

"That guy is not good enough for you," he adds.

My eyes shoot open. I swipe a hand across one cheek. "What? Are you kidding me? I'm the one who's not good enough. I'm the one who can never live up to the amazing Bang brothers."

"That's not true."

"Jensen. Yes, it is. It's always been like that. I'm not mad about it. I'm just realistic."

"That's bullshit."

Anger flares in my chest. "You're invalidating my feelings? Seriously?"

He's silent.

"I'm telling you how I feel," I nearly shout at him.

"Okay, okay. But my point stands. He's not good enough for you. He's a dickwad."

"Argh!" My molars grind together. "He's not!" I take a breath. "I know you feel that way, and I get why. But I've gotten to know him better and that's not who he is. There's a lot more to him than you know."

"It's not just about me. He had the most penalty minutes on his team last year."

I did not know that. But I know how hard he's working this year to change his style of play. "That was last year."

"You have to listen to reason."

"*You're* the voice of reason?"

"Yeah, I am."

"Phhht."

"Jesus Christ, Annie."

"I'm an adult, Jensen. I make my own decisions about who I date or sleep with or marry, for that matter."

"Marry! No!"

My bottom lip quivers. "Well, don't worry about that." It's looking like things are over between Logan and me.

"Mom said you lied to her about seeing him."

"Sort of. Because I knew everyone would freak out like this!"

"You need to think this through," he says tersely, and we end the call.

I hear from Kingston next. The oldest brother, the one who was always looking after the rest of us. Then Jakob, then Leif, then Tanner, all variations of the conversation with Jensen. Of all of them, Leif is the most laid back about it. As usual. He's the most easy-going person I know. Well, Dad's pretty even-tempered, too.

From Dad, I get a text that makes me cry.

> DAD: Hey Mini Bang you're probably getting shit from your brothers about all this and your mom is pretty cheesed off too, but just know it's all because we're worried about you. We love you and want the best for you and that includes any man that lays a finger on you.

I sit on my bed and tears slide down my cheeks. "Thanks, Dad," I whisper.

In my pajamas, I trudge out to the kitchen. I'm not hungry, but I want something. I don't know what, so I peer into the cupboard. Aha. A bag of marshmallows.

I put some into the microwave and wait.

Ivan comes out of his bedroom.

"Logan's gone?"

"Yeah." I pout down at the counter. "Maybe forever."

"What?"

With my head still bowed, I nod. "He thinks we should break up."

Ivan's hand lands on the middle of my back and rubs. "Why?"

The microwaves dings.

"What are you making?" Ivan peers at the appliance.

"Marshmallows."

"What? In the microwave?"

"Yeah." I take out the plate. "They get all chewy and crispy."

"That is fucking weird."

"I don't care."

"So why does he want to break up?" Ivan asks again.

"Well." I pick up a crispy marshmallow, my chest feeling

like Arctic tundra, barren and frozen. "Of course I think it's because he doesn't really care about me that much."

Ivan snorts. "I don't believe that. He's crazy about you."

"I actually don't believe it either. He's just not ready to trust in love." My heart feels like a corkscrew is twisting into it. "He has some stuff to deal with and he hasn't yet."

"Ah."

"I understand it." I chew on the marshmallow. "His dad is a piece of work. He's always been really hard on him about his hockey. Withheld affection to get what he wanted."

"That sucks."

"Yeah. So I get it. But...I wish he knew he can trust *me*." I swipe a hand over one eye. "I wish he knew how special he is. He said he knows how important my family is to me and that we should end things."

"Huh. So he doesn't want to come between you and your family."

I frown.

"What did your brothers say?"

"They all think he's an asshole and I should dump him."

"So Logan was right."

"No." I stare at him. "I mean, yeah, but...I wouldn't dump him just because they tell me to. I'm a grown woman. I make my own decisions. Jesus! Was he doing some kind of self-sacrificing bullshit?" I pout down at my plate of marshmallows. "I hate it that they don't really know him. I just realized tonight when Mom and I were having dinner that I'm in love with him." A tear pops out and slithers down my cheek. "Th-that was why I told her about him. I don't want it to be secret. I want them to know, because I care about him and he's not the monster they think he is. And I kn-knew there was going to be fallout, but I was prepared to deal with it so I could be honest."

I hiccup. "And then he wanted to end things. Or 'take some time.'"

"Because he didn't want to come between you and your family."

I stare at him, the sugary treat melting in my mouth. "Damn."

———

THE NEXT DAY I'm at the arena and I'm thinking about Jensen and our conversation, and for some reason I want to watch the video of Logan's hit on him. I go to the video room and sit down at the computer to search it out. Then I watch it. And watch it again. I slow it down and study Logan's skates. And Jensen's. Rewind and watch it again.

Wow.

———

I GAZE at the faces of my entire family on the screen of my laptop in front of me. "Hi, guys. Hi, Mom and Dad."

We're on a Zoom call that I've set up. Mom and Dad are sharing a computer, their faces close together.

"What's going on?" Mom says without smiling. Gak. She's still salty.

"I want to show you all something."

They all wear similar perplexed expressions.

I click my mouse to share my screen and start the video. It's the clip of the hit on Jensen, slowed way down. "If you look at Logan's skate blades...right here..." The video stops. "You can see he's lost his edge. This shows he wasn't trying to hit you, Jensen, like he said. He knew the play was dead and he was trying to slow down or stop. Like he always said. Watch it again."

They might not be trained to watch things like that as closely as I do, but they all know this stuff.

"If he'd been strong on that inside edge, it might not have happened." Giving myself a mental pat on the back, I add, "It probably wouldn't happen now, after the work we've been doing."

"Well," Dad says. "I think you're right there, Annie."

"I want to see it again," Kingston says.

I play it again for them. And I point out something else. "Jensen's not strong on his skates at this point either. Check out his left foot. See how he falls awkwardly, twisting his ankle as he fell? Honestly, I'd say you bear some of the fault for the way you fell."

"Fuck off," Jensen mutters.

"Jensen," Mom says.

He sighs. "I wasn't saying it to Annie. Shit. She could have a point."

"Have you thought about a job with the Department of Player Safety?" Leif asks me. "You're good at this."

I'm good that this. Heat expands in my chest.

"Yeah. Obviously you've found your calling," Tanner says.

"I've had a couple of guys ask me if you're doing one on one coaching," Kingston says. "It seems like everyone's heard about the results you're getting. And the Bears are playing great."

"Oh. Wow." I blink at that.

"I was like, that's my little sister," Kingston laughs. "All proud of you."

"We're proud of you, too," Mom says. "I'm sorry you didn't know that. That I don't tell you that enough."

"When we talked the other day..." Jensen pauses. "I never know you felt that way. That you couldn't live up to us."

I press my lips together.

"What?" Kingston frowns. "That's ridiculous."

"That's what I said." Jensen nods.

My throat feels like someone stuffed a hockey sock down it. "You don't know what it was like, growing up with all of you."

Silence floats from the computer monitor.

"What was it like?" Kingston asks quietly.

I sniffle in a breath, fighting back emotion. "I couldn't play hockey like the rest of you."

"You played hockey," Jensen points out.

"I played for fun. I couldn't play well enough to even be competitive, never mind as a pro. I was the only one of all of us who didn't. Then I found figure skating and you all thought it was stupid."

I gaze at the faces on the screen, all wearing identical looks of confusion.

"No, we didn't," Kingston says.

I sigh. "Yeah, you did. Mom and Dad, you didn't even want to pay for figure skating lessons."

Mom bites her lip. Dad rubs his face.

"But I loved it," I say. "But that didn't work out either. I just wanted to be good at *something*, even though I'd never be as good as my brothers."

Jakob makes a rough sound.

"I felt like no matter what I do in life, it'll never be good enough."

Jensen opens his mouth as if to argue with that but Bailey, off camera, elbows him and he shuts up. That almost makes me smile. I can't wait to meet her.

"Then I got this job in the NHL. I was proud but also terrified that I'm not good enough for this either. That I'd fail at this, too." I wave a hand, remembering Logan's admonishment.

"And I know I didn't fail at figure skating, that I couldn't help that I got injured, but still...it feels like a failure."

"But your job is going great," Tanner says.

"It is. Except for getting involved with a player. I knew it was a bad idea, but...I fell in love with Logan."

Another thick silence.

"You're in love with him?" Leif asks.

"Yes." I lift my chin. "But we're taking a break to think about things, so...s-so you may not even need to worry about that. But I wanted you to know the truth. That what he said about what happened was the truth."

"Jesus." Kingston shakes his head. "I had no idea you felt that strongly about him."

"Me either." Jensen frowns.

Mom's forehead creases. "You're taking a break?"

"Yeah. Ivan says it's because Logan doesn't want me to have to choose between you and him."

"Nobody's making you choose, Mini," Leif says.

"He...he would step aside so he doesn't come between you and your family," Mom clarifies slowly.

I nod, my bottom lip quivering.

"Well, that's..." She clears her throat. "That's admirable."

I stare at her image on the monitor. She looks like she's going to cry.

I thought Logan breaking up with me because my family hates him was stupid. But...she's right. If he really cares about me, doing that is very...honorable.

"Yeah," Jensen says, his forehead wearing a perplexed furrow. "It is."

Kingston rubs his jaw. "I'm kinda seeing this dude in a different light."

"Yeah." Tanner nods. "Same."

Jensen makes a face. "Me, too. What if I reached out to him? I could call him and try to clear things up."

I stare at my big brother. "You would do that?"

He makes a rough noise. "Yeah. We're family. Right?"

My heart squeezes then swells up. "Right." I draw in a breath. "But no. You don't have to do that. I need to handle this myself."

"Anyone who messes with one of the Bangs messes with all of us," Jakob says.

Love fills my heart. "Thanks, guys."

TWENTY-SIX

Logan

Mom and Dad were surprised by my invitation to come visit and go to a game, but they eagerly accepted. Which makes me feel bad that I don't do it more often. I avoid it because I know Dad would always be critical of me and we'd end up arguing.

We lose the game in OT, which sucks.

"You could easily have won that game," Dad rants on the way home. "What the hell happened?"

"We were doing all the right things," I reply, digging deep for an even tone. "Three pucks went off the goalpost or crossbar when we were trying to score."

"That turnover in OT, though." He shakes his head.

"It was three on three. That happens."

"We never had three on three overtime in my day. I don't like it."

I swallow a sigh.

Back at my place after the game, when I've changed out of

my suit and into sweats, I pause in my bedroom. I have to do this.

I have to think about Annie. About her courage and guts and determination. If she can be brave enough to do the things she has, I can do this.

I walk out to the living room where Mom and Dad are watching TV in my living room, a recap of the game on a sports channel. "Hey, could we talk about something?"

Dad barely looks up. Mom says, "Sure. What's up?"

I take a seat, wishing for a shot of tequila. Teemu jumps into my lap and I set my hands on his furry body. "I met a girl."

Shit. That wasn't what I was going to lead with.

Mom's eyes brighten. "Oh."

Dad still doesn't look away from the TV. "You're always with some girl or other."

"I think he's telling us because this one's special," Mom says.

"Yeah, I think she could be." I don't mention our "timeout." I search for the words I rehearsed. "But what I really want to talk about are my goals for this year and how I've been playing."

Dad frowns. Mom smiles with a perplexed notch between her eyebrows.

I launch into my spiel. About my goals, playing better, getting more minutes. Dad interrupts a couple of times and I quietly ask him to hear me out. Mom gets up and takes the remote control for the TV away from him and mutes the volume.

I shoot her a grateful glance.

"There's nothing wrong with being a fourth liner," Dad says. "Like I was. Hardworking, getting under the other team's skin, baiting them into penalties. Those guys set the tone for the game a lot of the time. They get the crowd into things with the big hits."

"Okay. So this is the thing. When you say things like that—trying to justify that I should be happy being a fourth liner—it makes me feel like you don't care about how I want to play. You want me to play the way *you* played. I feel like you don't support me."

Mom turns anxious eyes between us at my challenge to Dad.

"What's wrong with how I played?" He frowns at me.

"Nothing was wrong with it. That was you. I'm *me*. I want to play a different game." I pause. "I'm playing a different game. I'd like to have your support. I'd like to know..." Aw fuck. My throat closes up and I have to stop. I swallow hard. "I was thinking when I invited you here that I'd do it more often if I didn't have to listen to you criticize me after every game."

"Oh, Logan." Mom sighs.

"I don't criticize you after every game," Dad snaps

"Dennis." Mom gives him a look. "You do."

He scowls.

Again, I give her a look of thanks. "I think you do. I feel like you do. It's hard to listen to." I tell him how I felt as a kid. Never good enough. Worried about not being loved.

He looks at me as I talk, his eyebrows pulled down, like he doesn't quite understand what I'm saying. Maybe he doesn't. Maybe this is all news to him.

"I'm an adult now and I need to let go of my need for your approval. I've formed my own identity and my own values. I can't live my life to impress you. I have to live it for myself. I don't need your approval...but what I need...what I'd like...is your support."

"I do support you."

"I don't feel like you do," I reply quietly.

"We're here, aren't we?" he asks gruffly. "That's support. Support. Approval. It's the same thing."

"No. It's not."

He gazes at me.

"Support means giving me your blessing to do what I've decided to do, even if you don't agree with it. Maybe offering to help me. Not telling me I'm wrong."

"I've helped you your whole life!"

Breathe. "I know you have. And I appreciate it. I know you both have done so much for me and made sacrifices so I could play hockey." I hate whining about shit when I know that. They *have* done a lot for me.

"I'm glad you see that." Dad frowns.

"Oh, Logan. We're your parents. Of course we did everything we could to support you. And you don't owe us anything for that."

I gaze at her. "Are you sure?"

Her forehead puckers. "What does that mean?"

"I'd like to know that you love me even when I don't drop the gloves or make the hard hit."

"Of course we do!" Mom's head tilts. She sends a distressed glance at Dad.

I don't think Dad's ever said he loves me. Mom has, more so when I was young. Will he say it now?

He makes a sound in his throat. "Of course I love you."

"And we're so proud of you," Mom adds. "Look what you've accomplished. Right, Dennis?"

"Yeah." Dad looks away from me, at the TV still playing highlight reels. "You're a better player than I ever was. I'm proud of that."

Jesus. My throat constricts. I take a slow breath, then swallow, digging my fingers into Teemu's fur. "Thank you. That means a lot to me, to hear that."

"I was always proud of you. I just wanted you to be the best you could."

"Thanks, Dad." Okay, fuck, I'm going to lose it and start crying. I rub my nose. "I love you, too. And you, Mom."

I've tried to tell myself I don't care what Dad thinks about how I play. But that's a lie. I care. I guess the need for a parent's approval never goes away. I *do* want to know I've made them proud. I want to honor the sacrifices they've made as hockey parents. Because I know they made a lot of sacrifices. But I also want to be my own man. Make my own decisions. There's a tension between those things that makes it hard.

"We've had a lot of arguments," I say. "I haven't handled things as well as I could have. I go back to being a kid and argue with you. So I've been thinking about it and I'm going to try to not do that anymore. And I'd like it if you wouldn't jump in with your opinions or advice unless I ask you." I meet his eyes.

His Adam's apple bobs. He says nothing for a long moment and the silence in my apartment beats against my eardrums. I dig my fingers into Teemu's soft fur. Finally, Dad nods. "I'll try. I kind of like giving my opinions though."

Mom laughs softly. "Yeah, you do."

"We'll both work on it," I say, my voice rusty.

"It's like..." Dad hesitates.

I wait. I know it's hard.

"You doing your own thing, trying to be different...trying to be the new kind of player..." He coughs. "It's like you don't need me anymore."

I pull in a slow breath through my nose. There it is. Fuck.

The moment drags on forever as I absorb that and process it. Pressure builds in my chest, like someone has a bicycle pump attached to me and is pumping hard. I know how hard that had to be for him, to admit a vulnerability, a fear. I appreciate that he's gone that far...for me. It means so much.

I move my head up and down slowly and choke out, "I'll always need you, Dad."

Okay, Mom's crying. Dad and I are close, but she's full-on bawling into a tissue.

"Geez, Mom, don't cry. Please don't cry." I swipe my forehead.

"I'm sorry," she sobs. "I love you both. I wish we talked about this sooner. I wish you weren't the one who had to bring it up, Logan. But I'm proud of you for doing it."

It's messy and uncomfortable and disturbing. And I've never felt so strong.

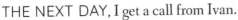

THE NEXT DAY, I get a call from Ivan.

My first thought is that somethings happened to Annie and my heart vaults into my mouth.

But I just saw her this morning at the practice facility and she was fine.

"What?" I bark into the phone.

"Uh...sorry to bother you..."

"Is she okay?"

"Who?"

"Annie."

"I think so?"

"What are you calling me about?"

I hear him chuckle. "You okay, bro?"

"Not really."

"It's okay. Chill. Annie's fine." He pauses. "Well, sort of. I need to talk to you about something."

"Okay. Go."

"In person."

I frown. I'm still at the practice facility and we're about to leave for the hospital to visit some sick kids. "I'll be home around five," I say. "Or do you want me to come there?"

"No, your place is good."

Because of Annie. "What's going on?"

"I'll tell you later."

My mind buzzes with curiosity, but at the hospital I focus on the kids, stuck in this place when it's nearly Christmas. Some of their stories are heartbreaking, like the little guy with Ewing sarcoma, a kind of bone cancer, so pale and thin and bald, but wearing a Bears jersey and a huge smile.

Maybe it's being around these kids that makes me anxious and fear the worst. But Ivan said Annie's fine. And surely she wouldn't send Ivan to dump me...would she?

At home, I tell the doorman to send Ivan up when he arrives and a moment later he knocks on my door. I let him in, but I freeze in place at seeing who's with him. Stella Bang.

She scares the shit out of me.

A woman who's raised five hockey playing boys and one headstrong girl who likes to be thrown up in the air—on skates —is not someone to mess around with.

My breathing quickens and sweat breaks out under my arms. "Uh. Hi, Mrs. Bang."

"Call me Stella."

I swallow. "Uh. Come in." I give Ivan a what-the-fuck look. He grins. "I'll let you two talk. Bye!"

"What?" I glare at him, then turn back to Stella as Ivan leaves. "Okay."

What more do we have to talk about? She's probably going to dejunk me.

"Can I offer you a drink?" I ask politely, wiping my palms on my jeans. "Coffee? Tea? Water?"

"I'd love a cup of tea."

"Oh. Wait. I don't have tea."

She laughs. "A glass of water, then."

I get us both one and we sit in the living room.

"Your place is nice," she says. "Great view."

"Thanks."

"So." She fidgets with her hair.

I'm not the only one who's nervous. I wait.

"Annie was a bit rebellious in her teenage years."

I nod slowly. "She told me."

She cocks her head. "Did she? That's surprising. But mature."

"Rebellion is a sign of a kid who's fighting to be seen as who she is."

Stella gazes at me. Her tightly schooled features shift as her bottom lip quivers and her eyes go shiny.

Jesus. Another crying mother. Panic flares in my gut. I rub my mouth, not sure what to do.

"Yes." She sniffs. "You're right. I know Annie always felt overshadowed by her brothers. Star hockey players. I knew that and I tried to make sure she knew she was special. But it was difficult when she was always arguing with us and acting out."

"I argued with my dad a lot, too."

"Because you wanted to be seen as who you are."

"Yeah." I pause. "Exactly."

"We try. Parents. We don't always get it right. But we love our kids and want the best for them."

"I know." Didn't I just hear this from my own mom?

"I'm sorry I kept pushing her and Ivan together."

Whoa. I gaze at her speechlessly.

"It truly came from a place of wanting Annie to be happy. But I also thought that maybe she was being so obstinate about it because...that's her. If I wanted her to wear pink, she wore black. If I hated tattoos, she got three of them."

I slowly nod.

"I don't believe she was with you because she was being defiant. I shouldn't have said that. She's not like that now. She's grown into an amazing young woman. Strong. Determined. Resilient."

A thick feeling tightens my throat. "Yeah."

She bite the inside of her cheek, looks away, then back at me. "The other thing I'm sorry for is that I did misjudge you. We all did."

I stare at her.

"Annie got us all together on a video chat and showed us the video of when that hit on Jensen happened. She slowed it down and played it for us a few times and pointed out where you lost your edge and fell. But you fell on Jensen with your stick out."

My head goes empty and I can only stare at Stella. After a moment, I say, "Annie did what?"

She smiles. "It was interesting. Also she showed us where Jensen wasn't completely solid on his skates either, and that probably contributed to how he got hurt."

My head turns slowly from side to side, trying to comprehend this. "When did she do that?"

"A couple of days ago."

So it was after I lost my goddamn mind and told her we should break up. Even after that...she defended me. To her family.

I think my heart stops. Then it explodes into a rapid banging.

She believed in me. Even when I was an asshole to her. I don't even know what to do with that...with that kind of love. Love that expects nothing in return. I want to believe I deserve it. I want to believe I can have that. But, holy shit... "I really screwed up."

"No. Well, maybe."

I squint at her.

"That's why I'm here." Her smile has faded and a troubled

notch has formed on her brow. "I want to help make things right."

I haven't felt like such an idiot in a long time. I don't understand what's happening.

"Do you love Annie?"

My eyes widen. I swallow. "Yes."

She pulls in a shaky breath, her lips pushing out and her eyes shining. Christ. More tears. I'm still sweating. "I knew it." Her lips curve into an unsteady smile. "All I wanted for my kids is love. Like Lars and I have. I messed up, pushing Annie and Ivan together. I've been interfering a lot lately. But things have worked out pretty well for my other kids. I want things to work out for you and Annie. But I can't do it myself. Annie's not going to listen to me right now."

"I need to talk to her." I'm seized with a sense of urgency. "Right now. I fucked up...er..."

She waves a hand. "Don't worry. I've heard it all."

No doubt. She's a hockey mom.

"I messed up," I try again. "I told her we should end things between us."

"I know. She told us. But it's not too late." She pats the air in a calm down gesture. "I think she feels the same about you. Let's talk about what you can do."

"Uh...okay."

An hour later, I'm calling Ivan. "Okay, dude. You owe me. Big time."

"Yeah. Sorry about that. She wanted to talk to you."

"Well, here's how you can pay me back."

TWENTY-SEVEN

Annie

"You need cheering up."

I shove my hand into the bowl of popcorn. "No, I don't."

I'm wrapped in a fuzzy blanket on the couch, binge watching *Night Stalker* on TV. What better way to distract from a crushed and bleeding heart?

Dramatic much, Annie?

"Come on, you've been moping for days."

"So? Let me mope."

"No. You're coming out with me. Come on, get dressed."

"I don't want to go out. It's cold. It's snowing. I want to eat popcorn and watch true crime shows."

"Let's go skating."

I lower my chin and give him a look. "We skate every damn day."

"Not at Bryant Park. Come on, it's a New York Christmas experience. It's all decorated and there's shopping kiosks and food and music. It'll be fun."

I pout. It does sound kind of fun. "But I don't want to have fun. I want to wallow in misery."

"You can do that later. Get your skates. We can show off and impress people."

Okay, he got me. "Fine." I heave a sigh and throw the blanket off. I'm wearing flannel pajamas at one in the afternoon on a Sunday. I go into my room and change into black fleece leggings and a pink turtleneck sweater.

I eye my reflection in the mirror. I don't care how I look at all right now, but it's not like me to go out without at least a little makeup. So I brush my hair and slap on some mascara and lip gloss. Then, bundled up and carrying our skates, we set out walking toward Bryant Park.

"It's actually not that cold." I turn my face up to the few softly falling flakes. "I guess."

"It's nice. Very Christmassy."

It definitely is. Christmas decorations are everywhere. As we walk down Sixth Avenue, we pass Radio City Music Hall, extra bright with its lit-up tree, and the giant red Christmas ornaments. White lights strung in trees twinkle in the low afternoon light. I have to pause to take in the sight since it's my first time in New York at Christmas. It's beautiful.

We arrive at Bryant Park and I marvel over all the kiosks set up with food and shopping, more strings of white lights everywhere. People throng through the space and as we near the big skating rink, music reaches our ears. I have to admit the sight of a skating rink does lift my spirits.

We lace up our skates and hit the ice. At one end, a colorful Christmas tree sparkles and glows, and blocky skyscrapers tower around the park. The pale sky feels low and a few gentle snowflakes drift around us. Ivan takes my hand and we set out on a brisk lap around the ice.

I'm still sad and worried and hurt. But the ice under my

blades and the chill air whooshing on my face feels good. I love skating so much.

As we head back toward the Christmas tree, I see an unusual sight—a hockey player in a jersey and hockey skates.

"You can't play hockey here," I say out loud.

"Nope. You definitely can't," Ivan agrees.

I recognize the Bears logo on the jersey, and then I recognize the size and shape of that player...it's Logan.

My heart leaps into my throat. Open mouthed, I glide toward him as my feet stop moving.

Ivan keeps skating, tugging me along.

"What is happening?" I stare at Logan and our eyes meet as we draw nearer together.

He smiles. That beautiful, tempting smile that melted me from the moment I met him years ago. "Hi."

"Hi."

Ivan releases my hand. I glance at him but he's skating away. "Hey..." I turn back to Logan. "What are you doing here? And dressed like..." I gesture.

"I want to skate with you."

"Oh." I blink.

"Will you skate with me, Annie Bang?"

"Um...okay."

He takes my hand and a new song starts. It's Calum Scott's "You Are The Reason."

I remember this song. I remember dancing to it at Club Crystal. With Logan.

Logan moves beside me and slides an arm around my waist, taking my other hand like he knows what he's doing. I'm gazing up at him as I set my hand on my waist, over his, and we start skating forward.

"I learned a few things," he says as he leans forward and lifts his right leg into a spiral.

Mystified, I follow him, lifting my own right leg as we glide. I remember the first coaching session, where I got him to do a spiral. He was so pissy and resistant. And wobbly. Well, he's still wobbly, but better.

I follow his lead as he slowly lowers his foot back to the ice and we skate again. Then he does a half swizzle to face me and change our hands so his right hand grips my right and his left holds my left, our arms crossed.

"Waltz jump," he says.

I laugh out loud as I take the hop, then tighten my core as he tries one. And he does it! We do a few of those, then he releases one of my hands and moves to the side. I watch him as I pump and swizzle in small moves, again following his lead, and then he turns toward me into a spread eagle and takes my hand and we spin together. Yes, it's slow, yes, it's wobbly, but it's figure skating and he's doing it and I love him.

We come out of the spin and he skates backward doing some crossovers, focused but smiling at me. "Waltz jump," he says as he releases my hands, and I do a small solo jump. Then he does the same, feet actually leaving the ice, and, arms outstretched, he lands it! I laugh again with delight. He does a small turn, takes my hand, and holds it up so I can turn as well.

He skates backward again, arm outstretched and holding mine and he does another spiral as he faces me. I lift my leg too, so amused and yet proud as he glides backward, leg not high but definitely off the ice.

As we skate, I improvise a few more turns and we free-style a bit to the music until the song ends and he pulls me into him. I spin and he wraps he arms around my waist and I lean against him. I tilt my head to look up at him, smiling so hard my face hurts.

Applause breaks out around us, and I come out of my fog of enchantment and glance around. "Oh my God." People are smiling and talking and I realize everyone stopped their own skating to watch us. And a lot of them are holding phones up.

Logan grins. "We're popular."

"No one knows who *I* am." I cover my face with a mittened hand. "But everyone knows who you are."

"That's okay." He shrugs, takes my hand, and we skate to the boards where Ivan is waiting. With a phone in his hand that he apparently just used to video record us. He's grinning, too.

I shake my head at him. "What did you do?"

"I only did what Logan asked. It was all his idea."

I look up at Logan. "You wanted to learn to figure skate?"

"Yeah. Just enough to do a little routine with you. Ivan taught me."

"He's a fast learner," Ivan says, pocketing his phone. "Well, I gotta go. Bye!"

Wide-eyed, I watch him leave, then look back at Logan.

"Did you listen to the song?" he asks.

"Sort of. You know I like that song."

"It's an apology. But I want to say the words, too. I'm sorry, Annie."

Something spins in my chest, hot and soft. "About what?" I whisper.

"You were right. I was a coward."

My eyes are fastened on his face. For him to admit that he was afraid...a rush of emotion swamps me.

"I hated how upset you were about your mom's reaction to us being together. I knew you didn't want your family to know about us. And...I was scared I wasn't good enough for you. I'm sorry I hurt you. Christ. Don't look at me like that." He reaches out and pulls me closer, pressing my face to his chest. I hear his heart thudding rapidly. "I'm sorry. I thought it was for the best."

"I know," I mumble into his jersey. I pull back and look up at him.

"You do?"

"Well, I dad have the thought that maybe you didn't really care that much. Or you didn't want to be mixed up with Bang family shit."

One corner of his mouth quirks up. "Too late for that."

"But I know how your dad made you feel. I know you didn't believe that you could trust me." I eye him warily, still not sure if he does trust me.

"I do trust you," he says in a low voice. "Your mom told me about the video you showed everyone. About how you showed them I lost an edge and actually fell on Jensen."

What? My mom told him? When? I stare at him.

"And I realized you didn't have to do that. And I realized I was a fucking idiot." He leans his forehead against mine. "I trust you."

I nod slowly, my throat thick.

"I talked to me dad," he continues.

My eyes widen. "You did? Oh wow."

"Yeah. I knew I had to do it. I told him why it bugs me so much when he criticizes me." He recounts details of his conversation and ends with the heart-wrenching revelation that his dad felt like Logan didn't need him anymore. "And I guess I sort of don't need him. But then again..."

"We always need them," I finish for him. "I know. I feel like that about my mom. She's been interfering and making me crazy, but...that was why I told her about us. Because she's my mom and I wanted her to know that I was falling in love."

We gaze at each other for a long moment, oblivious to people skating around us. "You're falling in love?" he asks quietly.

I nod.

Eyes still locked, he says, "So am I."

Then we're kind of surrounded as people tell us how great that was and ask for autographs. Logan's autograph.

"Hang on," he mutters. "We'll get out of here as soon as we can."

"But I want to do that again."

"Uh..."

I laugh. "Kidding." I just want to hear him tell me again that he's falling in love with me.

When we can finally escape, we find our boots and change out of our skates. Logan takes off his jersey and folds it into a bag he has. "Sweating like a pig." He pauses. "I'm not actually sure that pigs sweat."

"Did you know that sweating is a human superpower?"

His smile is slow and sweet. "No."

I nod. "It is. It allows us to survive almost anywhere. It's an evolutionary wonder. A highly efficient way of cooling. And it's way better than how vultures stay cool."

He chokes on a laugh. "Okay, how do vultures stay cool?"

"They poop on their legs."

"Okay. You're right. It is better than that." He regards me with fond amusement. "Thanks."

"So you have another superpower."

"Along with making you come so hard you see Saturn?"

I grin. "Yes."

He leans in closer. "I love doing that."

Heat flushes through me, making me nearly as sweaty as he is. "I love it, too."

"Let me buy you a hot chocolate somewhere."

"How about we take it back to your place?"

"Great idea."

We take a taxi to his place and on the way I open Spotify

and read the lyrics to the song we skated to. My throat squeezes up and my eyes sting.

"I wrote that song," he says.

I laugh-sob and lean against him.

"Well, I could have. It says what I want to say to you."

At his apartment, I'm greeted by an ecstatic Teemu. "Hello! Hello!" I crouch down to greet him. "How's my favorite pupper? Have you been a good boy?"

He licks my face and I laugh, and then I go with them for a short walk to the park. Back in Logan's apartment, it's warm and cozy, and we (all three of us) snuggle up on the sectional with our hot chocolate and lots of kisses and more talk. He tells me about talking to his teammates and how they got him to see what was going on inside him. "And your mom helped, too," he adds.

"Oh yeah! My mom! When did she talk to you?"

"She came to see me."

"What? When?"

"A couple of days ago."

"She flew to New York to see you? And never told me?"

"Yep. She also apologized." He strokes my hair. "For interfering and trying to fix up you and Ivan."

My head jerks up. "She apologized to you? And not to me? Jesus!"

"Settle down, I'm sure she'll talk to you about it, too." He smiles. "She also apologized to me for misjudging me."

"Oh." I stare at him wide-eyed. "Really?"

"Yeah. She says the family will give me a chance because they love you and they want you to be happy. So I'd better make you happy."

I bite my lip on a smile. "I agree." Then I touch his face. "You do make me happy."

"You make me happy, too." He catches my hand and kisses

my fingers. "That's when I realized how badly I fucked up. Because you went to all that trouble to try to convince your family I'm a decent guy even though I told you we should break up. I was an idiot."

"Yeah."

He laughs.

"No, you weren't. You thought you were doing it for me, to save me from the wrath of my family. That was actually very noble of you."

His face softens.

"Just misguided," I add.

He chuckles, then sobers. "You were so upset after your mom found out about us. I thought...you didn't want your family to know about us. And that wasn't enough for me. Anymore."

"I *did* want them to know. That's why I told my mom. Yeah, I didn't like it that she was mad. But that wasn't about me. I was mad for *you*."

"She said you defended me to your brothers. Showed them that video."

"I didn't want them to hate you for something that you don't deserve. Even if we never got back together, I wanted that for you."

"Yeah." He exhales. "Yeah, that. Christ, Annie. You make me feel like maybe I am worth it. Like maybe love is real."

"It's real." I look into his eyes. "I love you. No matter what."

"You know what made me love you even more?"

I blink. "What?"

"Ivan told me where you were when Jensen got hurt."

"Ohhhh. Yeah."

"Seoul."

"Yeah. At the Four Continents Championship." I drop my

gaze to his throat. "Ivan and I were about to compete when I heard Jensen was hurt and in the hospital."

He makes a rough noise in his throat.

I lift my eyes to his again. "It's okay. We went on. We did fine. It was hard, but part of being a champion is being disciplined."

"I hate that. I'm sorry."

"I know you are. Now."

"You are an amazing woman. So strong. I watched you getting thrown across the ice, spinning in the air, letting Ivan lift you over his head while he's twirling on skate blades. Jesus." He swipes his forehead. "You are absolutely fucking fearless."

My heart swells up so huge in my chest it's in my throat and I can't breathe.

"I figured if you could do shit like that, if you could compete after finding out your brother's in the hospital, if you can get over injuries and concussions, and start a new career, then I could talk to my dad about not being an asshole to me."

I break into a huge smile. "I inspired you."

"Yeah, you did. And I love you for it."

"I love you, too. I know that was hard. And I love how brave you are. How strong you are to set your own path." I set my fingers on his cheek and lean into him for a long, slow kiss. His mouth moves on mine, firm and confident, and my belly flip flops with need. He does this to me every time. Just a kiss...a touch...a word.

"I love that I can be myself with you," he says in a low voice. "And feel safe."

My eyes sting. "Yeah. I feel the same."

"You told me once you trust me. And I wasn't sure why. But want to deserve your trust. I'll do whatever I can to deserve that."

"Me, too." I blink back wetness. "I missed you."

"Me too." He kisses me again, then takes our empty cups and sets them on the table. He reaches for me and pulls me onto his lap and I snuggle in closer, as close as I can get, and it's never close enough. I press my breasts against him, open my mouth to his seeking tongue, and slide my hands under the collar of his sweater to find warm, smooth skin.

"I love how you turn me on."

"Mmm. Me too." I tip my head back so his mouth can move over my throat. "I need you."

He picks me up and carries me into the bedroom, then sets me gently on his bed. I pull my sweater off and wriggle out of my leggings as he undresses, too, right in front of me and I drink in the sight, his body a strongly muscled shadow against the faint light coming in the bedroom door.

He moves over me, kneeling between my legs, his hand on the middle of my chest pushing me to my back.

"I need you inside me." I lift my knees for him and watch him, my gaze traveling over his broad chest, tapering down to a narrow waist, his abs defined, his thighs big with his knees spread wide on the bed. I reach for him now, wanting to touch him again, to feel that male arousal, and he watches with heavy-lidded eyes as I stroke him, then let my fingers slip beneath to cup him.

"Aw, Annie." His jaw tightens.

"Fuck me. Please, Logan."

His eyes flare with heat at my words and he takes himself in his hand and slides the head up and down where I'm wet and achy. Oh yes, this is what I need, him inside me, joined together in the most intimate perfect way we can be.

"Maybe we don't need a condom?" I say. "If you're okay with it. I've had tests done."

"Me too." He nods slowly. "Are you sure?"

"Yes. I trust you." My body lifts toward him and then he

slides into me, easing in bit by bit, his girth stretching me wide, filling me with the most consuming, satisfying bliss.

A groan rises in my throat and I watch him, watch his face tense as he pushes in farther, taking in the sheen of perspiration building on his chest and rippled abs. So beautiful, I could look at him forever. I want this to last forever.

When he's fully inside me, he pauses, takes a couple of short, sharp breaths, then lowers himself over me. His arm slides beneath my head and he kisses my mouth, my cheek, the side of my neck, breathing me in. His panting breaths are rough at my ear, and I inhale the scent of his hair, lift my hands to his body, so big and solid, run my hands down his sides over satin skin to his hips.

"Annie." His mouth brushes my ear. "Annie."

The weight of his body, the thrust of him inside me is everything in this moment. I hold on to him, my eyes burning with tears, as he touches something so deep inside me it almost hurts with an unbearable sweetness. It's so beautiful, so softly sensuous, so deeply moving being with him like this, now that we're both sure of who we are...and who we are to each other.

"I love you." I slide a hand back up his body and into his hair. "I love you so much."

"I love you too, Annie. Love...you..." He rolls his hips against me with each word, thrusting up into me, so deep, so achingly lovely. "Forever."

My heart expands and aches at the wonder of it as we rock and sigh and ride soft surging waves of sweet pleasure, filling my body, my mind, my soul. He rises onto his knees, holding my thighs as he gazes down at me, his eyes dark and hot. Our eyes meet and hold, a connection drawing out between us that shimmers and glows, surrounding us in luminous pleasure and brilliant heat. It's intense, almost *too* intense, but I can't look away.

"Annie. You're mine."

I smile, a slow, rapturous smile. "Yes. I'm yours." And he's mine, all mine. Pure joy and gratitude and overwhelming love for him rush through me, so huge and hot.

His hand slides up between my breasts to rest at the base of my throat in a possessive yet utterly protective gesture. We stare into each other's eyes as he thrusts once more, and again, and I lift my body to meet his, taking him deep, as deep as I can. Tears leak from my eyes at the expression on his face, the devotion and worship, the gratitude and appreciation, and I reflect it back to him, giving it all to him, giving him everything I have.

Heat pools in my core, thick and liquid, sensation surging across my skin, swirling inside me, tightening every nerve ending. A ragged groan tears from his throat and his body goes rigid. "Annie. Christ, Annie. I love you."

And he falls over me again, his hand on my forehead, holding my hair, tipping my head back so he can kiss my mouth as he pulses inside me in wrenching spasms that set off my own orgasm, burning through me in violent, exquisite flames. I hold on to him, clasping him with my arms and legs, our mouths fused.

Then we lie curled beneath the covers of his big, beautiful bed, languid and lazy and blissful. I smile when I hear his breathing change. He's asleep. I listen to his heartbeat, so strong and steady. Like him.

I felt a connection with Logan from the first day we met, years ago. I felt seen and heard with him. I felt valued.

In my life, I've felt imperfect and afraid. And Logan has, too. Maybe we didn't share our deepest, darkest fears in Peongchang...but we have now. We trusted each other enough to do that...to tell our truth, without fear of judgment. To be brave enough to show up and be honest. And that's where connection comes.

TWENTY-EIGHT

Annie

"I really am sorry."

I roll my lips in because my bottom lip is quivering and I might start crying. Mom is nearly in tears and I can't handle that.

I never saw Mom cry over anything until her best friend Diane was diagnosed with cancer. It was a roller coaster of ups and downs until Diane's cancer came back last year and she passed away. It hit Mom hard, losing her best friend.

"I know," I choke out.

"I feel terrible that I said that."

"It's okay."

She sighs and wipes one eye. "I was disappointed and worried about you being with someone not good enough for you. I want you to be happy, above everything else. Truly."

"I know, Mom."

"That's all I want for my kids. Happiness. Love. Trust."

I nod.

"And I'm also sorry that you feel like you're in competition with your brothers. It's not a competition, sweetheart."

"Mom. Everything's a competition."

She smiles. "I know sibling rivalry is a normal thing, to an extent. But the thing is...you all are different. Even the boys have their differences. I don't expect Kingston to be as laid back as Leif. *You* are different from your brothers. It doesn't mean you're not as good—you're just different, with your own unique qualities and talents. You're fearless and determined and loyal. And a truly beautiful skater. I admire you for how you moved on from the disappointment of having to give up figure skating. I know how hard that was for you. You've done amazing work here with this team and I can tell they all respect you."

Yes. I'm different.

Now the tears do brim over and slip down my cheeks. I use both hands to wipe them and Mom and I move together for a long, tight hug. "Thanks, Mom. I love you."

"I love you, too, my special girl."

As we draw apart and I reach for a Kleenex, my phone buzzes.

It's a couple of days after Logan's figure skating debut and Mom's still here. She's making my favorite chicken and wild rice casserole and Logan's coming for dinner tonight. It'll be a real chance for her to get to know him better.

I pick up my phone and unlock it. There's a text from Logan that says,

Uh oh.

I frown. What does that mean?

Then he sends me an Instagram link.

I click through and it's a picture of him and me, at Bryant Park, skating.

I smile.

Then there's a pic of us kissing.

Uh oh.

Nobody's supposed to know about us.

Except...people do. Now my whole family. Logan says he told his friends about us because he needed advice. Ivan knows, obviously. And now...people who were there that day are posting pics of us.

My stomach tightens. "Oh shit."

"What's wrong?"

I tell Mom and show her the post.

Logan sends another link.

"Yikes." I sink my teeth into my bottom lip and stare at my phone.

> LOGAN: I'll be over in about fifteen. We can talk more

> ANNIE: Okay

I feel a relief that he's coming, because...facing this with him seems a lot less daunting than facing it myself. I can deal with it myself, and I will, but having someone who's got your back is...well, it's wonderful.

Ivan comes out of his bedroom. He wanted to give Mom and me privacy.

I tell him, too, about what happened.

"Well, shit." He lowers himself into a chair. "But duh...of course this was going to happen."

"I'm sorry," is the first thing Logan says when he walks in. "This is all on me."

I take his jacket and hang it up.

"Hey, Ivan. Hi, Stella."

She smiles at him. "Hi. Your figure skating routine was impressive."

He takes off his ball cap and shoves a hand into his thick hair. "Maybe so, but it was dumb." He sits on the couch beside me.

"I thought it was such a beautiful thing." She sighs, hands on her lap. "I shouldn't have encouraged you."

"No, no." He shakes his head vehemently. "This is not your fault at all."

"I've been poking my nose in too many places."

Logan looks at me and meets my eyes. "I promised you no one would find out from me."

"I feel responsible, too," Ivan says.

"No," Logan and I say at the same time. We smile at each other.

"I didn't post it anywhere," Ivan adds, hands up. "I swear. I just sent the video to you."

"I know. It wasn't you," Logan says.

"We would have to deal with this at some point," I say.

"True." Logan meets my eyes.

"It's okay." I lift my chin. "I've been thinking about this and I have a plan."

Mom smiles. "Of course you do."

"Are you going to tell us about it?" Logan lifts an eyebrow. "What do you need from me?"

"Or me," Mom says.

Ivan grins. "Or me."

I smile at them all. "Thank you. I appreciate your support so much. Especially if this doesn't work out. I'll need it, then."

"Of course we're here for you. Always." Ivan looks at Logan. "Just don't make any short jokes."

I blink at him.

Logan tries not to smile.

"They go right over her head," Ivan finishes.

Logan and Mom burst out laughing. I throw a cushion at him.

I love these people.

___

"THIS IS MY RESIGNATION." I push the paper across the desk to Brad Julian.

He pushes it back. "I can't accept this."

I go very still. I glance over at Jennifer Sattler, VP of People and Culture for the hockey organization, sitting in Brad's office with us. She nods.

"I thought you were going to fire me," I say.

"No." Brad shakes his head. "We saw the stuff on social media. I gather you and Logan are involved in a relationship."

"Yes." I keep my head up. "We are. We've been trying to keep things discreet, but we knew we would have to deal with it at some point. I don't want to cause any problems for the team. So I'm quitting."

"You don't need to do that," Jennifer says. "There's no real conflict. We just ask that you maintain a professional relationship while you're both working."

"Logan's overcome his attitude about the skating," Brad says.

Brad knows all.

"And he's been playing great. It's good to see."

I nod slowly. "Yes." I take a deep breath. "Okay." My mind is working. I like the idea I've come up with and still want to pursue it. "I won't quit right away. I'll finish the season. But next year...I have a proposal for you."

Brad frowns. "Okay. What is it?"

"I'm going to start my own coaching business. I've been

approached be a few players, from other teams. I think in this market there are enough professional players interested in my coaching services." There are three NHL teams near here, not to mention their affiliates. "And that would include the Bears." I tip my head. "I think our professional relationship would be more comfortable for all of us if I'm not an employee of the team, but rather a contractor."

Brad's face is inscrutable as he considers this. "Interesting." He looks at Jennifer. She gives a small shrug.

"That could work," Brad says. "I'll discuss it with the Hellers. Do you have information on how you'd be compensated?"

"I'm working on that and I can give you a written proposal in a few days."

Ivan has put me in touch with a contact at Chelsea Piers, where he works, so I can rent ice time. I'll need to figure that and other expenses into my business case and work out how much I'll need to charge to make money.

"Okay." Brad smiles. "I'm glad we're not losing you. You've been a huge asset to the hockey club this year."

"Thank you. I appreciate that." My confidence has grown.

They don't see me as second rate. I *am* good enough for this job. I *am* as good as my brothers—I'm just different. I'm doing this, something I love, and maybe it's not what I always dreamed of, but it's fun and rewarding.

As I leave Brad's office, I get a text. I pull out my phone.

It's a message in the WAGs group chat. They added me yesterday. There's a game tonight and I'm going to it with them, sitting with the wives and girlfriends of the players I coach. But I won't be there as a coach.

Okay, I can't let go of the skating thing entirely. Of course I'll be watching with a critical eye. But that'll be for a different time.

Tonight, I'll be there cheering on my boyfriend. My boyfriend who's currently playing on the second line.

Dear Diane,

Well, I almost messed this one up.

I came to visit Annie in New York, excited to see her and Ivan together again. You know I love him and have since they were partnered up when they were twelve years old. As they grew up, I always wished they would be a couple. They had so much chemistry on the ice it was hard to believe those feelings didn't exist off the ice! Remember the things people used to say about them? Remember that crazy conspiracy theory that they had a secret baby together they were keeping hidden? Oh my gosh, that was so funny.

But deep down inside—I wanted it to be true.

As I do for all my kids, I wanted Annie and Ivan to find their happily ever after. And I'm embarrassed to admit that I ignored what they were telling me—that they are just friends. I kept pushing and pushing. I had good intentions! I know you won't judge me.

When I found out that Annie is involved with Logan Coates, I just about had a heart attack. Remember, he's the one who hit Jensen a few years back, when he ended up in the hospital and out for months? We all thought it was a dirty hit and Logan should have been punished more than he was. I couldn't believe she was involved with a player like that.

And it's serious!

It was a hard thing to accept. Lars and I talked a lot.

He's such a reasonable man. One of many reasons I love him. He settled me down and got me thinking. And then Annie showed us video of the hit, showing that Logan didn't really intend to hit Jensen like that.

More than that, it showed me that Annie believed in him no matter what. And that she wanted us to know the truth about him, no matter what. She's grown up into such a mature, strong, determined woman. I'm so proud of her. I always have been, but I never realized how much she's tried to live up to her brothers. I should have made sure she always knew how talented and wonderful she is (except when she got caught drinking underage that one time and was almost kicked out of the skating club). (Well, maybe there were a few times she tested my limits...)

And when I got to know Logan a bit better, I saw how much he loves her, too.

And that is what I want for her. Plain and simple. To love and be loved by someone unconditionally, someone who's always got your back, someone who respects and worships you. And if that's Logan...I'm good with that. I'm more than good—I'm ecstatic.

After my missteps, do you think I've changed my mind about finding love for my last single child? No! I'm off to visit Tanner now, the baby of the family. He's still young, but I have a feeling he's ready for love.

I still miss you so much. I'll write again soon.

Love, Stella

THANK YOU FOR READING! I hope you loved Logan and Annie as much as I do! Want to find out more about what Mama Bang has in store for Tanner? Find out in HOOK 'EM

HARD. **She's all wrong for my boys and me, but tell that to my stupid heart...**

CLICK HERE TO READ HOOK 'EM HARD NOW>

AND IF YOU loved LIGHT 'EM UP and need more Bears Hockey hockey boys, check out MUST LOVE DOGS...AND HOCKEY, book 1 of the Bears Hockey series.

CLICK HERE TO READ MUST LOVE DOGS...AND HOCKEY NOW>

I SO APPRECIATE your help in spreading the word about my books, including sharing with friends! Please leave a review on your favorite book site!

You can also join my Facebook group, Sweet Heat Reader Lounge, for exclusive giveaways and sneak peeks of future books.

If you'd like to receive emails from me with all my news about sales and new releases, add your name at https://www. kellyjamieson.com/newsletter .

BANG BROTHERS HOCKEY SERIES

Meet the Bang Brothers—five hot hockey-playing brothers who are allergic to commitment.
The brothers are about to face off against their newly-retired mother...who suddenly has plenty of time to play matchmaker. Add in their baby sister and some secret dating, a single dad, an accidental pregnancy, a marriage of convenience, and a wrong bed—or two—and these siblings are not going to know what hit them!

Lace 'em Up
Show 'em How
Hit 'em Hard
Lock 'em Down
Light 'em Up
Hook 'em Hard

ACKNOWLEDGMENTS

Obviously, I have to first of all thank my Bang Brothers Hockey co-authors—Elise Faber, Jami Davenport, Kat Mizera, Gina Azzi, and Cathryn Fox. Its has been an honor (and also a lot of fun!) creating this world and these characters with you.

I also have to thank Kate Willoughby for your ongoing support, encouragement, and feedback. I am so grateful.

I am always thankful for the team I work with—my amazing assistant Stacey Price, rock star publicist Heather Roberts, and magician editor Kristi Yanta.

Thanks also to author friends near and far, for support, learning, and laughter, including those Friday afternoon Zoom sessions.

And as always, I am most grateful to you—for reading this book. I feel so lucky to have the support of readers in my Facebook group, those who read my emails, and those who buy and read my books. Thank you so much!

ALSO BY KELLY JAMIESON

HELLER BROTHERS HOCKEY
BREAKAWAY
FACEOFF
ONE MAN ADVANTAGE
HAT TRICK
OFFSIDE

POWER SERIES
POWER STRUGGLE
POWER PLAY
POWER SHIFT

RULE OF THREE SERIES
RULE OF THREE
RHYTHM OF THREE
REWARD OF THREE

SAN AMARO SINGLES
WITH STRINGS ATTACHED
HOW TO LOVE
SLAMMED

WINDY CITY KINK

SWEET OBSESSION

ALL MESSED UP

PLAYING DIRTY

BREW CREW

LIMITED TIME OFFER

NO OBLIGATION REQUIRED

ACES HOCKEY

MAJOR MISCONDUCT

OFF LIMITS

ICING

TOP SHELF

BACK CHECK

SLAP SHOT

PLAYING HURT

BIG STICK

GAME ON

LAST SHOT

BODY SHOT

HOT SHOT

LONG SHOT

BAYARD HOCKEY

SHUT OUT

CROSS CHECK

WYNN HOCKEY

PLAY TO WIN

IN IT TO WIN IT

WIN BIG

FOR THE WIN

GAME CHANGER

BEARS HOCKEY

MUST LOVE DOGS...AND HOCKEY

YOU HAD ME AT HOCKEY

TALK HOCKEY TO ME

THE O ZONE

GOOD HANDS

SCORING BIG

MERRY PUCKING CHRISTMAS

STANDALONES

THREE OF HEARTS

LOVING MADDIE FROM A TO Z

DANCING IN THE RAIN

LOVE ME

LOVE ME MORE

2 HOT 2 HANDLE

FRIENDS WITH BENEFITS

LOST AND FOUND

ONE WICKED NIGHT

SWEET DEAL

HOW SWEET IT IS

HOT RIDE

CRAZY EVER AFTER

ALL I WANT FOR CHRISTMAS

SEXPRESSO

NIGHT IRISH SEX FAIRY

CONFERENCE CALL

RIGGER

YOU REALLY GOT ME

SCREWED

FIRECRACKER

BIG WITCH ENERGY

HATE ME UNDER THE MISTLETOE

ABOUT THE AUTHOR

Kelly Jamieson is a best-selling author of over fifty romance novels and novellas. Her writing has been described as "emotionally complex", "sweet and satisfying" and "blisteringly sexy." She likes coffee (black), wine (mostly white), shoes (high heels) and hockey!

Subscribe to her newsletter for updates about her new books and what's coming up, follow her on Twitter @KellyJamieson or on Facebook, visit her website at www.kellyjamieson.com or contact her at info@kellyjamieson.com.

Made in the USA
Coppell, TX
28 August 2024